**What early readers think of "The Counterfeit Drug Murders**

**Great mystery that leads you into a new venue of illicit drug companies.**

Frank has written yet another terrific mystery. He continues to develop the main characters of the series and also to draw us in with new and interesting people. The story took me to many familiar places which is always entertaining. Frank leaves the reader wanting more knowing the latest character has a lot yet to do. Which way will Eve go? Only Frank knows for sure. By Diana McDonough on February 8, 2021

**A Police Procedural with a Very Real Issue**

The Counterfeit Drug Murders is another Hoffman and O'Hare Mystery that provides both an excellent police procedural, as do the previous installments, and an exploration into the world of counterfeit drugs, a serious and very much real issue. Although the story involves Hoffman and O'Hare, The Counterfeit Drug Murders introduces new characters into the mix around which much of the story revolves. As before in the series, the story takes the readers to a variety of locations. Both intriguing and educational, I recommend the book. By Jackson Coppley on January 10, 2021

**A New Type of Murder**

Frank Hopkins writes like Sergeant Joe Friday, "Just the facts, M'am" as the writer's fictional detective husband and wife team of Hoffman and O'Hare tackle a series of murders related to poison drugs. Carefully documented charts and tallies of deaths entice the reader to follow clues leading to other clues. At the same time, the author's expertise puts us into the head of an unknown person tracing down the killers, and we begin to cheer for success. The book is hard to put down as the killers try to escape justice in exciting attempts and the person, still not known by the law, hunts them down. Hopkins knows his subject and brings to light a growing problem of careless and criminal drug compounding killing many patients. No longer can a reader trust for sure the drugs in the little plastic bottles given out usually innocently at the pharmacy. By Thomas Hollyday on January 30, 2021

**Emotional read**

Very intense and very emotionally gripping experience. It develops in the way that surprised the hell out of me. But it was good. Well told for sure. By Nan on January 15, 2021

**A delightful read**

An interesting read the story revolves around a series of murders related to drug poisoning, and detective Hoffman and her husband O'Hare try to solve this mystery. The plot is well written, and the author very carefully plotted the cues and clues of the murders for the reader to hook them with the book. And the way the author explains every detail, like the procedure to find the clues and the methods they follow it actually ignites your imagination. This is one of the books in a series called "Hoffman and O'Hare mystery," but you can read it as a single book as well. The author also brings up a sensitive issue of counterfeit drugs and the underground world of pharmaceuticals that I was not at all aware of. So it is kind of educational for me as well. Overall it is a great book to read. I would definitely recommend this book to anyone. By JC on February 8, 2021

**Twisted Realism**

Heavy doses of realism and well-plotted twists make this police procedural a page-turner. By LindsVan on January 20, 2021

# The Counterfeit Drug Murders

A Hoffman and O'Hare
Mystery

by

Frank E Hopkins

Also by Frank E Hopkins

Fiction:
  *The Billion Dollar Embezzlement Murders*
  *Abandoned Homes: Vietnam Revenge Murders*
  *First Time*
  *The Opportunity*
  *Unplanned Choices*


Non-fiction:
  *Locational Analysis: An Interregional Econometric Model of Agriculture, Mining, Manufacturing and Services,* with Curtis Harris.

This book is a work of fiction. Names, characters, places, and incidents are the product of the author's imagination or are used fictitiously. Any resemblance to actual events, locales, or persons, living or dead, is coincidental.

Copyright © 2020 Frank E Hopkins
All Rights Reserved
ISBN 13: 978-0-9988200-4-0
Ocean View Publishing
Ocean View, Delaware 19970

FRANK E HOPKINS

# DEDICATION

Unfortunately, many Americans incorrectly believe that their country has the world's best health care system. The origins of this myth may be rooted in our citizen's nationalistic belief in the general superiority of the U.S. fostered after World War II and recently supported by conservative politicians, the medical establishment, and the pharmaceutical industry.

International data challenges this contention. A simple comparison of U.S. and other developed counties' COVID-19 infection and death rates are stark, deadly evidence of this contradiction. Two organizations ranking U.S. healthcare relative to other nations paints a dismal picture compared to ours. Numbro (https://www.numbeo.com/health-care/rankings_by_country.jsp) ranked U.S. health care in 2020 as number 30 out of 93 countries. *The World Population Review*, (https://worldpopulationreview.com/country-rankings/best-healthcare-in-the-world) ranked us 37 out of 100 countries. These poor rankings have implications for our life expectancy. World Data Info (https://www.worlddata.info/life-expectancy.php) reports in mid-2020, Hong Kong had the highest life expectancy with 82.3 years for males and 87.7 years for females. The U.S. ranked number 40 out of one-hundred and 66 countries with 76.1 years for males and 81.1 years for females.

The sale of counterfeit drugs and the opioid epidemic are contributing factors to our low life expectancy. This book examines a family torn apart by a premature death caused by a counterfeit drug, and the suffering of one female member who was ensnared into opioid addiction by an immoral physician.

First, I dedicate the book to the FDA staff, honest pharmacists, drug manufacturers, nurses, and physicians who strive to serve the public, and to keep us healthy and addiction free. Second, it is dedicated to those who have been unfortunate enough to be trapped into the scourge of opioid addiction. May both groups become safe and stay healthy.

## ACKNOWLEDGEMENTS

I am indebted to those who have written books and articles on the pharmaceutical industry and the Food and Drug administration that I used to research this book. *The Truth About the Drug Companies: How They Deceive Us and What to Do About It* by Marcia Angell, MD, shows how the drug industry games the FDA and the public to make obscene profits by developing new drugs with minor improvements over existing drugs. *Dangerous Doses* by Katherine Eban shows how counterfeit drugs are produced and how law enforcement combats them. *Dopesick: Dealers, Doctors and the Drug Company that Addicted America* by Beth Macy describes the growth of the opioid crisis in the Appalachia, and its impact on drug dealers, addicts, and family life. *Compounding and Manufacturing* by IML Training describes how compounding pharmacies produce drugs. The reader should access the FDA website to learn about the successes and failures of the legal pharmaceutical industry and illegal drug manufacturers, https://www.fda.gov/drugs.

I thank the early readers of the first draft for advising me on how to improve the book: Kari Horner, Diana McDonough, and Sally Scarangella. Mary-Margaret Pauer performed the development editing that improved the structure, plot, and rhythm of the novel. Thanks to the beta readers who read late drafts and provided comments that significantly improved the novel: Mary Lou Butler, Jackson Copley, Walt Curran, Mary Dolan, Carl Pergler, and Ruth Ziemniak. 99Designs produced the excellent book cover.

## Chapter 1 Death of a Friend

Monday, April 23, 2012

Exhaustion overcame Dr. Jean Bennett. She winced hearing the announcement calling her to the fourth medical crisis since the Kitty Hawk General Hospital had admitted Mary Jewel nine hours earlier. Mary's heart had stopped again. When Dr. Bennett arrived in her room, the resuscitation team had already started the defibrillator.

Mary's body jolted as the electricity surged through her heart. Dr. Bennett watched in resignation, thinking this may be their last try. After twenty minutes, Dr. Bennett motioned for the team to stop. She looked at the wall clock and declared Mary dead at 7:35 p.m.

Earlier at Mary's request, Dr. Bennett called her son, Brian, in Alexandria, Virginia. He left work in the afternoon and drove four and a half hours to the hospital on the Outer Banks in North Carolina.

Dr. Bennett did not look forward to telling Brian his mother had died. She met Brian in the ICU waiting area, and said, "Sorry, we couldn't revive your mother after her fourth cardiac event. Her heart suffered too much damage from the earlier failures."

Tired from the drive, Brian became nauseous and started breathing rapidly because of what he had just heard. He said, "She had told me her heart had recovered since her ablation surgery corrected the irregular heart rhythm three years ago. How did this happen? It's too soon." He ran his fingers through his hair in desperation. "I'm not ready to have her leave us. My kids loved her and talked about giving her great-grandchildren when they married. How am I going to tell them and my brother and sister?"

Dr. Bennett mentally reviewed Mary's medical history. "We

assumed we had corrected her heart problems, and I can't understand how her heart failed so rapidly. If you give me permission, I want to have the medical examiner conduct an autopsy to make sure the hospital didn't make a mistake. But, I'll understand if you don't want her death investigated."

"I can't believe she's dead at sixty-four. I'd like to find out why. Yes, perform the autopsy. Please send the results only to me. I don't want the rest of the family to hurt more by reading how she died. I'll tell them what happened. When can you release her body, so we can schedule the funeral?"

"By Friday, unless the medical examiner has too much work. I'll send you the autopsy results." Dr. Bennett relaxed since she didn't have to talk to all the relatives.

"Good, I was afraid it would be longer." Brian said, believing his mother's death will crush his brother and sister. They depended on her.

After Dr. Bennett left, Brian called his wife, Sandy, at home and told her what happened, including Bennett's request for an autopsy. "Perhaps, we should leave our children home. A funeral might be too traumatic for them."

Sandy had interrupted her accounting career to care for her two grade-school kids. She heard the anguish in her husband's voice, "I've talked to my mother. She's on standby and said she'll watch the kids if we need her. When is the funeral?"

"Dr. Bennett told me the medical examiner might hold her until Friday, so not before Saturday."

His halting voice told her don't leave me to suffer alone. "I'll be there tomorrow."

"Thanks. I'd appreciate that. I'm numb now, and I don't know how I'll cope now that she's gone." His heart's rapid beating slowed as he talked to his wife.

"What did the doctor say caused her death?"

"Dr. Bennett didn't know, but expressed concern it could be a hospital mistake which she wanted to identify," Brian said.

"I still remember the bitterness of your mother's ex-boyfriend, John Short, when she rejected him. He stalked her in person and on email. You should tell Dr. Bennett,"

"I will." He had suppressed that memory, but his wife's mention of it caused him to grimace and recall his earlier desire to physically hurt Short.

After the call ended, Brian drove to his mother's beach house in Duck, a small summer resort located on Bodie Island, the northernmost peninsula of the Outer Banks, nine miles north of Kitty Hawk on Route 12. Duck is a new town incorporated in 2002. Duck's permanent winter population numbers in the hundreds, but swells to over 20,000 during the summer months.

Mary Jewel purchased a new beach-front home because of the warm climate compared to upstate New York and the beauty of the hilly narrow barrier peninsula bordered by the Currituck Sound on its west side and the Atlantic Ocean on the east. Mary liked the easy access to Route 12 which runs through the middle of Duck, and south to Kitty Hawk, with access to the North Carolina mainland, over the Caratoke Highway Bridge.

After he let himself in, Brian started crying when he suddenly realized the finality of her passing. She would never again greet him when he visited Duck, he would never talk to her on the phone, nor watch her play with his young children.

When he composed himself, he called his relatives so they could plan to attend the funeral. Since Brian had not decided the date and time of the funeral, he requested their email addresses to notify them when he had scheduled it. After talking to his sister Eve, his brother Stu, his uncle and two of his aunts, and a few friends, he stopped calling because of the time and his emotional exhaustion.

Brian despaired for his children who had liked staying with their grandmother, without their parents, for two weeks for the last five years. Starting in spring, they looked forward and talked about their summer vacation. How would they react to the passing of their grandmother?

Brian knew he had to sleep to control his emotions so he could make the notification calls and arrange for the funeral. But sleep didn't come easy. He felt his heart's palpitations as he thought of how he would continue his life without the steadying presence of his mother. He fell asleep after an hour of tossing and turning. He woke up at sunrise, exhausted, but ready for the day.

In the morning Brian phoned Paul O'Hare. "Paul, it's Brian Jewel. I'm afraid I have sad news. My mother died last night of heart failure."

Paul, speechless for a moment, knew Mary, her husband Gary, and her children well. Gary had taught in the History Department at Binghamton University with Paul. He said, "I'm sorry. Last time I talked to her she told me her health was great. Margaret and I had plans to visit her in July. We'll both attend her funeral. Let us know when and where. I hope Eve and Stu are not too depressed."

"I'll email you when we schedule the funeral," Brian said.

Dr. Bennett waited until Tuesday morning to call the medical examiner, Dr. Simpkins at the Brody School of Medicine at East Carolina University in Greenville. "Joe, Dr. Bennett from Kitty Hawk. Mary Jewel, a patient of mine, died last night. I didn't sign the death certificate because I don't know why she died. I'd need you to do an autopsy. During the last week, two other mysterious deaths occurred at the hospital. I'm concerned we might have made a mistake and want to find out."

"Send me Mary Jewel's corpse and her medical records. Are the other two cadavers available?"

"No, their relatives buried them."

"Too bad. Send over their medical records and bodily fluids taken during their treatment. I'll see if the three deaths had anything in common after I complete Mary Jewel's autopsy."

"When can you release Mary Jewel's body?" Dr. Bennett asked.

"Have the funeral home pick her up on Friday afternoon."

Dr. Bennett called Brian, "The medical examiner agreed to autopsy your mother. He expects to release her body by Friday. However, he won't be able to release the full report on the cause of her death until after the lab completes the toxicology tests."

"Thank you Dr. Bennett, I'll schedule the funeral for Monday. I don't know if the medical examiner will consider homicide as a cause of death, but my wife and I want you to know about the behavior of her ex-boyfriend, John Short. He dated my mother for six weeks. When she broke it off, he threatened and stalked her. He even went so far as to email her he might kill her if she started dating someone else." Brian felt relieved to tell someone of Short's behavior who could make a difference.

"Thanks for telling me. Perhaps, you should call the police."

Dr. Bennett hoped Short and not a hospital mistake killed her patient.

Brian asked Dr. Bennett, "Please have the hospital call the Monroe Funeral Home, to tell them of my mother's death and ask them to pick up her body after the autopsy."

He wanted to plan for her funeral including burial next to his father. They scheduled viewings at the funeral home for Sunday and the burial for Monday morning, April 30 at the Austin Cemetery in Kitty Hawk.

Twenty-five years ago, the Jewel family left the cool spring climate of Binghamton, NY, in June, after the Binghamton University spring semester ended to spend two weeks vacationing in warm Kitty Hawk. They liked the stores and restaurants of the 3,000 plus population town. After fifteen years of visiting Kitty Hawk, they purchased their Duck house.

Following Dr. Bennett's advice, Brian called the Kitty Hawk police department. He spoke to Dave Conner, "My mother Mary Jewel died yesterday. Dr. Bennett told me she wasn't able to determine the cause of death and has requested an autopsy. My wife and I suspect she might have been murdered by an ex-boyfriend, John Short, who had threatened to kill her."

"Thanks for the information. When is the funeral?"

"Monday morning at the Austin Cemetery."

Sandy called Brian a little after 11:00 a.m., "Hi Brian, I'll be leaving in a few minutes. Mother's here. It's raining, so it may take over five hours."

"It hasn't started here. I'll be waiting. Drive carefully." He needed her and waited patiently for her arrival.

After finishing his phone calls, Brian cleaned the house to prepare for his family's visit. His first impulse was to throw everything out he didn't enjoy. But he decided not to since he knew his siblings liked some artwork, rugs, and furniture he detested. Since they'd arrive by Friday, he called his mother's lawyer and scheduled a reading of the will for Saturday morning.

After a tasteless lunch, he tried to read several draft contracts he accessed on his law firm's database. Even though he loved being a lawyer, after a half-hour, he realized he couldn't continue. He sat on the front porch and kept recalling memories of his mother guiding him through childhood, her encouragement for him to enter law school, and her support for his marriage. He alternatively smiled or cried while waiting for Sandy.

When he saw her pull into the driveway, he wiped his eyes hoping to disguise his sorrow. The sight of her long black hair, beautiful smiling face, and slender body as she left the car revived him. While still distraught over his mother's death, he knew his family gave him a reason to continue.

He rushed down the porch steps and embraced her as she left the car. Her warmth reassured him.

"Brian, you look exhausted. How are you?"

"Until you arrived, tired and sad. I didn't get much sleep last night."

"Rather than talk, let's go inside so you can take a nap."

They entered his bedroom and fully clothed they crashed on the bed. Her embrace reassured him, his tension left, and he fell into a deep sleep.

## Northern Outer Banks North Carolina

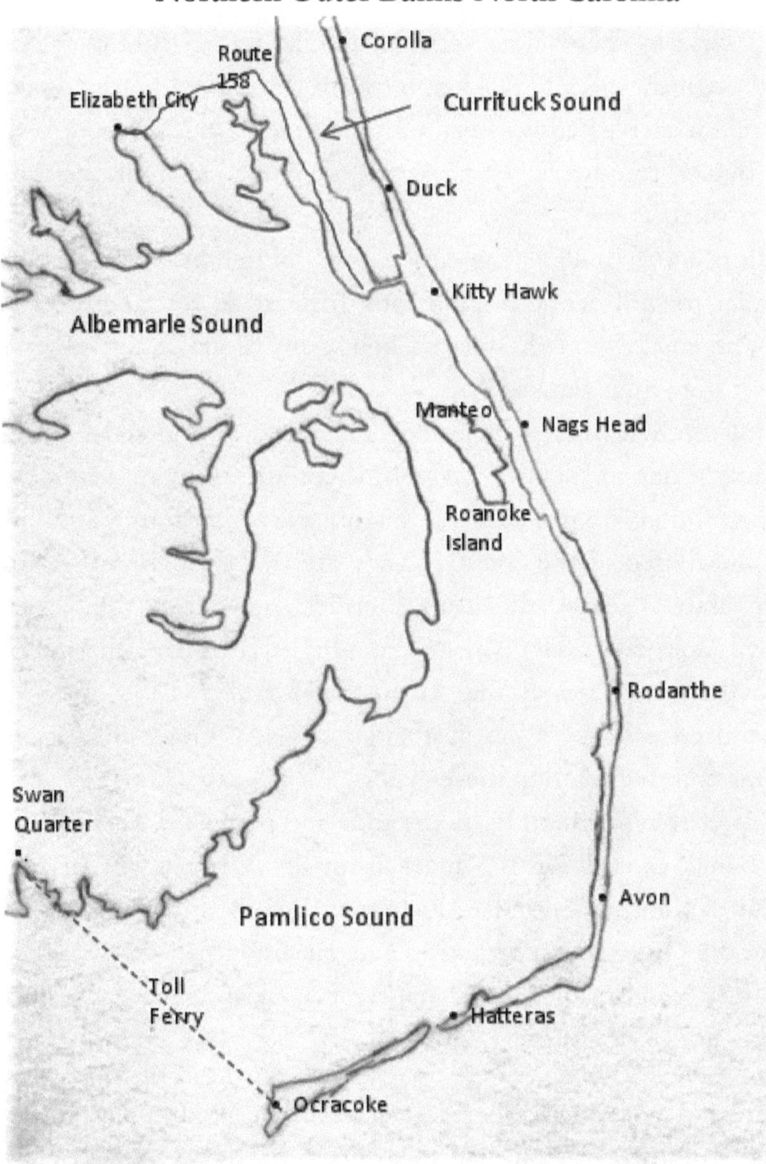

# Chapter 2 Return to the Outer Banks

Tuesday, April 24, 2012

Waking up, Paul O'Hare said, "Angel, as a long-term friend of Mary Jewel, I need to spend time with the family before the funeral to help them though their grief. But I don't want the trip to be depressing for you. Brian hasn't scheduled his mother's funeral. I'd like to drive to the Outer Banks, tomorrow. If we arrive early, we can tour the areas we haven't visited."

"Hon, I was thinking the same thing," Margaret Hoffman said. She felt tender toward her spouse. "I look forward to returning to the safe house, the site of your heroics in killing my attacker, and driving the length of the Outer Banks."

Paul reached over to her side of the bed and kissed her, put his arms around her and said, "I know how you can really thank me."

The Outer Banks are a historically important and unique geographical area of the country. They are the site of the first English colony, pirate Blackbeard's death, a critical site during the Revolution and Civil War, the first flight of the Wright Brothers, charming light houses, the graveyard of the Atlantic, the reality TV show, Wicked Tuna, and growing vacation destinations. The Outer Banks has many museums commemorating these events.

The narrow northern barrier islands and peninsula of the Northern Outer Banks extend for 100 miles from the Virginia border to Cape Lookout. Currituck Sound, Albemarle Sound, and Pamlico Sound separate the Outer Banks from the mainland. Warm waters of the Gulf Stream are responsible for their semi-tropical climate, perfect for attracting northern visitors.

After an early breakfast, they left at 8:30 on Wednesday and drove south on Route 113 from Dagsboro until it merged into Route 13 at

Pocomoke, Maryland. They loved the drive south to the Chesapeake Bay Bridge-Tunnel. In Maryland they passed through park-like woods until they reached Pocomoke near the Virginia border. Then they drove through a series of small villages in Virginia's eastern shore, reminiscent of a period fifty years earlier in most of the country's farm regions. The highlight of the drive began as they drove onto the over twenty-mile-long Bridge-Tunnel connecting the Eastern Shore of Virginia to Hampton Roads on the Western Shore. Both loved to drive and view the wide open unimpeded water and Eastern and Western shoreline.

They left early so they would arrive for lunch at the rest stop, restaurant, and six hundred and twenty-five foot long fishing pier. They took their time walking on the pier, talking to the fishermen and women, before they looked for a table. Occasionally, they watched a fish being hauled from the bay. They considered the views from the restaurant worth the trip.

Usually on road trips, the couple talked about the case they were investigating, a potential case, or the book they were writing or promoting. This trip they had no case and had completed their last domestic book tour so the driving and sightseeing had its own rewards. They spent time reminiscing how they survived in Duck and looked forward to the most of the trip except Mary's funeral.

After arriving in Kitty Hawk, Paul said, "It's early. Let's go to Mary's house, Brian expects us. We can check into the hotel later."

Paul turned left at Route 12, which runs through the Outer Banks from Corolla south to Ocracoke They drove north, passing the ocean front beach houses on his right, ranging in size from bungalows to recently constructed mansions. The driving tension left Paul as they entered the town limits of Duck.

Brian and Sandy greeted them at the front door of Mary Jewel's three-story cedar-sided home.

"You're the first of our friends from Binghamton to arrive. The others planned to show up during the day on Friday."

Paul listened to the waves lapping against the shore a few hundred feet away.

Sandy led them into a sunroom in the back of the house overlooking the ocean. They sat in white wicker chairs in front of a coffee table with plates of fruit, cheese, and crackers. Brian offered them wine, which they accepted. They snacked on the appetizers, as Brian summarized the events of the last several days. Margaret put down her glass of Chardonnay, when Brian told them of the planned autopsy.

"Dr. Bennett showed concern over a hospital mistake, but I assume they'll look for drugs and poison, since her heart appeared in good shape the day she died. I complicated matters by suggesting my mother's ex-boyfriend may have murdered her," Brian said. He told them of his concerns about John Short's behavior.

Paul raised his eyebrows, surprised Mary had any enemies.

"Short owned a drug company. He had the means to poison her." Sandy said. She didn't disguise the hatred in her voice.

"I want to learn more, but we have to leave to check into the Hilton Garden Inn. Can you tell us tomorrow?" Paul said. His heart raced in anticipation of discovering if a good friend had been murdered and if they may have a role in solving the crime.

"Yes, we'll tell you all our suspicions then. I enjoyed reading your book on the billion dollar embezzler. Can you show us the safe house in Duck where you killed him?" Brian asked.

"We'll take you to it, but I only acted instinctively implementing Margaret's training on how to use a gun. I didn't have a great mental or moral debate before I pulled the trigger," Paul replied.

"Yes, but you saved your wife's life."

Margaret experienced the warm sensation she always did when recalling Paul's fearless behavior and modesty and couldn't wait to get him alone in the hotel room.

"We'll pick you and Sandy up at 9:00," Paul said.

When they left to go to the Hilton, Margaret said, "Mary's death looks like a safe case to investigate with no professional criminals waiting to attack us."

"I thought the same thing. But, just in case, I'll keep practicing my target shooting."

On Thursday morning Margaret and Paul began their tour of the Outer Banks. In addition, to visiting the safe house in the morning they planned to spend the afternoon at the site of the first flight by the Wright brothers in 1903 at the Wright Brothers National Memorial in Kill Devil Hills, south of Kitty Hawk.

The sight of the remaining damage of Hurricane Irene on August 27, 2011 in Kitty Hawk surprised Paul and Margaret. They learned that inlets in the islands created by the storm had either been filled in or covered by temporary bridges, so traffic could proceed south on Route 12.

After picking up Brian and Sandy they drove south, and Brian handed Margaret a USB drive. He said, "We included emails between my mother and John Short. Read them and see if they interest you."

"Thanks, we will." Margaret said. She put the USB drive into her purse and looked at Paul, who, like her, wondered about their content.

Paul pulled up in front of the safe house and said, "We haven't been here since the attack. It's been repaired and looks new."

"Is it still a safe house?" Brian asked.

"No, the TV and newspaper's publicity of the crime and the publication of our book gave it too much notoriety. The Berkeley and Jones accounting firm use it as a company conference and training center. The building to the right of the house has the new lecture rooms," Margaret said.

Paul gave them a tour of the facility, its grounds, and described the gun fight, repeating what he and Margaret had written in the book.

Paul explained the fear everyone in the house had during and after the rocket-fired-grenade attack and how he stalked the serial killer before shooting him through the head.

Sandy and Brian loved their guided tour which took two hours.

They returned to Mary's house, they enjoyed a light lunch on the deck, which Sandy had prepared. Since Brian and his wife had visited the Wright Brothers National Memorial many times, they didn't join Margaret and Paul in the afternoon.

That night Paul inserted the USB drive into his laptop. They both read the email exchange. Paul said, "It's incriminating if Mary was murdered." His instinct told him to start investigating.

Margaret sensing his emotion said, "Let's wait until the autopsy report before we invest time examining her death." As an ex-police detective, she learned not to get excited by every piece of potential evidence.

On Friday they drove to Roanoke Island. In the morning they visited the Elizabethan Gardens, and the North Carolina Aquarium. They had lunch at the Avenue Waterfront Grill in Manteo. In the afternoon, they took a driving tour of the island, including the commercial fishing areas in Wanchese in the island's south end. At night as they promised themselves, they enjoyed a great seafood dinner at the Sunset Grill in Duck.

On Saturday, they took the seventy-mile drive south on Route 12 to Hatteras. They observed the repairs on Route 12 and the new temporary bridge over the new inlet on Pea Island created by Hurricane Irene.

They climbed the Hatteras light house. While waiting for the ferry to Ocracoke Island, their last stop on their drive, they attended the free North Carolina Graveyard of the Atlantic Museum. They marveled at exhibits representing some of the more than 2000 ship wrecks on the Outer Banks, including 86 ships and 4 submarines sunk during World War II. They purchased a print of the Outer Banks displaying the locations of the sunken ships. They planned to hang this print next to that of the Delaware shore that presented its ship wrecks. Before taking the ferry to Ocracoke, they stopped for lunch at the Wreck Tiki Bar.

Sunday, tired from their tour, they met with the other mourners, and prepared for Monday's funeral. Paul introduced Margaret to Eve and Stu.

Each day leading up the funeral, they discussed the potential murder of Mary Jewel and debated whether it would be a case of enough complexity to warrant their time investigating. They both agreed the autopsy had to report Mary's death a homicide before they would discuss pursuing the case with Brian.

## Chapter 3 Mary's Autopsy

Wednesday, April 25, 2012

Dr. Simpkins started Mary Jewel's autopsy at 8:00 a.m. Since the body had not experienced a traumatic injury, such as a gunshot wound, a beating, or an accident affecting her external appearance, the autopsy would start with an external examination. He restricted the internal investigation to the state of her vital organs and circulatory system.

The hospital had followed standard protocol in preparing the body for transport to the autopsy site, marking their incisions so Simpkins would not assume they were external and a probable cause of death. The life support medical tubes remained in the body. Besides Mary's corpse, the hospital sent blood samples taken during Mary's hospitalization, her clothes, and medical records. While Dr. Simpkins performed the autopsy, the Toxicology Laboratory at the Office of the Chief Medical Examiner in Raleigh tested the blood samples for poisons or unexpected levels of minerals and proteins.

After Dr. Simpkins performed the external examination, he removed and examined the organs. Since Mary had been hospitalized with heart disease symptoms, he examined the heart in more detail than the other parts of the body. He didn't find evidence of coronary artery disease; but she had a slightly enlarged heart, showing that myocarditis could have caused her sudden death. An infection, toxic poisoning, or inflammation could cause myocarditis. His initial examination did not identify the cause of death.

Dr. Simpkins sent multiple sectional slices of the myocardium, the muscular middle layer of the wall of the heart, to the toxicology lab for examination. Since he didn't discover another likely cause of death, he sent samples of all organs and tissue samples to the lab which expected to return the full test results in a week.

Dr. Bennett believed in the admonition "to do no harm." as a medical student. She realized doctors and hospitals made mistakes, but tried to minimize hers, and support hospital procedures that reduced the organization's errors. Early, in her medical career, she read the 1999 publication by the Institute of Medicine that hospital mistakes caused 98,000 deaths annually. This appalled her. Dr. Bennett realized mistakes occur because of the uncertainty of diagnostic procedures and patient errors reporting symptoms. In 2010 the Centers for Disease Control reported there were 715,000 deaths in hospitals. According to the Institute of Medicine study, hospital mistakes amounted to 13.7 percent of hospital deaths which she thought way too high to be acceptable or believable. She found the 98,000 number was developed from extrapolating evidence from a small number of records and not from hospital death data attributable to their mistakes. While some hospitals did review unexplained deaths to determine their cause, Dr. Bennett hoped hospitals would develop a more universal and accurate death reporting system.

Leapfrog, an independent organization, provided hospital safety ratings. Dr. Bennett had started her research hoping to preserve Kitty Hawks Hospital's "A" rating.

After Dr. Simpkins had completed the autopsy, he called Dr. Bennett. "The results of the physical autopsy were inconclusive. The toxicology lab should provide more information."

Dr. Simpkins explained his findings to Dr. Bennett at their noon teleconference. He summarized the autopsy and stated a toxic substance or an infection caused her myocarditis and her death. He concluded the cause of death could be an accident, homicide, or a hospital error, but they wouldn't know until they learned the final toxicology results.

# Chapter 4 Reading the Will

Saturday, April 28. 2012

Wayne Watkins, Mary's lawyer scheduled the reading of her will for 10:00 a.m.

Wayne arrived at 9:00 at the small office in a strip mall on Route 12 in Kitty Hawk to review the will and prepare for questions. He thought the reading should go well, except for the paragraphs on Mary's daughter Eve. Wayne waited for Mary's children, confident he could answer whatever they asked to their satisfaction.

Gloria, Wayne's Administrative Assistant, moved a small rectangular mahogany conference table to the front of Wayne's desk. She placed white ceramic cups, saucers, glasses, and three beverage containers on the credenza. They contained hot regular coffee, decaf, and cold water. Gloria placed a new legal tablet and a pen in front of each chair at the table. She put the signed original will plus three copies on Wayne's desk. When she finished the preparations, she sat at the receptionist desk in front of the door waiting to greet the attendees. Gloria loved working on will readings on weekends, since Wayne paid her time and a half, and she had spare time to read her latest mystery novel.

Mary's three children, Brian, Eve, and Steward, drove to Watkins's office in Brian's SUV. The wives of Brian and Stu stayed at Mary's house.

They remained silent until they reached Watkins office.

As they walked into his office, Eve smelled the strong coffee and rushed to pour a cup. The others chose their beverage, took random seats, and shook Wayne's hand, and introduced themselves.

"It's unfortunate to meet under these circumstances. This won't take long. Your mother has divided her assets equally between you three and set aside a small amount for administrating the will."

Brian looked at Eve whose face had changed. She tried to hold back a smile. Eve knew she didn't deserve an equal share for the pain and sorrow she had inflicted on her mother and had thought she might be left out of the will.

"I worked with your mother for ten years. My wife, Jane, and I have become her friends, so we were saddened by her loss. Jane played tennis with your mother at least twice a week for the last nine years. While we had a social relationship, I helped her professionally with her real estate investments, the extent of which you might not be aware, and the will. Mary liked financial secrecy. While I'm sure you would rather have you mother alive, she amassed a fortune of over $10 million."

Eve's heart throbbed. Could she keep clean with a share of that much money?

Wayne continued, "You inheritance should enable you and your families to avoid financial hardship as long as you don't squander it. Those are your mother's words, not mine, and she insisted I include them in the will."

Stu knew his mother aimed that sentence directly at him, since he had started two unsuccessful retail businesses in Cape May. The first, a print and art gallery went bankrupt within three years of its incorporation. The second business, a tee-shirt and inexpensive souvenir store lasted longer, closing its doors five years after opening. He and his wife, Gayle, had to declare personal bankruptcy to keep their house. While he didn't want to work for a salary, he had to turn over control of his finances to his wife to keep her. He hoped he had the brains and maturity to let her invest the new unearned money rather than try and control it.

Stu at thirty-six, a muscular six feet, had a charmed high school and college athletic career. He earned nine varsity letters in high school in football, basketball, and baseball. His blue eyes, black hair, and good looks made him a target of the coeds. Unfortunately, for them, he had started dating his future wife during junior year in high school. He never cheated on her.

With the arrogance of youth, he expected to be chosen as best in the league, all-star, and most valuable player. Stu won a football scholarship to the University of Maryland with stiff competition for the position of wide-receiver. He finally started in his third year of college. He majored in business administration hoping to be as successful in his own firm as he had been in high school and college sports.

While he excelled at organized athletics, he did not share the same fate in business. Stu soon learned mental competition was more critical in life than in the small physical world of sports. Anyone with a decent mind, with a body of undetermined size and speed could enter the business arena. With two failed businesses, Stu had an immense fear of repeating bankruptcy. He committed to let Gayle manage their inherited money without interfering. He'd be happy working at his job, being a parent, and living with his loving wife.

Wayne handed copies of the will to each heir. "Let's review the will. I won't read each word, but I'll summarize its main points. I prepared a diagram of your mother's bequests and the responsibilities of the heirs, so you don't have to read the will now. You can read the details after we adjourn.

"Your mother named Brian executor. He will implement the will's provisions. I know this won't happen, but if he engages in questionable activity violating the terms of the will, please call me."

Christ, Brian thought, while Wayne told me of this possibility, it sounded colder when he read it. I'd never cheat my family.

"She followed my advice and placed her assets into three trusts. Brian will administer the first two while I will administer the third. The first trust only includes your mother's home in Duck. The second trust and third provides for the distribution of her non-residence assets.

"The Duck home trust has money to pay real estate taxes and maintenance for ten years. I will modify the house deed to a property-in-common ownership, with each of you owning one-third of the home. Upon the death of the first heir, the joint ownership will increase to half. The final survivor will own one hundred percent of the home.

"There are no restrictions on siblings using the home. In the event of a scheduling problem, Brian will resolve all conflicts to the mutual satisfaction of each heir." Brian knew his mother chose him since he was the oldest, a lawyer, and the other had traits his mother hoped would resolve problems in executing the will. Brian had no problems with her decision, but had concerns he might make enemies of his siblings.

"Your mother's remaining assets will be distributed equally between the three siblings. The second trust will provide for the distribution of two-thirds of her remaining assets between Brian and Stu, who will have immediate control of their inherited assets. The second trust will expire after these assets are distributed."

"Your mother established an individual trust fund for Eve's share. I will be the trustee and give Eve adequate money for living expenses and capital expenditures for real estate and transportation. Within two weeks, Eve must send me financial accounts of her expenditures and income for the last twelve months so I can determine the monthly amount the trust fund should send her. After twenty years, provided she doesn't revert to illegal drugs and test negative in her monthly drug tests, the funds in the trust will revert to her control and this trust fund will end. If she uses drugs, the twenty-year period will restart from the time of a medically recognized date when she is certified clean of drugs."

Eve silently thanked her mother for setting up the trust and keeping her from accessing her inheritance unimpeded. With millions, she feared she'd return to drugs and either kill herself from an overdose in a few years, or a drug pusher would steal her wealth.

"Brian is in charge of selling the non-Duck house real estate assets over a five-year period. I will be the real estate lawyer for the real estate transactions. Brian will divide the money from the real estate sales equally between each of you. I will deposit Eve's share into her special trust."

Wayne completed his discussion of the will and ended by asking, "Are there questions?"

They shook their heads and murmured, "No."

Brian drove home. Speaking first, he said, "While we won't recover from losing mom soon, she wrote a great will. I don't think any of us want to contest it."

Stu and Eve nodded in agreement and began reading the details of the will.

Eve turned toward those sections affecting her. She remembered ten years earlier at twenty-one, her drug addiction followed her recovery from a car accident occurring two months after graduating from college with a computer science degree. The accident had shattered her left leg, but left her beautiful face, blonde hair, blue eyes, and figure intact. She had four operations over a year, including a knee replacement, before she regained walking without a severe limp. Eve had to resign from her job and didn't work for twelve months because the opioid pain-killers clouded her judgment and fogged her memory.

Since she couldn't bear the pain after the first operation, the surgeon, Dr. Cleary, prescribed a thirty-day supply of 80 milligram OxyContin tablets. Eve developed an addiction after a week. Dr. Cleary renewed her prescription monthly until after her recovery from the last surgery.

Eve didn't expect to experience withdrawal symptoms, since she had read in the drug company's literature that OxyContin was non-addictive. After a week of abstinence, she knew she would die if she didn't receive another pill. During the first two days, she sweated profusely during sleep when she slept. When awake, she had a runny nose, minor muscle aches, and became frantic about her ability to stay off the drug. Her condition worsened by the third day. She experienced nausea, diarrhea, and vomiting. Eve couldn't bear to live with such pain. On the fifth day of not using the drug, she waited outside Dr. Cleary's office. When she saw him walk to his car, she rushed toward him. "Doctor Cleary, please give me another prescription. I can't stand it. I'm sick without it."

"I can't because of hospital policy. However, I have some drugs at home. If you follow me, I can give you a few pills."

Ten minutes later, she parked a few car-lengths behind his and joined him as they entered the building and took the elevator to his condo in Rockville, Maryland.

The living room impressed her. It contained a black leather couch, two matching blue upholstered chairs, and a gray marble coffee table. Filled bookcases leaned against the wall opposite the door. Original modern art adorned the open walls. Two large windows to the left of the door showed an expansive view of the hills to the west.

"Have a seat. I'm having a glass of white wine. Please join me?"

She nodded "Yes," trying to survive the nausea racking her.

He handed her the glass and watched her hand shake as she moved it to her mouth for a drink, which she partially spilled. "How bad do you want the pills?" Cleary said, with the steady gaze of a predator ready to make an easy kill.

"I need it and will die without them."

"Will you do anything for it?" He said, trying not to leer and scare her away.

Eve didn't answer.

"I'm single, work hard, and don't have time to date. I have needs and I'm looking for a sex partner, someone cultured and educated, to enjoy the good life with me." He opened his arms and moved his shoulders pointing at his possessions.

Eve remained quiet staring at the pill bottle, her doctor kept twirling in front of her.

"I have a proposal that can solve both our problems. You visit me once a week and I'll give you a week's supply of what you need," Dr. Cleary said, as he carefully reeled in his prey.

Eve's fear increased as she waited.

"This way you don't have to walk the streets or steal from your family to survive. Since I don't have any STDs, you'll stay healthy as long as you don't see anyone else. Most addicts die after a few years on the street. This way you'll have no danger. If you need an escort, I'm acceptable and will be happy to oblige."

Eve didn't talk and started shaking. She hadn't decided how to respond to the doctor's proposal. Her fear of the pain continued. Withdrawal overwhelmed her.

He reached out and touched and stroked her arm. She liked his warmth. "Let's try it once, and I'll give you a week's supply. If you don't want to continue next week, I'll have no problem. Why don't you go in the bedroom, and I'll follow you." He smiled as he watched her curvaceous body move. He knew he would enjoy her.

Cleary's behavior surprised her as he took his time trying to arouse her with passionate foreplay to help her enjoy the experience. She didn't, but loved the relief the pills gave her for the next week.

Eve returned in seven days. They continued their relationship for five years. In the second month, his efforts at arousing her worked, and she enjoyed the sex and didn't think of herself as a prostitute, but as a surviving consenting adult. They socialized. Eve introduced him to her family. Since she only took drugs to keep from being sick and didn't require high doses to combat pain, she held a steady well-paying information technology job.

Eve later learned Cleary had two other drug-addicted sex slaves. One had an unforgiving husband, Tim Stables. Eve thought she had defeated OxyContin until the jealous spouse shot and killed him and the pain of withdrawal returned.

Not wanting to repeat her loss of freedom to another man, or worse, she confided in her mother and Brian. They enrolled her in a drug treatment program, and she remained clean and sober for the last five years.

When Brian stopped the car at their new joint property, she knew without him and their mother she would have died. Now she had a new financially secure future if she never returned to drugs.

Eve initially thought positively of Dr. Cleary. He took care of her and kept her off the streets and alive. A month of sobriety made her realize she had just been rationalizing their liaisons. Eve developed a deep hatred for him that expanded over the years to others who ensnared the helpless into a lifelong addiction – doctors, illegal drug pushers, and most vehemently pharmaceutical companies who lied through advertising to trap the unwary.

## Chapter 5 Attending the Funeral

Monday, April 30, 2012

In the will, Mary directed she should be buried at the Austin Cemetery, on Tillett Street on the bay side of the island in Kitty Hawk. That Monday the sky was clear and temperatures in the high 60s. Mary's three children, Brian's and Stu's spouses arrived fifteen minutes before the 10:00 a.m. funeral's start. Wayne Watkins walked in five minutes later.

Margaret and Paul scouted the area a half hour before the funeral. After parking, they walked holding hands the short distance to the bay. They enjoyed the view of the bridge from the mainland to the north and boats moving on the Inland Waterway. Looking around, Margaret said, "This place is a perfect location for a cemetery."

Paul said. "Yes, but I don't want to be buried. I want to be cremated."

Over one hundred people attended the funeral which surprised Brian, Eve, and Stu who didn't know their mother had that many friends on the Outer Banks. They only recognized thirty-six of the attendees. The unknown mourners amplified their new appreciation of their mother.

Brian asked, "Wayne did the size of the crowd surprise you?"

"No, she was very popular, volunteered in many civic groups and donated to charities that helped the poor. The Democrats tried to get her to run for local offices, but she declined. A local reporter will cover the funeral."

"I know, her paper will publish her obituary I wrote," Brian said.

"Good, I'll read it," Wayne said, wondering what unknown facts he'd learn about his former client.

Unknown to the siblings, three cops attended in plain clothes. Detective Dave Conner did not want to wait until Mary's autopsy to start collecting information on the potential homicide of one of Kitty Hawk's prominent citizens. Detectives Conner and June Devin arrived early. During the funeral, the police collected information on the attendees. Patrolman Jim Stone stood one hundred yards away from the burial site and used a small camera, with a telescopic lens to take photos of every attendee. The detectives gazed at each mourner, making mental and written notes, on their facial expressions.

Margaret and Paul approached Brian. "The funeral is about to start, we'll talk later at the house," Brian said.

The funeral staff gave Brian a microphone. He presented the initial eulogy describing the importance of his mother to him. She had financially supported him when he attended Georgetown Law School. During his speech, he spotted John Short at the periphery of the crowd. While Brian wanted to discuss his mother's death with Short, he decided not to ruin the funeral. Brian told the crowd of several memorable humorous incidents he experienced with his parents.

Stu thanked his mother for her love and financial support when his businesses when bankrupt.

Eve thanked her mother for rescuing her from the depth of drug addiction, stating that without her mother's help, she might not be alive today. Eve's words testified to Mary's parental strength.

Margaret gradually understood that Mary's children had more complex experiences than revealed in her short introduction to them before the funeral.

Several local Outer Banks residents, including her lawyer, Wayne Watkins, said a few words in praise of her.

Before the funeral, Margaret told Paul, "Hon, her children seem very nice and well adjusted. Not the type of children I used to meet as a cop."

"While they're normal, they've had difficulties."

After the speeches, Paul took pains to talk with Eve and Stu who he had watched grow from infancy to college graduates. Paul said, "Angel, let's talk to Eve."

After they walked over to her, Eve said, "Congratulations, Paul. You've picked a winner in Margaret. I've read both your books. Very exciting and realistic."

"Glad you liked them," Margaret said. "That was a great speech extolling your mother's role in your life."

"Everything I said was true. Without her and Brian, I'd have overdosed."

"Eve, I heard you had a drug problem, but I wasn't aware it was that serious," Paul said.

"Every drug problem is serious. Families are good at hiding the darkness of addiction. You still don't know the depths of my life, but I am okay now. Now, I have a successful career and a new boyfriend."

They discussed her current life for ten minutes never referring to her earlier situation.

Margaret saw Stu, walked over to him, and said, "Great, but funny speech. I didn't understand being in the private sector could be so difficult. Paul and I always worked for a public institution and didn't face the risks you did."

"It's not the risks. It's how you handle them, and I didn't do very well." They spent another fifteen minutes discussing Stu and his wife's financial plans.

At the end of the funeral, Brian invited everyone to Mary's house.

The three cops went to the station to review the photos, compare notes, and identify anyone they thought suspicious.

Mary's friends and their spouses had prepared a buffet of cold and hot foods which they placed on tables on the lawn, between the back pouch and the ocean, as soon as they returned to Mary's house. Brian had hired a bartender and a server to attend to the guests' needs. The celebration lasted for three hours. Brian relaxed when he realized John Short didn't come. He hadn't decided whether to ignore, confront, or attack him. Thankfully, he didn't have to choose.

Later in the afternoon while sitting alone on the back porch, reminiscing about his mother with his wife, Brian received a call.

"Detective Dave Conner of the Kitty Hawk Police Department here, we're investigating your mother's death as a possible homicide based upon what you told us, and Dr. Jean Bennett's request for an autopsy."

Brian's adrenaline rose, hoping he'd receive closure on her death. His chest tightened, and the room tilted as he tried to steady his focus. He wanted to find out the status of the investigation and how he could help.

"We need to talk to you at the police station at 9:00 tomorrow morning."

"I'll be there." Brian said as he grasped the back of the chair, hoping to learn why she had died so young.

## Chapter 6 Police Interview Brian

Tuesday morning, May 1, 2012

As Brian parked in front of the station the next morning, he looked forward to helping the police. After he introduced himself to Detectives Conner and Devins, they ushered him into an interview room.

Conner started the conversation. "We're not sure someone murdered your mother, but we needed to collect data before everyone leaves Duck. Tell us why you believe your mother's death involves John Short."

Brian reviewed his mother's history with Short, including her complaints when they dated and of being stalked by John after they broke up. He handed the USB drive to the detectives to support his story. Conner inserted the USB drive into a laptop. Neither detective changed their expressions as they read. When they finished, Detective Conner said, "Useful information, thanks for bringing it to us."

"Did John Short attend the funeral?" June Devins asked.

"Yes, but he kept to himself and didn't talk to anyone in the family. Short skipped the gathering at my mother's house."

"Is this John Short's picture?" Conner asked, showing him the image of the white hair, slightly overweight, handsome man.

"Yes."

"Thanks. One of our officers took photos of ninety-six individuals. Please try to identify the thirty-eight we can't, especially your family and friends. We're interested in those you don't know as well," Detective Conner said.

"As I display the photos on the laptop, tell me their name and relationship to your mother. If you only recall their name, tell me. If you don't recognize the picture, tell me. I'll enter information as you go through each picture," Detective Devin instructed.

Brian identified twenty-nine, including family members and a few of his mother's friends. He suggested, "Since I don't know all my mother's Duck friends, ask her lawyer, Wayne Watkins, and Dr. Jean Bennett, to review the pictures. Both might recognize those I didn't."

"Brian, you've been a great help. Thanks for coming. We'll look into Short's treatment of your mother and other women. But, I caution you, it will take a while before the medical examiner completes the autopsy and determines the cause of death. It might not be a homicide."

Brian drove home with mixed emotions. Thankful that the police had started an investigation but frustrated at the time it might take. He worried the autopsy might report his mother died of natural causes. He asked Sandy, Eve, Stu and Gayle to meet him on the deck where he recounted his meeting with the police. He expressed his dissatisfaction with the pace of the investigation.

"I'm concerned if they don't find anything in the autopsy, they'll never investigate our mother's death. If Short murdered her with an untraceable poison, he'll go free."

"Hopefully that won't happen," Stu said.

"Do you think Margaret and Paul would investigate our mother's death?" Brian asked.

"I'm not sure. Paul was a close friend of our family. Ask him. He might," Eve said.

# Chapter 7 John Short

Monday, April 30, 2012

John Short led a carefree life with his wife, Liz. They both met at the University of North Carolina and married after graduation. She earned an M.S. in Pharmacy and worked at CVS supporting them as John earned a Ph.D. in Chemistry at Duke University. The Chemistry Department at East Carolina University in Greenville, North Carolina hired him as an assistant professor.

Liz transferred to a CVS in Greenville and worked until two months before the birth of their first child. They had two children during his first four years of teaching. Initially, they lived in a small two-thousand square foot ranch house on a four acre, semi-wooded lot north of the Greenville downtown area and the Tar River, the perfect place for raising children. After they became established, they planned to build a larger house. They planted a garden on a cleared quarter-acre and ate organic vegetables.

In his second year of teaching, John realized on a professor's salary he couldn't live the life style he had promised his wife and wanted for his children. After enjoying teaching and writing academic papers, he decided to abandon the tenure quest and chose a career to make him rich.

The corporate life attracted John. The multi-million dollar salaries of executive management excited him. But, he soon discovered, after talking to fellow Ph.D. chemistry graduates that those with his technical background seldom achieved high management positions. Rather, they spent their time in labs researching the next profitable chemical product for their company. If the Ph.D. made a discovery, the company and not the researcher owned the patent. They would only receive a salary, not royalty generated wealth. He abandoned the search for a corporate position.

John rejected a government career for the same reason as he planned to abandon academia – poor salaries.

In the first week of his fourth year of teaching, he confided to Liz, "I'm searching for another career. I don't get paid enough." He tried not to smile as he revealed his long-held secret dream to his wife.

"We live a comfortable life. Look around." She cleared her throat and wondered why her husband didn't realize how they prospered compared to others who didn't have incomes allowing them to save for the future.

"We'll need a new and bigger house as the kids get older. Even if I get tenure, we won't be able to afford one." Brian lost his battle of not smiling and reached over and kissed her, wanting her to join his new quest.

Liz thought him wrong about a new house, unless he had grandiose plans for a mansion. She wondered if he had decided on a specific job change and planned to tell her.

"I've concluded we'd have to start our own business. But I haven't decided what type." His eyes beamed and body became rigid as he continued to tell his wife.

If she could divert his plans by suggesting time-consuming activities, maybe he'd forget his fantasies and become a happy tenured professor. "Before you quit teaching, find out how to run a business. From working at CVS, I learned technical skills aren't enough to make a company thrive. You should learn accounting, finance, business law, and organizational behavior before we incorporate," Liz said. She doubted he would follow her advice.

"Isn't running a business common sense?" He thought chemistry had difficult processes to master compared to the non-intellectual activities required to run a company.

"No, it's legal processes, business procedures, and managing people. That's why they have a business school at the university. I suggest you audit business courses in the time you have left teaching. Running a business includes hidden costs and laws we can't ignore."

He remained quiet for a minute, thinking over his wife's advice. "Perhaps you're right. I'll start with George Smathers, an accounting professor. He should let me sit in his introductory course."

Liz hoped he would tire of studying non-chemistry topics.

While learning business procedures, he investigated the type of company a Ph.D. chemist could form and expect to make a six- or seven-figure income. He analyzed a consulting firm, a chemical company, and an import/export firm. He understood he didn't have enough of a reputation to charge high consulting fees. Formation of a chemical company and the infrastructure to produce chemical products exceeded the $200,000 they had saved from their salaries and had inherited from Liz's parents. John realized without a patentable molecule he couldn't borrow from a bank or raise money in financial markets. He rejected an import/export company since he didn't have time to learn the mysteries of international chemical trading.

As they ate lunch on a Saturday afternoon a year after he had first mentioned changing his career, he asked his wife for advice. "I reviewed several options for forming my company but other than it having something to do with chemistry, I haven't decided what to produce and sell. Do you have any ideas?"

Liz had watched with amazement as John had taken the courses she had recommended. She became caught up in his entrepreneurial spirit and suggested a company that would involve her. "We could be successful by starting a compounding pharmacy." She smiled, as she reached for her glass of ice tea.

"We can't compete against the chains." John wondered if asking her was smart.

"Correct. A compounding pharmacy is not the same as a drug store that sells directly to the public. They change the delivery system of an FDA-approved drug, a pill for example, for a patient who cannot take it in this form to one they could take. If a patient can't take the pill form of a drug, we could create a liquid for injection. Compounding pharmacies sell directly to regular pharmacies, not to individuals."

"How do we start?" John had changed his mind on his wife's participation. Knowing her habit of giving long answers he raised his roast-beef sandwich to his mouth.

"Get approval by the state. It should be easy since they require a qualified pharmacist to manage the drug part of the business. I'll fill that position. Since you're taking management courses, you can handle the business end. Your chemistry Ph.D. will help. As we get bigger, we can become an outsourcer to the large drug companies and sell them the FDA-approved drugs for which they own the patent. You have the skills to develop the chemical process to produce the drugs."

"You're the expert in pharmaceuticals. How long will it take and what will it cost?" He sipped ice tea waiting for her response.

"I'll draw up a plan, schedule, and cost estimates to find out. Then we can proceed if it is reasonable. We can start sooner than you might think. Our land is perfect for building a small drug processing plant. We don't have to wait until your six-year teaching contract ends. I can begin working as soon as we decide to start." She took a few potato chips from her plate.

"So you supported me through graduate school and now you'll support me through a career change." John realized he had underestimated his wife throughout his marriage.

"Of course. We have a great marriage and forming a business partnership will strengthen it." Since they had finished eating, he stood up, kissed her and led her into the bedroom.

In 1982, during his fifth year at the university, they applied to the state to incorporate as Greenville Pharma.

They used their savings to start the company. Liz imported inexpensive generic ingredients from India and China. She tested them to ensure their quality. Liz used her personality and contacts to market the company to the pharmacies in Eastern North Carolina. Her skill in creating the compounds at a lower cost than their competitors ensured a rapid growth for the firm. Greenville Pharma's revenues increased twenty-five percent annually for the first twenty years, starting at $75,000 in 1982 and ending at $6.5 million in 2002. With John's help, the company grew, but Liz was the principal force behind its success.

As a reward for their accomplishment, Liz and John agreed to build a large, modern house in 1993. John took on the responsibility for its design and hiring the builders. They decided on a six-thousand square foot two-story brick home with five bedrooms, an indoor pool, studies for each parent, a fully equipped gym, and a three-car garage. Liz convinced her husband, they will need the extra bedrooms in less than fifteen years, when their kids visit with the grandchildren. She told him they needed the gym and an indoor pool to stay healthy. It took a year to build and furnish the new home.

Since Short enjoyed teaching and the opportunities it presented, he became an adjunct professor when he left his full-time job at the university. He taught one course per semester.

While he had a good marriage with Liz, he thought it okay to cheat with coeds who wanted higher grades without studying. He didn't see a conflict with his marriage vows as long as he didn't hurt his wife and kept her sexually satisfied. While he loved his wife, he couldn't resist the willing coeds and became addicted to them.

Liz caught him, in 2002 with an employee of Greenville Pharma and threatened a divorce. She hired a private detective who discovered his multiple past transgressions. While a successful adulterer for twenty-six years, he discovered being caught once could ruin his life.

Liz fumed, since she considered the concept and success of their company driven by her, not him. Liz demanded he give her control of Greenville Pharma. When he objected she said, "It's the best solution for you. Even though you took a few management courses, you don't have the skills or drive to grow the company. When I take over, you'll still stay rich. If you run it, we'll be bankrupt and poor in a year."

John bristled at her comments, but realized they were true. He had a greater interest in coeds and divorcees than money.

Liz died on Monday, June 3, 2002, after being rushed to the hospital with pain in her chest and numbness in her arms and legs. John heard she had an appointment with a lawyer on Wednesday to discuss filing for divorce. Her physician cited heart failure on the death certificate. John had her cremated two days later.

Short knowing he didn't have the technical skills to supervise manufacturing the compound drugs, promoted David Winthrop. He overlooked that Winthrop had argued with his boss, Liz Short. Winthrop championed rapidly expanding the company, while she preferred a conservative steady growth to minimize the risk of bankruptcy.

With the new chief pharmacist the business continued growing. Short had more free time to pursue his main hobby – women.

After his wife's death, he decided it was too dangerous to find lovers in the firm. If caught, the company Board of Directors might force him to resign to keep the scandal away from the company.

Short used the internet to search for his next relationship. Being good-looking and wealthy, he had no trouble getting dates. Since he now had homes in Greenville and Duck, he enrolled in four internet dating sites and tried to develop unique relationships in both areas.

Mary Jewel had married in an era when many women were virgins or had only made love to their husbands before they wed. Becoming a widow shocked her. Her sex life had ended and loneliness consumed her. When she went to bed at night or woke up in the morning, she had no one to talk to. Desperate for companionship she responded to John Short's internet post nine months after the death of her husband.

On their first date on a Saturday in 2011, John met her at the

Sunset Grille in Duck, one of her favorite restaurants. John's conversation and looks thrilled her. She readily gave him her phone number. After the date, she felt inadequate, not knowing how to act on her first date in forty years with a man not her husband.

John liked her unblemished smooth complexion, blue eyes, and shoulder-length blonde hair. They were the same height. He couldn't wait to cuddle with her and press her large breasts against his chest. He took her to dinner at the Black Pelican in Kitty Hawk the next weekend. John became confident as the dinner progressed that he would have sex with Mary that evening. However, she didn't invite him in after the date. He drove home crestfallen and eventually angry. When he arrived home, he poured a Scotch to help him relax.

The next day, Mary surprised him by calling and asking, "Would you like to play tennis next Saturday afternoon and have dinner at my house?"

She had asked advice on dating from a widow friend who suggested she should reciprocate John's dinner dates to show him she was interested.

"Yes. What time?" His aggravation with Mary changed to anticipation.

"Pick me up at my house at 4:00. My development has tennis courts."

They each won a set, surprising them both. Mary liked that they had equal skills in tennis, since it should help them develop their relationship slowly.

John wasn't as happy as Mary, since he liked to dominate his women.

After they walked back to her house, she said, "Care for a drink? I have water, soda, beer, and wine."

"Beer, I need to replace the potassium I sweated out playing tennis." He smiled as he stared directly at her chest.

Mary handed him a Heineken and took one, "Can I give you a tour of my home?"

"Yes."

John followed her, staring at her sensuous hips as she walked upstairs to the second floor, and showed him the four bedrooms and a view of the ocean from the second story deck. "The master bedroom is on the first floor. I hardly ever come up here. The third floor has two more bedrooms and a large game room. We don't have to go there."

"The house is nice and spacious. I guess you need it when your children and their families visit." John assumed this would be his last visit to this floor.

"Yes, I do. Often two families show up at the same time, and the younger kids sleep on cots in the game room." Mary walked him downstairs and showed him her spacious bedroom.

"It's big. I love the shower and Jacuzzi," John said hoping he would experience them that night.

"I've prepared lasagna." She put it in the oven. "It should be ready in thirty minutes." She also served a garden salad and rolls. They sat at a dining room table in the great room, since the house didn't have a separate dining room.

John discussed his marriage and how he missed his wife. He tried to and gained her sympathy. They each had several glasses of Chianti with dinner. She told him about life with her late husband and how she missed him. Mary enjoyed the dinner conversation.

After she placed the glasses and dishes in the dishwasher, Mary asked, "Do you have time for coffee or brandy?"

"Brandy. Even decaf, keeps me awake."

"Have a seat, I'll get us some."

He chose a loveseat.

Mary sat in a chair next to him. They continued talking. John became impatient and asked, "Mary, why don't you sit next to me?"

"I want to go slow and get to know you before we get physical." She looked at her watch, "It's getting late, and I have to be up early to play tennis tomorrow morning." Mary thought her lack of sexual desire for a man that attracted her normal after having a husband die so recently.

Rather than argue, John stood up and said, "I'll call you to schedule our next tennis match."

Mary said, "I'll look forward to it," as she walked him to the door. He bent toward her lips to kiss her, but she turned her face so he kissed her on the cheek.

Driving home, he thought what a challenge. John's competitive spirit grew as he vowed to seduce her.

The couple played tennis and had dinner four more times in the next two weeks. On the last two dates, she had consented to a good-night kiss. John wondered if he should give up, especially after she won both sets in their last match.

Mary consulted with her widowed friend, who said, "Never win both sets, if you want to keep dating him. Men have fragile egos. Also it won't do any harm to make out with him as long as he stops when you ask, and you enjoy it. If you aren't thrilled after knowing him this long, you should drop him."

Their next date ended with dinner at Mary's house. After dinner he sat in the love seat, Mary sat next to him and handed him a brandy. They talked for fifteen minutes. John placed his glass on a lamp table and kissed her. She enjoyed it and deepened the kiss. John became uncontrollably excited as her breasts pressed against his chest.

They continued kissing and embracing for another five minutes. John then confident started to caress her breasts. She froze and said, "Let's slowdown," and wiggled out of his arms.

Dejected, he complied.

Mary said, "I'm new to this. I like you and want to keep seeing you, but I'm not ready for sex." Mary wondered why she liked John, but had no desire to make love to him.

"Sorry, I misinterpreted you. I want to see you again. You'll set the pace of our relationship."

John behaved himself on their next date, never progressing beyond making out. When alone, he detested himself. He couldn't stand being dominated by a woman and planned long and hard how he could seduce her. Once they had sex, he believed she would act normal. Others had, why not Mary?

As they kissed and cuddled, the next time John sat with Mary on the loveseat, he maneuvered his body so he was on top of her. He planned to immobilize her.

"Stop, let me go."

"No, just enjoy it."

As he searched for her lips for a kiss, he felt a sharp pain in his genitals that grew when he moved. She had kneed him. He released her, and she attacked him three more times. He withered in pain on the loveseat.

"No one is going to rape me. I should call the police. Just leave."

The pain intensified as he tried to stand. "I'll leave, but give me a few minutes."

"Hurry." She went to her desk opened a side drawer and took out a Glock. She disengaged the safety and pointed it at John. "You have two minutes. If you ever tell anyone in Duck about us, I'll have you charged with attempted rape."

When alone, she locked the doors and engaged the house alarm. Still shaking, she walked into her bedroom.

Mary, disgusted at his behavior, sick of ever having known him, wondered why she had spent so much time with him. She wanted to remove any odor or touch of his from her body. Mary took a hot shower.

Mary poured herself a double-Scotch and soda and sipped it, hoping to end her tension headache. She put the gun on a bedside night table, went to bed, and read. If he returned, and tripped the alarm, she planned to be ready. Then she'd have an excuse to shoot him. She didn't sleep for two hours.

As he walked to his car, John Short wanted to kill Mary Jewel. He sat behind the wheel for several minutes before he drove away. On the short trip to his Duck beach house, his emotions changed from anger to fear. If she went to the police and accused him of attempted rape, she'd end his Don Juan life style.

Why wasn't she the same as other women who either continued to be his lover or kept quiet after he forced himself? After he arrived home, he poured himself a large Scotch on the rocks, and decided to obey Mary's threat. He'd never mention their relationship to anyone.

Two weeks later his fear turned to vengeance. While he still resented her treatment of him, and lost his lust for her, he wanted to make her life miserable. He sent her an email, ordering her not to date anyone else, threatening her life if she did. When in Duck, he visited places she frequented. He wanted her to feel the fear of being stalked. Short sent different versions of the first email to torment her on a weekly basis. Short had no intention of carrying out his threat. He just wanted to make her wretched and depressed.

He knew his terrorizing game had worked when he received emails from her asking him to stop. He never answered them directly but kept sending her poison emails. After a month, Short quit contacting her when she threatened to go to the police.

# Chapter 8 Brian Asks Margaret and Paul to Investigate

Tuesday, May 1, 2012

After telling his family about his police interview, Brian called Margaret.

"I need to see you and Paul before you leave. Can we talk over coffee in a few minutes?" Brian asked.

"Let me check with Paul," Margaret said.

Paul said, "Okay."

"I can be at your hotel in fifteen minutes."

"Let's meet in the breakfast room," Margaret said.

Brian rushed in looking harried and face drawn.

"Brian, are you okay?" Paul asked.

"The police interviewed me this morning," Brian said. "I gave them a copy of the USB drive that I gave you with Short's and my mother's emails. They seemed to take them seriously, but said they declined to investigate Short until the medical examiner concluded that Mom's death was a homicide. I don't want to wait. I'm asking you to investigate Short before the medical examiner issues his report."

"Do you mind if we discuss our answer alone. We'll give you a call in ten minutes," Margaret said. She looked at Paul, concerned she had upset Brian.

Brian bracing for disappointment said, "That's fine. I'm driving to my mother's house. My cell phone will be on."

After Brian left the hotel, Margaret said, "Hon, I don't think we should interfere with the police, especially when we don't know if someone murdered her, but you knew the family. You decide."

"Brian could be reacting to his mother's death, wanting to blame someone since he felt cheated losing her early. It's easier to believe someone murdered her than thinking she had an unexpected natural death. Of course, he could be right. Even if he's correct, I agree, we don't have the local backup resources this time we had with the Delaware State Police in our last two investigations. Let's enjoy our visit here. I think we should wait until the autopsy states death by homicide before we accept his invitation. If someone murdered her, as a long-time friend of the family, I want to help catch them."

"I'll call him, and tell him our decision," Margaret said.

When Margaret called Brian he said, "I understand. Is it okay if I keep you informed if the medical examiner reports her death a homicide?"

"Yes, if she was murdered, we want to help you find the killer." Paul said.

When he arrived at the beach house, Brian summoned Eve, Stu and their spouses to meet on the rear porch He summarized his discussion with Margaret and Paul.

Stu spoke first. "Let's not do anything. I agree with Margaret and Paul, we should wait for the autopsy. If it's homicide, let the police handle it. We can't expect Margaret and Paul to work for free."

"I support Stu. Let's not involve others. We need to grieve Mother right now." Eve said.

Brian, disappointed, said, "Okay, perhaps it's best. However, since it might be a homicide, don't throw away any of her possessions until the medical examiner concludes she died from natural causes."

## Chapter 9 Leaving the Outer Banks

Tuesday afternoon May 1, 2012

Stu and Gayle drove to Wayne Watkins's office on their way home. Gloria, Watkins's admin, asked, "Can I get you something to drink?"

Both said, "Water."

Gloria led them to an empty meeting room. They sat at a round mahogany table. Gloria gave them bottles of water and said, "Wayne will be with you in a moment."

Wayne entered and said, "Stu, I enjoyed your tribute to your mother. She was an exceptional woman. What can I do for you?"

"After listening to the trust fund you set up for Eve on Saturday, we want you to set up one for us so my wife, Gayle, not me, controls our inheritance," Stu said.

"Okay," Wayne said. "But you have to tell me how you want it structured."

"I've gone bankrupt twice and want to preserve our inheritance. We need a small monthly stipend to supplement our income, and we want to set up a college fund to finance our kids' education without them going into debt."

"That's easy." Wayne said, "I'll write a trust fund for you and Gayle and set up accounts for your children. We can transfer money from the annual earnings of your fund into the kids' college accounts so we don't affect your trust fund's principal. With those contributions and normal growth, your kids will be set. How much of a monthly stipend do you want?"

"Enough to pay off our mortgage in ten years," Stu answered.

"Send me the amount of your remaining mortgage, interest rate, and remaining term so I can figure out what you need. You might want to refinance since you should get a lower rate for a shorter term," Wayne said.

"What happens if I die?" Gayle asked Wayne.

"Do you and Stu have wills?"

"No," Stu said.

"Then, we'll draw up wills for both of you and include identification of a new trustee to replace Gayle if she passes."

"Make sure it's not me. We want to name my brother Brian," Gayle said.

"After our meeting, I'll write a draft. Since you live in Cape May, New Jersey, we'll develop the documents via email. The final documents which I'll mail you have to be signed and notarized by each of you for the wills and both for the new trust. Gayle, you'll have to get Brian's permission in writing for him to be named a trustee. Have you considered how you want to invest? I could include instructions in the trust so you could restrict placing your funds in specific investments." Wayne said.

He smiled, knowing he had helped save Stu and Gayle from a third bankruptcy. This session, helping his friend's children, was one of the reasons he had become a lawyer.

"We want to eliminate risk so we don't lose part of the inheritance. No stock market speculation. Invest the money in areas yielding risk-fee growth," Stu said in a strong voice, showing the confidence he had acquired from recognizing and overcoming his financial weaknesses.

"Tax-free municipal bonds are your best bet," Wayne said.

"I plan to enroll in a Finance Master's program to learn asset management," Gayle said, her eyes beaming at her husband's recent behavior.

Wayne said, "I have the information I need to structure the documents."

Stu and Gayle left Watkins's office confident in their financial future. "That was easy," Stu said.

"Yes, and it's time we have a personal lawyer and signed wills. I can't wait to start my finance courses. They have to be more exciting than the education classes I've taken over the years."

After the meeting, they drove home to Cape May.

Eve met with Wayne Watkins at 3:00 p.m. to discuss her trust fund. She was adamant to adhere to the restrictions of the will and stay sober.

The addiction had cost her too much. After Dr. Cleary's murder and before the police arrested him, Tim Stables had stopped her on Park Avenue in Friendship Heights near her apartment. He said, "I discovered your relationship with Cleary."

"How?"

"Let's go to Starbucks and I tell you."

They both ordered a grandee Americano.

"I've been following him and saw you together. He had the same relationship with my wife, unknown to me, and gave her gonorrhea. Since there are few symptoms in women, the infection grew until she became sterile. I suggest you get tested. Maybe it hasn't progressed as much in you. He won't bother you anymore."

Eve didn't immediately respond. Cleary had led her to believe she was his only lover and therefore safe. Since he hadn't answered his phone for three days, and because of the tone and certainty of Stables's voice she knew she never see him again.

"Sorry to shock you, but I thought you should be aware of the disease."

"I'll see a doctor." She left the coffee shop. "Thanks for the warning."

Eve panicked at her initial reaction to Cleary's death and the potential disease. At least she had a month's supply of opioids, before withdrawal pains wracked her body. Cleary trusted her after two years and changed the drug disbursement from weekly to monthly, since Eve never missed showing up at his condo, when summoned.

Eve used the same family doctor as Brian. No way would she ask Dr. O'Conner to test her for an STD. She feared Brian might find out.

She decided to use Planned Parenthood, based upon what she had read about them in maintaining patient confidentially.

Eve tested positive and received a prescription for antibiotics. The attending nurse told her the doctor, by law, has to fill out a form and send it within one day after the test yields positive results to the Maryland Department of Public Health. Eve didn't know about this requirement. She had no problem answering the question on listing her sexual partners. Cleary was the only one. She smiled when the nurse asked for his contact information. Eve replied, "He is dead." Her only pleasant thought during the testing.

Two weeks later, Planned Parenthood tested her fertility. Eve learned she could never have children, something she had wanted since being a teenager. She cried for a week and thought Stables killing Cleary justified.

Eve's bitterness grew during four years of sobriety as she learned how the pharmaceutical companies who sold opioids escaped prosecution, but the lowly heroin pushers received long prison terms.

Eve continued to build resentment against anyone who helped trapped innocents into addiction, especially after she became sober.

After her mother's death, she decided to replace Stables's revenge with her own by murdering others responsible for mass opioid addictions and thousands of overdose deaths.

Eve accepted a bottle of water when she arrived at Watkins's office.

"Thanks for emailing your income figures and expenses," Watkins said, "They show you live well. Since you've been at Information Management Associates for four years, can I assume your salary will continue to increase in the future?"

"Yes, IMA is a medium size IT firm with twenty-two years of steady growth. The company expects to grow at least ten percent annually. While I can live on my salary, my car is seven years old, and I hate paying rent for my apartment."

"That seems reasonable. Have you decided on a new car or location?"

"No, I'll start looking tomorrow when I return to Chevy Chase."

"Since my role is to make sure your inheritance lasts, please don't buy a luxury car or an expensive house."

"Don't worry. I prefer a Toyota over a Lexus. They're a waste of money. I'd rather pay cash for the car than take out a loan. I'll look for a condo, not a house. We have the same goals. I'll select the condo so I only need the down payment from the trust fund and can make the monthly mortgage payments from my salary."

"Send me what you want. If they're reasonable, I'll send the checks for the car to the dealer and a down payment for the condo. "

"I'll send the car specs soon. The condo will take a little longer."

"The will requires you to take a drug test monthly. Dr. Bennett will write an order for the drug test. I have contacted a LabCorp testing office near your apartment and scheduled monthly tests. When you move, I'll find a testing location near the new condo."

Eve returned to the Duck house, planning to drive to Chevy Chase in the morning. She did not look forward to the tests and realized she had to be careful and stay away from food, such as poppy seed rolls, that might result in a positive test.

On the drive home, Eve smiled as she remembered she had told Margaret and Paul, she had a boyfriend. Six months ago, she didn't have one. Eve reflected how much had changed in her life since she became sober. After realizing how Cleary had used her, she had vowed never again to give herself to a man for drugs and suppressed her sex drive. Eve refused relationships with men for three years. Counseling helped her realize all men weren't the same as Cleary and her libido slowly returned.

Since she had given up drinking as part of her recovery, she never went to bars. Like most lonely American single adults, she joined internet dating sites. Being attractive she had no trouble being inundated with invitations. However, she found most of the men had either tobacco, alcohol or drug addictions; or were players interested only in sex and not a permanent relationship. Some were uneducated, poor, or had lied about their background.

Eve did meet several men who interested her and went out on enjoyable dates. Her fear and hatred for men died gradually so no relationship lasted more than three dates. She never reached the point of being sexually interested in her dates. After a year and a half, she quit the internet dating scene.

Several of her friends told her that work is the best place to meet someone. She realized it could also be the worst if the relationship ended badly, and her fellow employees knew both partners. So, she tended to stay away from the advances of her co-workers.

On a warm December Saturday, six months earlier, Eve decided to ride her bike on the C&O canal tow path from Georgetown in DC to the Great Falls Tavern Visitors Center in Maryland. She planned to complete the outbound leg of the seventeen-mile journey in less than an hour. As a reward she planned a relaxed picnic lunch of homemade chicken salad, chocolate-chip cookies, and water.

The thought of a bike ride to Great Falls, a portent of the end of fall excited her. Eve planned to stay in shape during the winter by exercising outdoors in the Washington metropolitan area. Each weekend, she planned to travel to different locations between the Atlantic Ocean and the mountains of West Virginia, unless it snowed, rained, or fell below freezing.

At Great Falls, she took her picnic lunch to a table overlooking the tow path and watched the runners starting, finishing, or continuing, the families strolling or picnicking, and everyone enjoying themselves.

The serenity of the moment ended when a voice she knew, but initially could not place said, "Eve, I see you had the same idea as we did, enjoying a picnic on the Potomac River."

She squinted looking into the sun and recognized the speaker as Joe Kelly who worked in the marketing department. Two young girls held each one of his hands.

"Hi Joe, great day to visit the park."

"It is. My daughters and I are walking south on the tow path to the Billy Goat Trail. Emma, the oldest, is holding my left hand, her sister Ruth the other. Kids say hello to Eve. We work together."

After they said, "Hi," Eve responded, "I'm on a short bike ride from Georgetown. I try to ride whenever it's warm."

The two fidgeting girls pulled at Joe's hands. "Eve, nice seeing you. My kids are impatient, I have to go."

Eve watched them leave thinking, strange I didn't know he had a wife. Joe doesn't wear a ring. Well that's another eligible man I'll have to cross off my list.

On Monday morning, Joe stopped by her cubicle, "It was nice to see you on Saturday. Too bad I couldn't stay and talk, but my daughters had begged me all week to take them for a canal walk."

"That's okay. I remember the importance of a daughter's time with her dad. I wasn't aware you were married."

"My wife died three years ago from cancer. I don't talk about her at work." He paused, trying to read Eve's reaction, which was a combination of surprise and sorrow. "I try to spend as much time outdoors as I can with my kids so they'll appreciate nature and exercise."

"Sorry about your wife," Eve said shocked and saddened, she knew very little about the person she had worked with for two years. "I grew up in upstate New York and nature was everywhere. Here in DC, one has to search it out."

"Sometimes my parents babysit for me. Would you like to join me for a walk on the canal tow path?"

"I'd enjoy that, but I can't." Eve noticed Joe's disappointment, "I had knee replacement surgery years ago, and I'm not supposed to go on long walks, which is why I bike."

Eve didn't want to offend Joe and give him the wrong idea that she didn't like him. "I'm having lunch at noon in the cafeteria today, why don't you join me?" The rapid change in Joe's facial expression from rejection to happiness surprised her.

"I'll meet you there."

Eve had amazed herself by asking Joe to lunch. She always thought him cute, but given her reservations on dating a co-worker, hadn't sought him out as a potential boyfriend. She liked his smile, handsome face, trim body, black hair, and blue eyes.

At lunch, they exchanged personal information on their likes and dislikes and aimed their conversations toward topics designed to impress the other. Eve learned he was four years older than she. It pleased her to hear, he had interests in classical music, the local Washington area stage, books, and liberal politics. She already knew and approved of his love of the outdoors.

Eve smiled when he told her, "I live in a development with large townhouses in Rockville on Tuckerman Lane."

He had answered the question of geographical desirability affirmatively, since they lived less than ten miles apart.

At the end of the lunch, he gave her a business card with his cell phone number on it. She reciprocated and gave him permission to call her.

That Saturday, they attended a Baltimore Symphony concert at Strathmore Center off Rockville Pike in Bethesda. He drove to the Willard Apartments in Friendship Heights, Maryland, arriving at 6:30.

Joe surprised her when she opened her door. As in most IT firms, she only saw him in casual clothes. Eve's eyes opened, she stood still and stared at him and couldn't resist saying, "Wow."

Joe wore a navy blue blazer, creased gray pants, a light blue oxford shirt, and a solid burgundy tie.

He laughed, and said "Sorry I didn't tell you I'll be dressing for the symphony."

"You look great. If any of my friends see us together, they'll be jealous," Eve thought I should have noticed him a few years ago. What a magnificent way to start our first date.

He stepped back as he took her in. "You look ravishing," Joe said, looking at her low-cut black cocktail dress. He never knew she had a sensual body, since at work she wore baggy slacks and loose shirts or sweaters.

"Come in," Eve said. "Let me get a coat." She tried not to stare at him.

As he walked past her, the aroma of her Red Door perfume further excited him. He knew they already had a successful evening, even if Beethoven's Ninth Symphony disappointed them.

They arrived at the concert hall early and had a light dinner before the music started. They enjoyed the phenomenal music in the acoustically perfect wood-trimmed hall.

On the drive home, she hoped he wouldn't pressure her for sex. Eve became apprehensive during the elevator ride to the eighth floor. When they reached her apartment, she invited him in for coffee, but he looked at his watch and said, "I want to, but I told my sitter I'd be home by 10:00."

Eve didn't know whether to be relieved not to have to face Joe's sexual hunger or be unhappy thinking he wasn't interested.

She wasn't aware that Joe shared similar fears of dating. Tonight was his first serious date since his wife had died, and he didn't know how to act.

Their relationship progressed at a Victorian pace, rather than the rush-to-bed speed of twenty-first century romances. They learned to like each other before they achieved the milestone of intimacy.

Brian and Sandy drove home to Alexandria, Virginia after they had closed up the Duck house on Wednesday morning.

As they started the drive Sandy said, "You look tired. Do you want me to drive?"

"Not now. I'm fine, but maybe later."

"You've been busy with the funeral and the will."

"Not to mention the time I've spent with the police, my family, and Hoffman and O'Hare discussing my mother's potential murder. Perhaps, everyone is right, I should leave it to the cops."

"Managing and selling your mother's assets may take more free time than you have. I'm willing to help. My first offer is to take over scheduling visits to your mother's house."

Brian's tense shoulders relaxed. He smiled. "You give me reasons every day to say, I love you."

Sandy smiled. "I'll keep giving you reasons never to stop saying it."

# Chapter 10 Review of Mysterious Hospital Deaths

Saturday April 28, 2012

Since completing Mary's autopsy would take longer than anticipated, Dr. Simpkins went to his office on a day off and opened the three medical records of those patients who had died mysteriously at the Kitty Hawk Hospital.

He didn't anticipate learning much from the three files, but moved ahead with the work since he believed unexplained deaths caused by mistakes were a stain on the medical profession. Dr. Simpkins thought if a homicide occurred, an autopsy should always identify it as the cause of death and provide evidence of how the individual died.

He constructed a table with the names of three deceased patients placed in the first row and their demographic and physical characteristics in the cells below the first row. He added rows for medical history, drugs applied, and probable cause of death. He noted that the deceased had three different doctors, who he decided to question on Monday. Simpkins planned to examine the hospital's Quality Assurance Department reports. They were responsible for verifying that the medical procedures used on the deceased adhered to hospital procedures and accepted medical practice.

The three women were over sixty. They had lived on the Outer Banks for over ten years. One had a husband, one divorced, and one a widow. Dr. Simpkins called the two doctors, other than Dr. Bennett, and found they each had heart problems, thought to be under control before they died. The women took similar drugs for lowering blood pressure, thinning blood, and reducing cholesterol as well as standard vitamins like D, $B_{12}$, iron, and niacin. Their kidneys functioned at level 3, at between forty-eight and fifty-five percent efficiency. However, unlike Dr. Bennett, their doctors entered heart failure on the death certificate.

Dr. Simpkins read the three quality assurance reports that stated in all three cases their doctors and the hospital followed accepted procedures.

He realized, with the pressure of last week's workload, he had not sent the other two patients blood samples to the toxicology lab, an oversight he planned to correct on Monday morning.

Dr. Simpkins called Dr. Bennett, who didn't answer, and left a message making a phone appointment for Monday at noon to discuss the comparative mysterious death results. He emailed Dr. Bennett his mysterious death table.

At noon, Dr. Bennett answered her phone, "Hi, Joe, nice table, but I agree we need the toxicology analysis of the other two to make the comparisons more substantial."

"The toxicology office promised to have the test results by next Monday."

Dr. Bennett, responded, "Good, but we should expand the table to include more mysterious hospital deaths in North Carolina where the patients share the same characteristics. We need more statistics to establish a cause-and-effect link."

"Great idea."

"I'll start Wednesday afternoon." She closed her eyes and thought of the cases she'd discover that would explain the causes of the rapid deaths of the three original patients.

They both agreed to talk again after the toxicology laboratory released the test findings.

Wednesday, May 2, 2012

Dr. Bennett normally worked Wednesday mornings, using the afternoon to play golf or tennis. This day, she skipped sports and updated the mysterious death table.

On Monday, Bennett had emailed the State Center for Health Statistics asking for April's list of individuals who had died in hospitals of heart failure within two days of being admitted.

She received a response the next day identifying seven new mysterious deaths fitting the search criteria, increasing the table to ten patients. Eight of the individual's hospitals were in eastern North Carolina within a hundred miles of Kitty Hawk. The others were in the research triangle near Duke, North Carolina University, and North Carolina State. The geographic concentration of the fatalities intrigued Bennett, convincing her they might share common causes. All the patients were over sixty, consumed similar prescription drugs, and died within a day of being admitted.

Bennett investigated whether the following hospital mistakes may have caused any of the mysterious deaths:

- Hospital acquired infections,

- Improper diagnosis,

- Technical staff inadequacies, and

- Improper drug administration.

She added four rows to the table reflecting the potential medical errors in the bullet list.

Emergency rooms admitted the ten patients and kept them in isolation until their death. Each hospital told her they didn't have any patients with a virulent infectious disease. Thus, Dr. Bennett believed none of the patients could have acquired a hospital-acquired infection and die within a day of being admitted.

Improper diagnosis may have been a problem, but since only Mary Jewel had an autopsy and the others didn't, Dr. Bennett had no way of knowing if the diagnosis for the others were correct.

Dr. Bennett called each of the hospitals involved and asked for the medical qualifications of the staff treating the patients. Since they were all superb, board-qualified physicians, and had trained and experienced support staff she didn't think staff inadequacies caused any of the fatalities.

She reviewed the patient's records to identify the hospital-administered drugs and compared them with the prescriptions taken by each patient. She didn't find any FDA documented interactions between the two groups of drugs that might lead to a fatality.

Since Dr. Bennett ruled a hospital mistake unlikely for the fatalities, she examined the potential for counterfeit or adulterated drug as the cause. Bennett learned about the dangers of counterfeit drugs since the growth in the generic drug industry in the 1990s. She had to get the patients prescription drugs to test the proposition that their drugs were counterfeit and fatal. She silently cursed the criminal elements of the pharmaceutical industry.

As a young doctor, she read about the case of the compounding pharmacist, Robert Courtney, who diluted the cancer drugs, Taxol and Gemzar, before distributing them to patients, many of whom died earlier than expected. Courtney received a prison sentence of thirty years for the counterfeit drug offense. He admitted to adulterating drugs involving 4,200 patients, 400 physicians, and 98,000 prescriptions. Dr. Bennett believed he deserved to die. Since then, she had been adamantly crusading against counterfeit drugs. She knew that despite her and other physicians' protests, the legitimate drug industry's opposition, and the FDA's expanded campaign to combat these killer drugs, counterfeit drug organizations had developed into a major international crime industry.

Dr. Bennett knew India and China produced most counterfeit drugs, and the U.S. imported over eighty percent of its counterfeit drugs. U.S. doctors purchased them directly from the manufacturers or from brokers and gave them to their patients. Brokers also sold them to the major drug stores. These illegally imported drugs had container labels, FDA imitation documentation, and pill labels hard to differentiate from the legal drugs. Sometimes patients not able to afford the high U.S. prescription drug prices ordered them over the internet from domestic or foreign drug websites.

# Chapter 11 Mary's Toxicology Report

September 1, 2010

At her last physical exam before her husband Gary's death in 2010, Dr. Bennett told Mary, "Your body is a testimony to exercise, proper diet, a happy marriage, and a successful heart operation last year for maintaining your health. I wish all my patients would follow your example."

"Thanks. Do I have any potential problems?" Mary asked.

"No, the MRI shows your heart is perfect. Your circulatory system shows no sign of blockage, your bones are strong, and you're not depressed, despite the situation with two of your children years ago. Your blood tests reported a healthy liver and kidneys."

Mary's husband died two weeks later. The shock of being alone didn't strike until after the stress of the funeral. Her children had returned to their homes, and she had to spend the night alone in the spacious, quiet, and isolated Duck house. Sleep came hard and crying easy. After four days, she called Dr. Bennett and asked for medicine to help her sleep and end her depression.

"Mary, I'll prescribe a serotonin reuptake inhibitor (SSRI) a new class of antidepressant drugs. It's different from what you took when your kids had their problems. SSRIs have fewer side effects than your earlier antidepressant, Imipramine. However, returning to your old athletic life-style, communicating and maintaining a relationship with your family and friends is the best cure for situational depression."

Dr Bennett didn't know using Imipramine could cause myocarditis disease and that stopping the drug would not repair the damage it had caused. Mary last took Imipramine in 2008.

Mary started taking the 60 mg pill of a generic version of Celexa.

The drug relieved her depression. But, Mary experienced the side effect of libido loss. She didn't enjoy being a widow, but she performed her required life-sustaining activities.

In August 2011, the FDA published a warning that daily prescriptions of Celexa should not exceed 40 milligrams, since a dose above 40 milligrams may lead to heart failure and death. Dr. Bennett lowered Mary's prescription to 40 milligrams.

Wednesday, May 2, 2012

Dr. Simpkins called Dr. Bennett, "Jean, I've received a preliminary report on Mary Jewel's blood toxicology report. I'll email you a copy. Call me after you've read it."

Dr. Bennett cringed when she read Mary had a high prevalence of Celexa in her blood, showing she might had taken the equivalent of 60 mg of Celexa daily. Mary had a blood alcohol content of .06 percent. Had she been self-medicating with alcohol and too much Celexa?

Concerned, Dr. Bennett called Dr. Simpkins.

Dr. Simpkins answered, "I've updated the autopsy, but I can't finish it until I resolve whether Mary Jewel overdosed with Celexa or if she took an adulterated drug. Can you get me her remaining Celexa tablets for analysis?

"I'll call her son, Brian. Hopefully they haven't thrown them away."

While the autopsy showed Mary Jewel had died of a drug overdose, to Jean Bennett's relief, it also proved the hospital didn't make a mistake since the staff had not given her Celexa during her short stay. Jean would be spared the ordeal of reporting the mistake to the hospital's quality assurance group and having to participate in an investigation of how to improve procedures so the mistake would never be repeated. The overdose information meant the hospital would keep its "A" safety rating.

While relieved, the hospital wasn't at fault; her medical curiosity drove Dr. Bennett to wonder how Mary had such a high level of Celexa in her blood stream. She thought Mary either took too many 40 mg pills or that they should investigate whether she had obtained and taken adulterated or counterfeit pills.

"Brian, this is Dr. Bennett. The medical examiner has told me he needs your mother's prescriptions to complete the autopsy report. Do you still have them?"

"Yes, they're in her medicine cabinet. I'll drive to Kitty Hawk tomorrow and give them to you."

"I'll be in my office all day. Call me tomorrow and tell me when you expect to arrive."

"I'll be there at 1:00. Why do you need the drugs?"

"I'll explain when I see you."

Thursday, May 3, 2012

Brian located his mother's weekly pill container. The pill bottles in her medicine cabinet contained eight drugs: Celexa, lisinopril (blood pressure), coumadin, (blood thinner), atorvastatin (cholesterol reducing), vitamins D, $B_{12}$, iron, and niacin. The first four were prescription drugs. He took the pill container and the bottles to Dr. Bennett, who said, "The medical examiner found your mother had a high level of Celexa in her blood. Only two things could account for this. She intentionally took too much Celexa or unintentionally ingested an adulterated drug. I don't think your mother would have knowingly overdosed. She didn't have an addictive personality."

Brian slumped in the chair, surprised at this information that confirmed his suspicions.

"We'll send all her drugs to the toxicology center in Raleigh to test them for purity and integrity."

"How long will it take?" Brian asked.

"Not long. It depends on their workload."

Before sending the drugs, Dr. Bennett counted the Celexa pills left, shocked the container had more pills remaining than her prescription indicated. Taking fewer pills would result in lower levels of Celexa in her blood than they measured in the toxicology test. She sent the prescription drugs to the toxicology center on May 3, fully expecting the Celexa to be counterfeit. She notified Simpkins by email. He called the center and asked for a rush on the analysis, since the tests would determine whether Mary died a natural death, or was a homicide victim.

Brian emailed his siblings a summary of his meeting with Dr. Bennett.

> Eve, Stu,
>
> I met with Dr. Bennett today. She informed me that our mother's blood test showed she had been taking a high dose of Celexa daily, rather than the prescription for 40 mg daily. Bennett told me that high levels had led to heart attacks in the past, and the FDA has advised against taking 60 mg versions of the drug. I gave Bennett mom's remaining drugs, labeled at 40 mg. The toxicology lab will test them to see if they are counterfeit containing 60 mg worth of active ingredients. If they are counterfeit, it means someone murdered our mother.
>
> I'll notify you as soon as I know.
>
> Love,
> Brian

Monday, May 7, 2012

The toxicology center examined Mary Jewel's Celexa drugs from the Avalon pharmacy in Kitty Hawk.

Dr. Simpkins received the center's draft report early in the morning. The report stated, "The tester verified that the appearance of the pill met the manufacturer's specification. They were white, oval, scored, and film-coated. The scored side had an imprint with 'F' on its left side and 'P' on the right. The imprint on the non-scored side was 40 mg. Next, he tested the pills for potency. Each pill held 60 mg of medication."

The tester emailed the results to Dr. Simpkins, stating that the Celexa Mary took was a counterfeit drug. He also notified the FDA hotline and the pharmacy that filled the prescription.

Dr. Simpkins, shocked by the results, had expected an absented-minded patient to forget she had taken a pill and involuntarily overdosed.

He called Dr. Bennett at noon and told her of the Celexa problem. "If Mary Jewel had an overdose, there might be thousands in the same plight. It doesn't make economic sense for the bastards to produce just a few counterfeit drugs."

"Christ," Dr. Bennett said.

"I've almost completed the autopsy. I'm finding her death a homicide because she should have died from the high level of Celexa. I'll send the draft autopsy to you and the Kitty Hawk police. Since I haven't completed the final autopsy document, I only sent the Celexa information to the FDA," Dr. Simpkins said.

The FDA contacted the Avalon pharmacy and directed them not to sell anymore Celexa from the lot that Mary purchased and to send the remaining drugs in the lot to them, and to identify their suppler. The pharmacy complied, stating they had purchased the drugs from one of the three major distributers.

The FDA sent the Avalon pharmacy drugs for testing to their Forensic Chemistry Center in Cincinnati. A week later they received the results, stating that every Avalon Celexa pill contained only 40 mg doses. The FDA notified the Avalon pharmacy and Dr. Simpkins of the test results. Simpkins concluded Mary must have purchased counterfeit drugs from another source. Simpkins, Bennett and the FDA had to determine how Mary obtained the 60 mg pills to stop others from dying.

## Chapter 12 A Slow Start

Monday, May 7, 2012

Since Mary's autopsy showed she had highly elevated Celexa blood levels, Dr. Simpkins called the North Carolina Toxicology Center in Raleigh and asked them to expedite the Celexa drug testing of the two mysterious deaths at Kitty Hawk General Hospital. The next day, the center reported both of the deceased patients had abnormally high levels of Celexa in their blood.

On Tuesday, Dr. Simpkins emailed the full autopsy report to Dr. Bennett and Detective Conner. Dr. Simpkins called Dr. Bennett and said, "The medical system in Eastern North Carolina may have a major counterfeit drug problem. We'll have to test the Celexa pills they took to be sure they are adulterated or counterfeit. Jean, you did an impressive job by expanding the mysterious death table and collecting the information. We need to examine whether the seven patients, not treated at the Kitty Hawk hospital, had elevated Celexa blood levels. I've contacted their hospitals and asked them to forward blood samples to the toxicology center."

Friday, May 11, 2012

Dr. Simpkins received the disturbing blood test results for the seven deceased patients. Three had high levels of Celexa in their blood and had taken real or counterfeit 60 mg Celexa tablets. He called Dr. Bennett. "Jean, the blood test results on six out of the ten on the mysterious death table, including three at your hospital, had fatal levels of Celexa."

"Did you contact the FDA and the police?"

"I'll contact both after our call and send the information to the FDA hot line."

"Joe, I'll take care of getting their prescription drugs for the others besides Mary," Dr. Bennett said.

Families of the patients retrieved the medications and sent them to their physicians, who forwarded the pills to Dr. Bennett. She delivered them to the toxicology center on Monday May 14, 2012. Relatives of the two deceased patients at Kitty Hawk replied they couldn't find the old prescription bottles. However, they remembered the prescriptions came from the Avalon Pharmacy, the same that Mary used. Dr. Bennett sent emails to Dr. Simpkins and Detective Conner, who forwarded the email to his FDA contact, Pete Dunlap.

Friday, May 21, 2012

A week later, the tester in the toxicology center emailed Dr. Bennett, Dr. Simpkins, and the FDA hot line to report his findings on the Celexa mysterious deaths. Their drugs, while labeled for 40 mg, contained 60 mg of Celexa. A dangerous drug was available in Eastern North Carolina.

"Detective Conner, this is Joe Simpkins. We have another complication on Mary Jewel's murder that you'll want to know about. Dr. Bennett had me investigate mysterious deaths at Kitty Hawk Hospital the week Mary died. Like her, an overdose of Celexa tablets appeared to have killed them both."

"Hope there isn't a serial killer in Kitty Hawk," Conner said. He realized they didn't have the police resources to catch one.

"I don't think so. The crime may be much bigger. Dr. Bennett and I believe someone is selling counterfeit drugs. I sent Pete Dunlap at the FDA office the same information I sent you. I suggest you coordinate your investigation with theirs."

# Chapter 13 Initial Police Investigation - John Short

Friday, May 11, 2012

Early in the afternoon, the Kitty Hawk detectives studied the draft autopsy report and met in an interview room to discuss how to proceed.

Dave Conner said, "I've been reading FDA material on criminal investigations. Their primary focus is to close the firms that produce counterfeit drugs. The FDA doesn't investigate the murder if the counterfeit drugs kill or injure someone, they leave that to their partners in the FBI, or the local, or state police."

Detective June Devins said, "Dave, I learned the same thing while we were waiting for the autopsy report. If the FDA identifies the maker, seller, or prescriber of the drugs, we can use their evidence to prosecute them if they murder or harm someone. Reading Short's emails to Mary convinced me he is our chief suspect, especially since he owns a drug compounding company," June said.

"Let's look at Short for murder and have the FDA search for drug counterfeiters. We can plan interviews of those who know him this afternoon," Dave said. He couldn't wait to devote real resources to investigate Short.

First, they decided to interview students, staff, and faculty at East Carolina University who might have remembered Short. Next, they hoped to canvas his neighbors in Greenville and Duck.

"We investigated a break-in a few years ago at Thomas Nelson's house in Kitty Hawk. He attended East Carolina, so I called him and asked, 'Do you remember John Short?'"

"Nelson said, 'Yes, very well. I was his graduate assistant in 1993 when I earned a chemistry master's degree.'"

June said, "I've called my cousin who works in the registrar's office at the university. She knows at least six employees and students we should talk to." She presented the interviewee list to Dave.

After looking it over, Dave said, "It's an impressive list: three professors, a former graduate assistant of Short, one current administrative assistant, and two female students. How did she choose the women?"

"Availability and vulnerability. They're both divorced, late forties, a decade younger than Short and attractive. If they didn't have problems with Short, maybe they recall who did," June said.

"I've typed a list of topics and questions we should ask. Did you develop an interview schedule?" Dave handed her the questions.

"Yes." June gave him the schedule.

> 1. Thomas Nelson, Graduate Assistant, 10:00 a.m. Monday, May 14 police station. He is staying in his summer house in Kitty Hawk.
>
> 2. Jane Sawyer, current graduate student, 1:00 p.m. Monday, May 14 police station. She lives in Manteo.
>
> 3. Professor John Summer, 9:00 Tuesday, May 15 at his office on the Greenville campus
>
> 4. Professor Stephen Ford, 10:30 Tuesday, May 15 at his office on campus
>
> 5. Professor Janet Gray, 1:00 Tuesday, May 15 at her office on campus
>
> 6. Peggy Andrews, Administrative assistant 3:00 Tuesday, May 15 on campus
>
> 7. Janis Benson, Former student 5:00 Tuesday, May 15 at Starbucks in Greenville.

June introduced herself to Thomas Nelson and escorted him into the interview room to meet Detective Conner.

Detective Conner said, "We need to talk to you about John Short. Detective Devins asked for your personal information earlier, but please summarize it so we can record it."

Nelson repeated what he had told Devins, adding, "I'm grateful to Short since his recommendation helped my application to earn a graduate assistantship at the University of North Carolina where I earned my Ph.D. in chemistry."

"Do you remember Short's relationship with coeds?" Dave asked.

"Yes, he propositioned many of his female students, or accepted their offers, even though he had a wife and two children. Back then, no one cared what a professor did as long as it didn't affect the university. Things have changed. At most universities, tenured professors can get fired for dating or propositioning students."

"How do you know this?" June asked.

"Short told me. Even suggested I approach those he rejected. He said our role is not only to teach students chemistry but how to lead a full life. That shocked me, I didn't think sexually exploiting students added positively to their life."

"Did you take his advice?" June asked.

"No, I was happily married then and have been for twenty-three years. I've always been faithful."

"Do you remember the women's names?" June asked.

"No, they weren't important to me."

"How was his temperament?" Dave asked.

"Short had a calm and steady personality. However, when he thought someone had wronged him, he could lose it. I worked for him during his last full-time year as a professor after he and his wife had started Greenville Pharma. They signed a contract to build their first independent drug factory. Before that Liz compounded the drugs in a sterile converted garage.

"Many times, when I was in his office, a contractor called with a problem or to announce a schedule slippage because of delays in receiving building materials. Short would be livid, raise his voice and tell the contractor, the situation was unacceptable, and they should correct it."

"He reacted that way in front of you?" June asked, incredulously.

"Yes, he didn't apologize, but told me in business you have to be firm with your vendors or else they'd take advantage and steal from you."

"Did he act that way with his wife?" Conner asked.

"I only heard him berate his wife twice. If I treated my wife that way, she'd divorce me."

They asked a few more questions to resolve dates and names.

Conner said, "Thanks for seeing us. You've been very helpful. If you think of anything else, please call us." They both handed him their business cards.

After they left, Dave told June, "That went well."

"Yes, he corroborated everything Brian Jewel told us. Short's behavior hasn't changed in years.

"I hope Jane Sawyer is just as helpful." Dave said.

After five minutes of discussing Sawyer's background, the detectives asked her to discuss her association with John Short.

Jane Sawyer said, "I've heard that Short played around with his students but have no first-hand evidence. However, when he asked me out, I remembered my friends warned me about his playboy behavior so I said no."

"How did he react to your refusal?" Detective Devins asked.

"Short took it in stride and didn't get mad."

"What had you heard?" Devins asked.

"That he was a player and to watch out for him."

"What do you mean, watch out for him?" Conner asked.

"Don't reveal my name, but two women told me he abused them. One said he had raped her."

This statement made both detectives move to the edge of their seats.

"Why didn't you tell the police?" Conner asked.

"They begged me not to. I had to respect their wishes."

"While we can't tell you the specifics of the crime, it's related to John Short harming women. We need you to give us their names. We won't tell who told us," Conner said.

Sawyer said, "I should have ignored Barbara Young's and Helen Morse's pleas not to call the police. Short raped Helen." She wrote their contact information on a note pad and handed the paper to them.

After a few minutes of questioning, Conner said, "Thanks for talking to us. You've been incredibly helpful."

Detective Conner said, "Call us if you think of anything new."

After Sawyer left, June said, "Christ! He committed a sexual crime. He may have killed Mary Jewel. We just have to find out how. We understand why."

"Call the two women Sawyer mentioned and set up interviews for Wednesday. You'll be better at getting them to talk to us than I might be," Dave said.

June wondered if her daughter would understand if she missed her 4:00 p.m. Wednesday soccer game.

Thirty minutes later, she told Dave, "We meet Barbara Young at her house at 10:00 a.m. in Greenville and Helen Morse at 1:30 at Starbucks in Manteo. Young wants her husband present while Helen doesn't want anyone in her family aware of the interview."

"Glad you scheduled them early in the day. I promised to take my two sons surf fishing in the late afternoon."

June smiled, knowing she would make her daughter's soccer game.

On Tuesday, Dave drove them to Greenville to meet Professor John Summer. He only answered questions related to Short's academic employment. Summer claimed ignorance of Short's behavior toward women.

The next interviewee, Professor Stephen Ford, responded to their questions the same way John Summer did.

As they left early and drove to lunch June said, "They coordinated their approach. I believe they're hiding something."

"Agree, but we have enough on Short. Let's not waste our time by talking to them again."

"Hopefully, Janet Gray will be more forthcoming."

Conner asked Janet, "How well did you know John Short?"

"Too well. For over twenty years, but I was better friends with his deceased wife. Are you here to discuss her death?" Janet said.

Both detectives' faces didn't flinch as they processed this shocking question. Detective Conner asked, "Please tell us what you remember."

"I think he murdered her."

"Why?" Detective Devins asked.

"Liz had caught him in an affair. He didn't react well when she told him she wanted a divorce and control of Greenville Pharma. One of her children came home from school and found her in pain lying on a couch and called 911. The ambulance's emergency medical technician (EMT) thought she had a heart attack. She died shortly after arriving at the hospital. The emergency room physician agreed and signed her death certificate with heart failure as cause of death. Short had her cremated two days after she died. There was no autopsy. I didn't believe she had a heart condition. Liz ran over twenty miles a week, and we played tennis often."

"Did Mrs. Short ever tell you her husband threatened her?" Detective Conner asked.

"Yes, she told me that while he appeared calm to everyone, when they were alone, he yelled and claimed she planned to ruin him. She said he scared her during the last two years of their marriage, and she sometimes feared for her life," Janet said. She felt relieved, finally having told her story to someone who appeared interested in doing something concerning Liz's death.

Conner, Devins, and Janet spent the rest of time discussing Short's potential for murdering his wife.

When the discussion ended, the detectives walked to an empty classroom to interview Peggy Andrews, an administrative assistant in the Chemistry Department.

"While Janet Gray might be correct that Short murdered his wife, I doubt if we'll find enough evidence to convict him, unless we test her ashes. Please verify that a local firm cremated her. We should get a warrant to seize the ashes. Until then, we should concentrate on Mary Jewel's murder, the abuse, and rape cases," Dave said.

The next two interviews with Peggy Andrews and Janis Benson yielded no results. Detective Conner terminated each after ten minutes. The detectives returned to Kitty Hawk more than hour earlier than planned.

Conner drove June to Greenville on Wednesday morning. The Young's house, a large two-story, cedar-shingled colonial on an acre of land, impressed them. Mrs. Young greeted the detectives from her porch as they walked toward as her. "Hi, I'm Barbara Young. You must be Detectives Conner and Devins. Hank, my husband, is in his study. We can talk there. Our kids are in school so we'll have privacy." She motioned for them to follow her inside.

The detectives walked through the gray-slate-floor foyer and followed Barbara into Hank's study. He sat at a large oak desk, facing the door, in front of a window with a view of their in-ground pool.

Hank stood up, introduced himself, and said, "Let's sit at the table. There's iced tea on the credenza if you're thirsty. Like being a cop, as a lawyer, my paper work never seems finished. I'm preparing for a case that goes to court on Monday."

Both accepted the drinks. Detective Devins said, "Thanks for agreeing to meet us. We'll try to be brief. As I said on the phone, we're investigating John Short, and we discovered your name as someone who can provide information on his behavior. We need to record the interview."

"Okay. How did you identify me?" Barbara asked.

"Through the University. You attended one of John Short's classes," Conner said. "What was your association with Short?"

"It started as a normal student-teacher relationship. Short was an outstanding teacher. The students loved him. He always invited them to see him during office hours if they had questions on his class material. I saw him several times. He was a professional and didn't express any sexual innuendoes or make any advances.

"Last year, he held a spring barbeque at his home on a Saturday afternoon after we finished the semester. That's when the trouble started. He congratulated me on being his best student and said he wanted to talk to me after the party ended about my career."

Both detectives looked at each other, realizing they had a new ally.

"We walked into Short's study, and he offered me a glass of wine which I accepted. He stayed behind his desk, while I sat on a loveseat. Short told me I had a brilliant future in chemistry if I wanted to pursue a Ph.D. He promised to give me a great letter of recommendation and mentioned five of his students who had earned doctorates. They teach at respectable universities."

"Now comes the sick part," Hank said.

"I thanked him, and said my husband has a successful law practice and that I wanted to raise my teenage children in Greenville. He said he understood but had another proposition," Barbara said.

Both detectives remained stoic.

"Short opened his desk drawer and took out a colorful portfolio titled Greenville Pharma and walked over to the love seat. He said he wanted to hire me. He offered me another wine which I refused since I felt tired. Short reviewed each page of the portfolio extolling the company's greatness. Short emphasized my rewarding future with stock options and a salary eventually higher than my husband's, if I accepted the job of deputy director of research," Barbara said. "I listened, but felt exhausted and wanted to close my eyes. Short must have noticed since he put my arms around me and asked if I was okay."

Barbara's husband, Hank, let out a muffled noise full of hatred. "She told me of his attack, last night. As her husband, I'm not happy. If Barbara told me then, I'd have driven to his house and broken his face and a few ribs. As a lawyer, I can't do that, but I wanted to stop him."

"Before I could answer, he began kissing me. I lost my fatigue, became enraged, slapped him, and pushed him away," Barbara said.

"Short asked, 'What's wrong? I'm willing to ensure your future at least you can show a little gratitude.' He moved to embrace me again. Short looked surprised when I punched him in the neck and pushed him hard off the loveseat. He fell and banged his head on the floor. Short looked up at me in fear. I'm an inch taller than him and in shape. He lacked muscle definition and had a beer belly. He looked liked he hadn't worked out in years."

Hank smiled, "I thought her karate classes were a waste. Barbara proved me wrong."

"Short stayed down, and I told him, if you ever mention this to anyone, I'll break your legs. My husband will sue and ruin you financially and professionally. The police will send you to jail. I walked out and drove home. I didn't tell Hank since I didn't want to upset him. After fifteen minutes of driving, my fatigue returned. I stopped at an Exxon station and purchased an energy drink, chugged it and when I became alert, I resumed driving."

Conner asked, "He committed sexual battery against you. Are you willing to testify against him?"

"Yes. Hank convinced me, it's my civic duty to protect other women." Barbara relaxed now that she told her story to the police.

"We plan to bring charges against Short, but he doesn't know the scope of the investigation so please don't mention our conversation to anyone. If he learns what he's facing, he might flee the country."

Barbara and Hank both agreed.

"Hank, you understand if you sue, you'll be more successful after he's convicted," Devins said.

"Yes, I do. We'll help you any way we can."

"Did you tell anyone of his behavior?" Conner asked.

"Yes, two of my girlfriends. I asked them not to repeat what I had told them to anyone. But, since you're here, one did."

"No comment." Detective Conner said, "We'll keep in touch. Call either of us if you remember anything new"

As they drove away June said, "Christ, he drugs his victims. I don't know if we have enough to arrest him, but we need to get him off the street."

"I agree and think we do. If we don't, he'll attack other women. But, the DA may tell us we don't have enough evidence to charge him. Short might counter Young's claim and say that she attacked him for no reason. Let's hope Short can't contest our next interview. Sexual battery is a Class A1 misdemeanor. As with every misdemeanor in North Carolina, it has a two-year statute of limitations. However, I believe we can convince the DA to charge him with sexual battery with malice, given his predatory history where the statute of limitations doesn't apply."

Helen Morse wore blue jeans and a gray sweater. She looked crestfallen with her eyes focused on the ground. She walked into Starbucks, having memorized the detectives' description and went to their table in an otherwise empty coffee shop.

Devins said, "Thanks for coming. We understand how difficult it is to discuss something you've kept secret from your family."

"I guess if I talk to you, it won't be a secret anymore."

"Correct. But, we have evidence you weren't alone in Short's treatment of women. We want to arrest him before he hurts someone else," Conner said.

"What do you want to hear?" Black half-circles bordered the skin below the lower part of her eyes.

"Tell us how it began and walk us through the actual attack." June turned on the recorder.

"I took his graduate class three years ago. His students loved him as an exceptional teacher and a professor concerned with their future. A month after the course ended, I met him by chance in the late afternoon on the street in downtown Manteo. Short suggested we have dinner since he wanted to learn about my life outside of the classroom. He complimented me on my intelligence, and said, 'I was one of the best-looking students he'd seen during his career.' I fell for his charm and accepted his invitation.

"We had a wonderful time, but he appeared disappointed when he took me home, and I only let him kiss me on the cheek and didn't invite him in for coffee. My ex-husband and I had split six months earlier, and we were going through a divorce. I didn't want him to accuse me of adultery, and I had no desire for sex with anyone.

"We saw each other four more times in the next month before I invited him in. John sat on my couch while I used the recliner. I placed coffee and cookies on my coffee table in front of him. After he picked up a cookie and began sipping his decaf, I excused myself to go to the bathroom. When I returned he took his second cookie and said, 'These are great.'

"I still wasn't interested in sex. Since he had never pressed me, I didn't fear him. After drinking coffee and eating a cookie, I felt drowsy. I saw him smile.

"He asked me, 'Are you all right?' I wasn't, and tried my best to stay awake. I said, 'No, I'm nauseous. You have to leave.' Short got up and sat next to me and put his arm around my shoulder and kissed me on the lips. I tried to push him away, but felt weak and sluggish, and he was too strong and kept kissing me. I screamed No many times, but he ignored me. He lowered the recliner, pulled my skirt above my waist, moved my underpants to the side, and penetrated me. He was too heavy and strong to push him off. When he finished, he asked 'Did you like it?'

"'Are you kidding? No woman enjoys being raped. Get out!' He did, and I haven't seen him since. While sore inside, I didn't go to the doctor and was too ashamed to report it to the police. I feared it would complicate my divorce." Helen, on the verge of tears continued, "He couldn't have picked a worse time to attack me without protection, since I was in the middle of my fertile period. I believed pregnancy

76

might have killed any property settlement I thought I should get. My husband might act the aggrieved and suffering spouse of an unfaithful wife."

"How did you handle that fear?" June asked.

"He made me feel so dirty so I took a long shower and douched myself to get any part of him out of me. I took a morning-after pill, so that if he made me pregnant, the pill would end it."

Conner listened to her and couldn't contemplate the horror of being violated. He said, "I vow to put Short away."

"Did you tell anyone right after it occurred, a friend or relative?" Detective Conner asked.

"No, no one," she said, but seeing the looks of disappointment on the detectives' faces, she continued, "I told a few friends six months later. It won't be a case of he said, she said. I remembered Monica Lewinsky's behavior and President Clinton's impeachment. I kept the underpants." She watched as both detectives kept a straight face, but revealed a hint of a smile.

"Would you be willing to give us your clothes and testify in court against Short?" Conner asked.

"Yes, that's why I agreed to meet you." Helen reached into her purse pulled out a paper bag and handed it to Devins.

"Let me get an evidence form for you to sign before I accept the bag," Devins said.

When she returned from their car, she filled out the form and gave it to Helen to sign.

"I kept the pants in the paper bag and in the freezer so mold wouldn't ruin the pants," Helen said.

"We're thankful you did," Conner said.

On the drive back to Kitty Hawk, June said, "He drugged her. That's second-degree rape. If we can match his DNA, the case is over. The judge can put him away for fifteen years if we can convince them Short is a sexual predator."

"That shouldn't be hard with the evidence we have."

"Agree. I don't want to wait to collect evidence on whether he murdered Mary Jewel and his wife before we arrest him. No sense leaving other women at risk," Dave said. "Rather than rush into interviewing his neighbors, let's analyze the information we have. If the DNA in Helen Morse's underpants is his, I'm sure the DA will indict him. There might not be a need to conduct more interviews, especially since we don't have expertise to investigate counterfeit drugs. Tomorrow, let's document our work and talk to the DA on Friday, even before we have the DNA results."

June Devins had located the local funeral home where they cremated Short's wife. They told June they had placed the ashes into three sealed vases and sent them to John Short and his two sons. She included this information and their addresses in her report.

Detective Conner called Shirley Sanders, the 1st Judicial District Attorney.

They drove fifty miles on Route 158 to her office in Elizabeth City for a 10:00 o'clock meeting on Friday morning. They gave her their reports and a summary briefing. When they finished, Sanders said, "We have a jurisdiction problem. The rape occurred in Manteo, which is in our jurisdiction, but the assault took place in Greenville in the 3rd Judicial District. I want to wait until the DNA results confirm Short raped her before we arrest him."

"We expect the results next Friday," Detective Conner said.

"What happened to the investigation of Short murdering Mary Jewel?" Sanders asked.

"We found the assault and rape evidence during Jewel's murder investigation," Detective Conner said. "While we haven't found evidence of Short murdering Jewel, we wanted to arrest him before he harms someone else."

"Excellent strategy, but until the DNA results are in, you need to continue the Jewel investigation. No need to inform the District 3 DA of the Short case until after his arrest. But arrest him as soon as you learn the DNA results are positive."

On the drive back Dave said, "I'll give you Short's neighbors' contact information. Call and schedule their interviews when we get back to the office."

## Chapter 14 Hoffman and O'Hare Help Brian

Tuesday, May 8, 2012

"Brian, this is Jean Bennett. I'm sending you your mother's final autopsy report. The medical examiner found multiple causes of death and ruled her death a homicide."

Hearing what he had suspected since her death, Brian felt vindicated. He now hoped the police would devote enough resources to arrest and convict John Short. Not wanting to completely depend on the Kitty Hawk Police, he planned to call Margaret Hoffman and Paul O'Hare for their help.

"Dr. Simpkins and I have been conducting a comparative study of nine others who died under circumstances similar to your mother's. We found they shared the same problems with the drugs they took. I'm sending you a summary of the results. The medical examiner has sent this information to the police department."

Brian printed two copies of the autopsy and the summary and gave one to his wife. After they finished reading the documents, Sandy said, "Did the autopsy satisfy you?"

"I thought I'd be happy to have my beliefs confirmed, but I'm not. While it proves someone stole her from us, it doesn't bring her back. If she died from natural causes, I might have felt better, and my hatred might have ended. Now, I want John Short arrested and sent to jail for the rest of his life.

"Short might be innocent. I researched his firm. Compounding pharmacies do not make counterfeit drugs. I examined Greenville Pharma's website. They do not sell Celexa.

"I still think it's him, but I'm concerned about the capability of the local police."

"Relax. Paul won't turn you down. Let Margaret and Paul work the case. They, the police, and the FDA should find the source of the counterfeit Celexa. You'll just go crazy trying to solve the case. You might be a great husband, father, and lawyer, but you're no detective."

Brian looked at his wife, realizing she was right. He couldn't move the investigation forward, and perhaps Short didn't commit the murder. "Maybe." Brian sighed and hugged Sandy.

Wednesday, May 9, 2012

Margaret and Paul had just finished two sets of doubles tennis, when Paul's cell phone rang. Paul saw Brian's name on his cell phone screen. "Brian, did you get the autopsy report?" Paul put his phone on speaker so Margaret could listen.

"Yes, it stated my mother's death was a homicide. She died from counterfeit Celexa which is circulating in the Outer Banks and the eastern part of the state. The medical examiner and Dr. Bennett found a similar situation with five other sudden heart failure related deaths. They took Celexa and had elevated levels in their blood at the time of their death."

"Brian, it's Margaret, please send us a copy of the autopsy and information on the other deaths."

"Okay."

"This is no longer a case of a simple murder of my mother-in-law, but a major health-care problem. It may require more of your time than a jealousy-induced murder." Sandy said.

Paul said, "Agree, we'll call with a plan to discover the source of the counterfeit drug after we read the material."

After the phone conversation ended, Margaret said, "Hon, I wonder if Short's firm created the counterfeit Celexa?"

Brian emailed his mother's autopsy report to his siblings.

Eve, Stu,

Please find our mother's autopsy report attached. The medical examiner has classified her death as a homicide. Margaret Hoffman and Paul O'Hare have agreed to look into her death and work with the FDA and the Kitty Hawk police to help find her killer. I will keep you informed of any developments as they occur.

Love,
Brian

On the way home, Margaret said, "Hon, if what Brian and Sandy claim is true, we'll need medical help to investigate Mary's murder."

"Brian told me Mary's cardiologist, Dr. Jean Bennett, is a counterfeit drug expert. We should speak to her."

When they arrived home, they rushed into their study. Paul started his computer and printed two copies of Brian's documents. They silently read them at their desks. Margaret finished first and waited for Paul to look up. When he did, she said, "This might be bigger than our first two cases if we can find out where the illegal drugs originated."

"Hon, I agree, but I hope Bennett can help us since we aren't experts in the pharmaceutical industry. So you want to do it?" Margaret asked.

"Yes. It's been two years since the embezzlement case. I miss the excitement."

"Let's hope no one tries to kill us this time."

"Angel, I'll Google Dr. Bennett's office number."

Margaret called the number she saw on Paul's computer screen. "Dr. Bennett, I'm Margaret Hoffman and have my husband, Paul O'Hare, on speaker-phone. We met you at Mary Jewel's funeral."

"Yes, I remember. I just finished your first book. Loved it. Your life is much more exciting than a beach doctor's. How can I help you?"

"Brian Jewel has asked us to look into the death of his mother and has sent us her autopsy report and your mortality table of similar mysterious deaths," Margaret said.

"Brian told me he had been talking to you."

"Do you have objections if we become involved? If not, can we talk to you to help us find the source of the drugs?" Paul asked.

"No objections. I'm flattered. It would spice up my life. Not that playing golf with my husband isn't exciting, but investigating the source of counterfeit drugs satisfies my urge to save lives." Jean Bennett smiled, her pulse increased, and she became excited as she realized as part of an investigation team she might do more than curse counterfeit drug distributers. She remembered Margaret and Paul always got results.

"How will the Food and Drug Administration investigate the counterfeit drugs?" Margaret asked.

"The FDA has an internet hotline doctors and hospitals use to report drug side effects. Different agencies have the lead depending upon the circumstances of the counterfeit drug. The FDA's Office of Criminal Investigation, working with the Department of Justice, takes the lead if the counterfeit drugs have a domestic origin. One of the FDA's major functions is to ensure new drugs are safe and effective, and that pharmaceutical companies produce pure drugs. Domestic rogue companies produce counterfeit drugs outside the regulated pharmaceutical industry.

The FDA audits overseas production to ensure they produce drugs to FDA specifications. However, the FDA doesn't have adequate resources abroad. The FDA inspects domestic drug manufacturers unannounced. To avoid the risk of being closed, domestic manufactures must maintain clean production facilities and develop production and testing documentation for their products.

However, the FDA has to announce scheduled inspections in India and China before they occur, in advance to comply with foreign laws and international protocols. Foreign manufacturers can repair faulty production facilities and produce missing documentation between the announcement date of the scheduled inspection and when it occurs. Thus, imported generics often included substandard and counterfeit drugs. Homeland Security is responsible for stopping illicit drugs from entering the country."

"Are there other drug situations harming the public?" Paul asked.

"Yes. The FDA publishes the cases on its website which I advise you to examine. Read material on the Office of Criminal Investigations or OCI website. While they investigate all violations of FDA regulations, they spearhead examining domestic production of counterfeit drugs," Jean Bennett said.

She continued, "One heinous case discovered the importation of the contaminated blood thinner heparin, in 2008. Before they removed it, dozens had died. We may have discovered a repeat of that problem with Celexa in North Carolina as the mysterious death table shows. Last year, a counterfeit version of the cancer drug, Avastin, was being imported from overseas internet sites by physicians and sold directly to their patients. Look at the FDA website. It's very informative and scary.

"I have patient appointments this afternoon and it might be better to call me at home in the evening." Jean gave them her cell and home phone numbers. "We can use Skype if you're familiar with it. I can show and send you information on counterfeit drugs that should interest you."

After the call with Dr. Bennett ended, Margaret said, "Hon, my husband's doctors treated him with Avastin. While I have no way of proving it, I wonder if he received a counterfeit under-strength drug, and didn't have to die as soon as he did. Let's catch these bastards."

Paul said, "No way of knowing if he could have lived longer. But, I agree let's find out who killed Mary and the others. I'm hungry. Let's break for lunch. I make tuna sandwiches."

"Thanks, Hon, I'm going to take a shower before we eat."

"Can I join you?"

After an afternoon viewing the FDA website, Margaret and Paul called Jean Bennett via Skype that evening.

"Dr. Bennett thanks for your time. From reading the autopsy and the mysterious death table, it appears counterfeit Celexa has killed at least six people in the state. We need information on the drug and the pharmaceutical industry so we can discover its source," Paul said.

"How can I help you?"

"Provide us technical support and identify reading material on pharmacy basics," Margaret said.

| Book Title | Author | Reason for Reading |
| --- | --- | --- |
| The Truth About the Drug Companies: How They Deceive Us and What to Do About It | Marcia Angell, MD | Shows how the drug industry games the FDA and the public to make obscene profits and by developing new drugs with minor improvement over existing drugs. |
| Dangerous Doses | Katherine Eban | Shows how counterfeit drugs are produced and how law enforcement combats them. |
| Compounding and Manufacturing | IML Training | Describes how compounding pharmacies produce compounds. |
| https://www.fda.gov/drugs | FDA | A description on how the FDA regulates drugs, its successes and concerns. |
| https://www.fda.gov/about-fda/fda-organization/center-drug-evaluation-and-research-cder | FDA. | Describes the FDA organization regulating drugs. |
| https://www.fda.gov/drugs/drug-safety-and-availability | FDA | Provided new drug safety warning and reviews past safety impacts. |
| https://www.fda.gov/drugs/development-approval-process-drugs | FDA | Outlines the FDA drug approval process. |
| https://www.fda.gov/drugs/guidance-compliance-regulatory-information | FDA | Provides a summary of FDA compliance and regulatory decisions |

"I recommend four books and the FDA Drug website. Read them, understand the successes and structure of the drug industry, and of its failings. I'm displaying a table on Skype identifying the sources I prepared for you this afternoon. I'll email you the table," Jean replied.

"In addition to educating you, I'd be happy to accompany you on interviews to drug companies. The interviews will reduce the time you need to collect evidence," Jean said, excited at the prospect of working with Margaret and Paul.

After Margaret ended the conversation, Paul said, "We should call Brian."

"Let me order the books before you do." Margaret accessed her email to display the table.

Paul said, "I'll continue reading the FDA website."

"Brian, it's Margaret and Paul. We've started to investigate your mother's murder," Paul said.

"I don't want you to do if for free. The family will pay you." Brian said.

"Don't worry, Margaret and I have enough money, and we expect to earn more on the book we'll write which will cover our time and expenses. We have to plan our approach and get resources to help us. We'll visit you in a few days."

After the call ended, Margaret reviewed the USB drive Brian had given them earlier for the second time. They both read the Short and Mary Jewel emails. "Christ, he tried to rape her and threatened to kill her." Margaret said.

When they finished reviewing the emails, Margaret said, "Short implicates himself. We'll have to prove he's a murderer and not just a talker."

## Chapter 15 Eve's Revenge

Wednesday, May 9, 2012

Since she left Duck, Eve had spent most of her free time with her boyfriend, Joe, or at her Friendship Heights, Maryland apartment thinking of her past. Eve had suppressed the memories of her terrible years before she became sober, but they came flowing back after her mother's death, especially after she received Brian's last email. To her, criminals appeared to hold most of the marketing and management positions in the legal opioid drug industry. Eve accessed CDC data that reported over 15,000 died in 2011 from prescription opioids compared to 4,300 from illegal heroin overdoses.

Eve also hated the illegal non-opioid producers. Her mother who kept her alive might have died from a counterfeit drug. She didn't understand why the drug industry didn't police itself.

Discussing her mother's will with Wayne Watkins on her requirement to stay sober didn't bother her. Eve understood that with her strong addiction to opioids, she had to have limits placed on her behavior. She couldn't stop thinking of those in the legal opioid industry that caused so much misery and death. It kept her from sleeping, and when she fell asleep, terrifying nightmares woke her.

Recalling the past began to affect her relationship with Joe. To maintain her sanity, she needed to extract revenge from her tormentors, since society and the police didn't. Eve didn't fear getting caught since the FBI reported in their 2011 Uniform Crime Reporting Program that arrests were not made in one-third of murders and non-negligent manslaughters. From watching TV crime shows, she learned most of the arrests were family members or friends, and the majority of unsolved murders were committed by individuals not related or not friends with the victim.

After Eve had decided on her course of revenge, the nightmares stopped, restful sleep returned, her fear of resuming her addiction ended, and her satisfying relationship with Joe restarted.

Eve, a student of spy novels, decided tasteless and odorless Ricin was the ideal poison for getting even. The pushers would die a slow painful death. She purchased castor beans for cash from several large seed stores in the Washington, DC area. Eve used a recipe she had found on the internet to produce Ricin in her kitchen.

As she prepared the poison, she decided on how to perform her first execution.

Eve detested Dr. Cleary's Oxycontin salesman, Ron Avon. Cleary forced her to have sex with Avon when he wasn't in town. Avon never shaved, had alcohol on his breath, and demanded oral and anal sex. She felt every time they met, his goal was to demean her for being an addict.

While it had been five years since she last saw him, she decided he deserved to die. She assumed he had caused many overdose deaths without fear of retribution.

Eve decided to meet him and suggest they get together. She wore a red wig, sunglasses, and large falsies in a tight pink sweater and waited outside his townhouse one morning. When he left, she followed him till he entered a doctor's office carrying a brief case. At 11:00 he drove to another office.

He continued this process until 5:30 when he entered a bar in Bethesda, Maryland. She sat at his table, where he sipped a glass of red wine. She introduced herself as Jennifer Staunton. Eve told him that her boyfriend had left her, and she was lonely. She ordered a glass of club soda and he another Merlot. They talked for thirty minutes. He excused himself and said, "I'll be back."

She dropped a Ricin pill in his glass after he closed the men's room door. When he returned, they continued their conversation as he sipped the wine.

After he emptied his glass, she said, "I'm enjoying our

conversation but I have to go. I'll be here tomorrow at six, if you want to see me again."

He winked and smiled displaying a conqueror's arrogance, and said, "Jennifer, it's a date."

They both left the bar separately at the same time. Eve, watched as the salesman walked to his car, hoping the Ricin did not attack him before he reached home.

Avon drove to his townhouse in Rockville, Maryland, had a light dinner and retired early. Eight hours later he woke up and vomited. Soon after, he experienced bloody diarrhea. He stayed home, skipping work, thinking he had contacted the norovirus, since he had the same symptoms a year earlier. Because he remembered it ran its course in two days, he didn't call the doctor.

He passed out the second day from dehydration, even though he tried drinking water to combat his thirst. Five days later, the development's maintenance staff entered his townhouse because of neighbor's complaints of horrendous odors. They found his decaying body lying in his own dried excrement.

When Eve read in the *Washington Post* that Avon had died, she believed the drug pushers had paid one small debt.

Two weeks after returning from Duck, Eve had trouble with her car's brakes while leaving Joe's house. Rather than have them fixed, she drove to a Toyota dealership in Rockville, Maryland and signed for a tan 2012 Toyota Prius. Several of her friends drove them and loved the hybrid's gas mileage and its smooth ride.

She called Wayne Watkins and said, "As we discussed at your office, I purchased an economical Toyota hybrid and need a check to pay for it.

"Fine, email me the bill, and I'll send a check to the car dealer. I'll send it overnight mail."

Two days later, she left her old car as a trade-in and drove away to her apartment. Finding a condo was her next trust fund task.

Eve dated the start of her relationship with Joe Kelly on the second Saturday in December 2011. She looked fondly on their courtship and the five weeks it took before they overcame their shyness and fear of intimacy.

That morning when they woke up together in Eve's bed, they shared a small amount of embarrassment, not knowing how to react to their new relationship. They looked at each other, embraced, and started foreplay. After they finished making love, they relaxed on the bed. Eve spoke first, "I can get used to this."

Joe said, "I hope you will. Don't worry you'll get pregnant. After our second child, my wife and I decided I should get a vasectomy."

"So you can't make me pregnant. That's okay at thirty-one I'm getting too old to become a mother. I'd rather be your lover."

Eve thought, now I don't have to worry that I'm sterile, if we married. She realized the only hypothetical impediment to their developing a full relationship had vanished, except for her opioid background.

They enjoyed each other physically as least two nights a week. Eve looked forward to the Saturday after they first made love since they had made a date to go to the Washington National Zoo with his children. She had planned to get to know them and make his family a part of her life.

After enjoying the zoo, the foursome drove to Joe's townhouse for a cookout dinner. Joe and Eve both understood she would stay over after the kids went to bed. She planned to cook the family breakfast: waffles, scrambled eggs and bacon. Joe told her they were his children's favorites.

A week after the discovery of Avon's body, the police released a summary of his autopsy report. He had died from Ricin, almost always a fatal poison. Eve decided never to use that poison again to avoid being portrayed with a standard method of avenging her past.

Using Ricin, a unique killing procedure, would make the police's investigation easier. They would question vendors of Castor beans to discover who purchased them – finding her. The next day, she disposed of her remaining stocks of Ricin and Castor beans.

Eve had to use a different method to eliminate her next victim. She realized even if she eliminated one Oxycontin salesperson a week she'd never stop the problem. Only elimination of the high level management decision makers at Simmons Pharma would, when they realized the danger to themselves of continuing to push drugs

Her actions benefited every potential patient with a painful condition. The opioids they produced could turn anyone into an addict.

# Chapter 16 Stewart and the Celexa Drug Overdose

Wednesday, May 9, 2012

After his wife went to bed, Stu began reading the autopsy report.

Horrified at its contents, he decided not to make any decisions on how to respond before morning. His mind would not relax. After an hour of restlessness, he took a sleeping pill and crashed next to his love, his peaceful, steadily breathing wife Gayle.

Waking in the morning after his wife roused him, he panicked. He had killed his mother. She had asked for the Celexa after she heard his doctor had weaned him off them. He feared the police might charge him with murder. They would claim he killed her to get his inheritance. Depression returned and overwhelmed him. He didn't tell his wife for three days until she prodded him to explain his standoffish behavior.

While Gayle sympathized with his problems, she convinced him to call Brian.

Saturday, May 12, 2012

"I've read mom's autopsy report and have something to tell you," Stu said, shaking.

"What?" Brian said perplexed.

"After the doctor had taken me off Celexa, mom asked me to give her any pills I had left. She told me she had a prescription for Celexa because of depression from being lonely after Dad died. I said yes and gave her twenty-five pills. The label said they were 40 mg, but the autopsy said she died from taking higher mg pills. I must have had counterfeit drugs. I killed our mother," Stewart said in a high pitched voice.

Brian hesitated and said, "You didn't kill her. You did what she asked. The seller of the drugs killed her. Do you have the prescription container?"

Brian realized this meant John Short didn't murder Mary Jewel.

"No, I threw it out after Mom put the pills into her container."

"Where did you buy the drugs?"

"Pear Pharmacy in Cape May."

"I'll call Margaret, Paul, and the Kitty Hawk police. They'll investigate. We have to tell the police so they can contact the FDA. Relax. You shouldn't be in trouble."

After he ended the call, Brian asked, "Sandy, did you overhear the conversation I just had with Stu?"

"Yes. Poor Stu, he has had problems in the last few years. You're a great brother not getting mad at him and telling him what he did wasn't murder."

"I hope he realizes he did nothing wrong."

"His confession makes it unlikely Short killed your mother," Sandy said.

"I know, unless Short's firm sold the drugs to Pear Pharmacy. But, I'll ask Hoffman and O'Hare to find out. Since I love you, I'll follow your advice, remain calm, and stay out of detective work."

Sandy gave him an appreciative kiss and hug.

Before he called the police, Brian hoped Margaret and Paul would interview Stu in Cape May. He wanted to tell the police of the planned interview.

"Margaret, it's Brian Jewel. Stu, my brother, provided me more information about our mother's death after he read the autopsy report."

"Let me get Paul."

Brian repeated Stu's conversation. "Are you both available to talk to my brother and investigate Pear Pharmacy?"

They looked at each other and nodded. Margaret said, "Yes. Send us his cell number. We'll see him on Monday. We have plans for the rest of the weekend."

Paul looked at the ferry schedule from Lewes, Delaware to Cape

May, New Jersey. "We can get there by 11."

Margaret made an appointment to visit Stu and called Brian, "It's all set. We meet Stu at noon tomorrow at his home. Are you going to tell the Kitty Hawk police the information on the source of the Celexa and what we are doing?"

"Yes, in the morning."

"Tell them we'll record our interview with Stu and Pear Pharmacy and email it to both you and the police."

After the conversation with Brian ended, Paul said, "Angel, that's interesting. Perhaps John Short had nothing to do with Mary's death."

"Yes, unless he supplied the pharmacy where Stu purchased the Celexa." Margaret smiled, "Hon, his innocence makes for a more interesting and complex investigation."

"That it does." Paul looked forward to spending time with his wife on the hunt.

Brian called early Monday morning, "Detective Conner, we received new information bearing on my mother's death."

He relayed Stu's phone call and that Margaret and Paul would talk to him tomorrow to try to find the source of the drugs.

"I'm glad they're recording the interviews. After they finish, please have them call me."

Brian agreed, but he didn't like the tone in Conner's voice.

Conner wasn't upset at Brian. He and June had been investigating John Short as Mary Jewel's murderer. Now he realized Short couldn't have done it. But poor John Short, they had amassed enough evidence of his crimes to sentence him to jail for a long time even though he hadn't committed the initial crime.

The detective wondered if Mary's son killed her. He realized Stu had inherited over $3 million plus a third share in Mary's beach house in Duck. Reviewing the will was part of the initial investigation. As a bankrupt, middle-aged business man, he had a perfect motive.

Conner dreaded the emotional impact reopening the investigation would have on the Jewel family. He liked Mary Jewel's children. He briefed his partner, June Devins, on recent developments.

Margaret started Stu's interview after Paul turned on a recording device. "We need to document how and from whom you purchased the drugs you gave to your mother."

"I understand."

"How did your mother request the drugs from you?" Margaret asked.

"I sent her an email telling her my doctor believed my depression had ended, and that I didn't need to take Celexa anymore. She had supported my recovery. In a return email she asked me to give her my remaining pills. I replied yes and made plans to drive to Duck the next day."

"Do you still have the emails on your system? What date did you visit her?"

"Yes, I save all family emails. Saturday, March 31."

"Please forward them to me." Margaret gave him her business card.

"Where did you get the adulterated Celexa?"

"From Pear Pharmacy in Cape May on Tuesday, March 20."

"Do you have copies of the receipts?" Paul asked, and wondered if poor record keeping had contributed to his bankruptcies.

"Yes, I keep medical receipts for five years."

"Would you like to go with us when we talk to the pharmacist? We need copies of the receipts," Margaret said.

"When will we go?"

"As soon as you copy the receipts," Margaret said.

Paul turned off the recorder.

They drove to the Pear Pharmacy and agreed Margaret should lead the conversation. She had a copy of Mary Jewel's autopsy. The three entered the store and walked to the back to the pharmacy section. Paul secretly turned on the recorder.

"Hi, I'm Margaret Hoffman with my husband Paul O'Hare and Stewart Jewel, a customer of yours. We're private investigators looking into the death of Mary Jewel. I'd like to speak to the head pharmacist."

"I'm Jim Pear, the owner and head pharmacist."

Margaret said, "Stu is the son of Mary Jewel. He purchased 40 mg Celexa on March 20 from your store. When his doctor told him to get off the drug, he gave what pills had left to his mother."

"He shouldn't do that," Jim Pear said, frowning.

"You're right, since the pills were 60 mg counterfeit drugs. Mary Jewel died from the fatal level that the FDA has advised against prescribing." Margaret handed Pear the part of the autopsy that identified the higher mg doses of Celexa.

He read it and said, "How do I know the drugs came from here. Why should I believe Stewart Jewel?"

Stu stiffened but decided not to talk.

"Because he'll testify in court under penalty of perjury," Margaret said. "Can you look at your records and tell us the source of the drugs?"

"Since you're not the police, I assume you don't have a warrant?" Jim Pear said.

"No, we don't," Margaret said.

"Then I'll wait for them. I don't want to reveal my competitive secrets unless I have to."

"Don't you want to stop the sale of counterfeit drugs?" Margaret asked.

"As I said before, I'm not sure we sold the drugs. I have to get back to work. Have a good day."

The three left the pharmacy, dropped Stu at his home, and drove to the Lewes-Cape May ferry.

Monday, May 14, 2012

While waiting for the ferry to depart, Paul loaded the recordings onto his laptop, and emailed them to Detective Conner and Brian Jewel, and sent a blind copy to Dr. Bennett. Paul told them he'd call Conner after he had time to listen to the recordings.

Paul called Dr. Bennett who didn't answer her phone. He left a message explaining Pear Pharmacy was their latest step to finding the source of the counterfeit Celexa.

Before calling Conner, Margaret's cell phone rang, "Hi, it's Brian and Sandy, we listened to the interview. Thanks for showing Stu's innocent," Brian said.

"We just asked the questions, he proved his didn't commit a crime."

"What will happen to Pear Pharmacy?" Sandy asked.

"I assume the FDA will investigate them. It's the FDA's responsibility to identify the source of the counterfeit Celexa." Margaret said.

Brian said, "We all owe Stu, for identifying Pear. This might directly lead to finding who killed our mother."

Sandy looked at Brian, smiling and said, "See, it's working out."

"I agree and didn't even lose my temper at the Pear Pharmacy's responses."

After the conversation ended, Margaret phoned Conner. "Did you listen to the interviews?"

"Yes, both June Devins and I listened together. Where are you?"

"On a ferry that just left Cape May," Paul said.

"Is Stewart Jewel with you?"

"No. We left him at his home in Cape May," Paul said.

"Good, since he had become a suspect. Margaret, excellent interview, your retirement hasn't made you rusty. The emails helped to convince us, Stewart Jewel isn't a murderer. I'll call the FDA and explain what happened and get them to pressure Pear Pharmacy. I wish that bastard's business was in Kitty Hawk. He wouldn't be so cavalier about telling us where he got the counterfeit drugs. I'd threaten to have all his drugs tested and tell the newspapers and TV. He'd make a call right away," Conner said.

"Yes, sometimes I wish I was still a cop," Margaret said.

"Thanks for your help," Conner said, as he ended the call.

"Angel, our trip to Cape May has moved the case along. We've shown neither Short nor Stu killed Mary," Paul said.

"Hon, I look forward to finding out Pear's Celexa source."

"I hope the FDA tells us."

"Hoffman and O'Hare are working out better than I thought," Conner told June Devins.

"Margaret was an ex-detective, so she has experience. Be nice to them if you want them to write positively about us in their next book," June said.

Both detectives laughed.

# Chapter 17 Eve Aims Higher

Wednesday May 16, 2012

After dinner at her condo, Eve accessed the latest quarterly Simmons Pharma Financial Report on an anonymous internet connection and copied the list of company officers. She used personnel search software to develop a profile of each officer, including their address, vacation homes, hobbies, and marital status.

Eve reviewed three employees who lived in New Jersey. She read the marketing officer had a wife and two children which eliminated him from her potential victims list. She had no desire to make the wife and children suffer for his crimes. The Information Technology manager lived in Morristown in northern New Jersey, too far for Eve to drive in a day and return home after the killing.

Hal Ramon, divorced, the Simmons Pharma's general counsel, lived in Lincroft near the company's location in East Windsor, New Jersey. He became her next target. Murdering a lawyer, whose job was to keep the company from being prosecuted and sued, excited her. Ramon's efforts allowed the company to addict opioid users.

Eve left work on Friday and drove three and a half hours directly to Lincroft to plan for her next revenge. She went by Hal Ramon's house, a large five-thousand square-foot redwood ranch house on three acres of land. An in-ground swimming pool flanked the house on its left and a tennis court on its right. A twelve-foot high evergreen hedge bordering the land protected the home from the casual viewer. Eve had to drive slowly by the driveway several times to get a clear picture of the estate. The driveway curved toward the house and ended at a three-car garage. The opulence upset Eve. How many people had to die so he could afford this lifestyle?

Ramon left at 8:00 p.m. an hour after she arrived and drove to a plush restaurant where he joined a woman who Eve thought looked like a hooker. After the couple entered the restaurant, Eve walked over to his car and placed an electronic tracking device under the passenger-side rear wheel fender. On the drive home, her heart pumped pure adrenalin, anticipating her next assassination.

Eve woke up refreshed at 9:00. She recalled the events of the day before but decided not to dwell on them but to prepare for her date with Joe. They planned to go to the early showing of *Silver Linings Playbook* with Bradley Cooper and Jennifer Lawrence. Eve's friends loved it and recommended she see it.

Joe's parents had agreed to have his daughters spend the night at their home. Eve planned to serve him a late lobster dinner after the movie. She spent the morning shopping for the shellfish, baking potatoes, and fixings for a salad. That afternoon she relaxed. She cleaned her apartment, washed clothes, started reading the novel *Gone Girl* by Gillian Flynn, and tracked Hal Ramon's car.

Ramon left his house early and drove to a location where he remained for six hours. She learned it was a golf course. He then drove home and stayed there for the rest of the afternoon.

Eve and Joe enjoyed the movie, laughing repeatedly. They started eating their lobster dinner by 9 p.m.

After Eve started eating the tail, Joe told her, "I've rented a Sea Colony condo in Bethany Beach, Delaware during the first week in August. My kids and I always go to the beach then. Hope you can join us."

Eve smiled, "Yes, I'd love to. I'll put in for vacation on Monday."

They had an exceptional night making love twice.

## Chapter 18 FDA Investigates Counterfeit Drugs

Tuesday, May 9, 2012

After reading Dave Conner's email, Pete Dunlap called the Avalon pharmacy and asked them to email him information on the Celexa prescriptions for the two other patients who had died at the Kitty Hawk hospital.

"Let me look up their prescriptions on our computer. They both last purchased them over six months ago. Both either stopped taking the drug or purchased it from another source."

"Thanks," Pete said, thinking of foreign internet drug purchases. He emailed Dr. Bennett and Detective Conner his findings and suspicions.

Monday, May 14, 2012

Detective Conner called the FDA to tell Dunlap of the search for the source of Mary Jewel's drugs. He said, "I've sent an email detailing Pear Pharmacy's role in selling counterfeit Celexa to Stu Jewel and attached the recordings and copies of the prescription receipts." Dave summarized the contents of the attachments.

Pete Dunlap listened without comment.

On Wednesday, the FDA sent a query to Pear Pharma, ordering them to name their source for the Celexa.

A week later, Pear responded in a registered letter that his pharmacy had purchased the drugs from Orlando Distribution. He included copies of the receipts in his letter.

After reviewing Mary Jewel's autopsy report, the mysterious death table, and the medication test results, the FDA sent a warning to the Counterfeit Alert Network. The FDA told the Network's health care and consumer organization members to review the source and lot numbers of the Celexa they possessed and to compare it with the lot numbers of the counterfeit drugs. They instructed the doctors to tell their patients if the lot numbers matched, not to take the drugs.

As with most organizations, the FDA had resource constraints to satisfy mixed goals. Congress had pressured the FDA to maximize the importation of generic drugs since they cost less than pharmaceutical patented prescriptions. The FDA also had to protect Americans from counterfeit or adulterated drugs.

Monday, May 21, 2012

José Raino, President of Orlando Distribution, received the FDA letter on Monday. He panicked not knowing how to answer it. He sweated and trembled for seven days before calling Brad Winthrop, remembering his strict instructions not to sell counterfeit drugs. José feared getting fired or arrested. If Brad confronted him, he decided to deny knowing they had sold illegal drugs.

José Raino called Brad, "The FDA contacted me asking for our source of Celexa we sold to Pear Pharmacy in Cape May."

"Reply, we received it from India Drug Sales and attach our invoices. I don't understand what's wrong with the drug, but don't sell anymore and destroy the remaining batches that came from India Drug Sales," Winthrop said. He wondered if Raino sold counterfeit drugs, even though he ordered him not to.

José Raino responded to the FDA the next day. The FDA sent an inquiry to the Indian firm but never received a reply. The FDA discovered the company had gone bankrupt two weeks earlier. Powerless to obtain information from the non-existent company, the FDA abandoned the investigation.

## Chapter 19 Eve's Unexplained Assassinations

Sunday, May 27, 2012

When Joe left after breakfast, Eve accessed her car-tracking software. She recorded each location where Ramon's car stopped. Eve continued this process every evening after she came home from work. By the end of the week she had fifty-five locations. Excluding his house, fourteen locations had multiple stops.

At 6:00 on the next Saturday morning, Eve put on her red-wig disguise and drove to New Jersey. Three hours later, she stopped at the first location, a sports bar that appeared four times.

Eve opened the tracking software on her laptop and found Ramon's car hadn't left his home. She located the remaining thirteen multiple entry locations on a map and planned her route to minimize driving time. Eve drove to the second location, the golf course and country club. She parked outside the entrance and turned on her tracking software. Ramon's car was headed for her location.

After he entered the club, she realized he'd be busy for at least four and a half hours playing golf. Rather than wait for him to complete his round, she proceeded to the third site. Eve hoped to visit them all in a few hours.

As she drove by, she discovered a home with Ramon's dinner-date from last weekend, wearing blue jeans and a blue sweatshirt, working in her garden. Eve revised her guess of Ramon friend's profession and jotted her address on a note pad. She discovered the other multiple locations included gas stations, restaurants, drug stores, supermarkets, and Simmons Pharma headquarters.

Eve drove back to the golf course. By noon she opened a small cooler and ate a chicken salad sandwich she had prepared. An hour later, Ramon left the club and drove to his blonde friend's home.

Rather than follow and risk being detected by Ramon, she returned to Friendship Heights. Eve paid the tolls in cash on the Delaware Memorial Bridge and Route 95 after leaving her EZ-Pass at home.

Eve arrived by 5:00, rushed into her apartment, showered, dressed, looked radiant and greeted Joe two hours later at her door. He handed her a bouquet of spring flowers as he walked in, giving her a lingering kiss.

"You look beautiful," Joe said. He handed her a DVD of the movie *Casablanca*. Eve had never seen it. "Wonderful news, Emma and Ruth are staying with my parents tonight, so I don't have to go home."

"You're handsome and smell great," Eve said, giving him another kiss. "Wait." She put a dish of lasagna she had prepared yesterday, in the oven. She added a salad and Italian bread to the main course. After dinner, she served him his favorite ice cream – mint chocolate chip.

At 8:30 she turned on the DVD player and started *Casablanca*, hoping it would not disappoint her after listening to all its praise. It didn't.

On Sunday after Joe left, Eve accessed a reverse phone directory on the internet to identify Ramon's dinner partner. Surprised, but pleased, Eve found the name, Ann Pace, and place of employment, the same as Ramon's. She accessed the data on the Simmons Pharma corporate officer directory and found she was the company's Chief Scientist.

Smiling, Eve said to herself, I can eliminate two at once. If I find a safe and isolated location, I'll use my Glock 9.

Eve drove to Ann Pace's house on Sunday afternoon and waited. After an hour, Pace drove to a strip mall and entered an Italian deli. Eve followed her and walked toward her car. When next to the car, Eve faked falling, and as she stood up placed a tracking device inside Pace's passenger-side rear fender.

Friday, June 1, 2012

Eve checked her tracking software after she returned home early from work at 3:00 on Friday. Both her prey's cars hadn't left Simmons Pharma.

Eve donned her disguise, wore black slacks, loose navy blue sweater, cap, and shoes, packed a roast beef sandwich, water, her gun, and drove to New Jersey arriving at Ramon's home at dusk. She checked the tracking software and found Ramon's car gone and Ann's in his driveway. The software showed Ramon's car parked twenty minutes away in a downtown restaurant area. Eve drove her car around Ramon's neighborhood using her laptop to monitor his car.

In an hour, she saw Ramon's car move toward his house, and she parked a three-minute walk away. She entered the driveway and walked toward Ann's car and hid behind several four-foot tall, blue blossoming hydrangeas.

Fifteen minutes later, Ramon's car pulled in the driveway and stopped next to Ann's car. Ann left Ramon's car and opened her back driver's side door and took out a small carrying case and returned to Ramon's car. He opened the garage door. Eve jumped from the bushes and fired at Ann's torso. As Ann fell, Eve opened the passenger-side door, and shot Ramon in the chest. When he slammed against the closed driver-side door, she put a bullet in his skull. Eve moved back from the car and shot Ann in the head as she lay on the ground. She picked up the shell casings. Eve's fingers shook a little, but the tremors hadn't affected her aim. Adrenaline surged through her veins.

Eve ran down the driveway and reaching the sidewalk, walked to her car. She drove home, driving within the speed limit, satisfied. Eve reached the Susquehanna River in Maryland around 1:00 a.m. She pulled off the highway, drove down a side street, parked the car next to the river, left the car, and threw her gun and shell casings into the Susquehanna River. On the rest of the drive home, Eve relaxed and felt safe.

Saturday, June 2, 2012

Fifteen minutes into the Philadelphia morning news, Eve stopped preparing bacon and scrambled eggs as she listened to a report on the double killing.

The announcer said, "This morning Hal Ramon's maid discovered two high-level executives of a major pharmaceutical company shot and lying by and in their cars on his palatial estate in New Jersey. The victims were Mr. Ramon and Ann Pace who he had been reportedly dating since her separation from her husband. Police have no comment on the murders. Her ex-husband was unavailable for comment."

Eve thought, too bad, noting the announcer didn't mention their role in the opioid crisis. Their deaths might not stop other drug executives. It was Eve's only regret.

While she enjoyed having Joe stay at her apartment last Saturday, she'd rather stay at his townhouse as she planned to do this Thursday. Eve liked the expanse of his townhouse, its four floors, furnished basement; formal kitchen, living and dining room, and two floors of bedrooms and a study. Eve realized any condo she could afford would pale in comparison with Joe's townhouse. She started to fanaticize about moving in with Joe.

She arrived at 5:00, greeted Emma and Ruth, and looked at Joe fondly. He cooked hamburgers on the grill. The baby-sitter arrived at 7:00 and they drove the short distance to Strathmore Center to hear the Baltimore Symphony.

The next Saturday morning, she visited a private gun dealer in Virginia to replace her Glock, in a no-background-check investigation purchase. Eve also acquired a silencer for the gun, fully aware she hadn't yet completed her quest for justice.

# Chapter 20 Hoffman and O'Hare Investigate Greenville Pharma

Friday, May 25, 2012

After Margaret and Paul finished a morning kayak run and had breakfast, Paul called their medical expert, Jean Bennett. "We need to go to North Carolina to meet the local Kitty Hawk police and visit Greenville Pharma. Do you have any free time next week?"

"I can join you on Wednesday."

"Perfect. We've almost finished reading the books you recommended," Margaret said, "I'm two-thirds of the way through, *Compounding and Manufacturing*, very informative. I've read many of the FDA webpages, including those you didn't reference, and *The Truth About the Drug Companies: How They Deceive Us and What to Do About It.* I didn't realize the extent and importance of the drug regulatory process."

"Make sure you both read them for the Greenville Pharma interviews so you'll understand their answers," Jean said.

Paul said, "We will. I've finished *Dangerous Doses*. It's amazing how the FDA and state investigators continue working without adequate resources against the power of illicit foreign drug companies."

"The FDA and industry relationship is scary, especially since it has been estimated 100,000 die annually from errors in hospital mistakes including prescribing legal drugs. When are you driving down? We should meet before the interviews," Jean said.

"Sunday," Paul said. "Can you meet us for dinner at the Sunset Grille in Duck? It is our favorite restaurant."

"Yes, at 7:00. I'll tell you my plan for Greenville Pharma."

After the call ended, Margaret said, "Hon, I can't wait to hear Dr.

Bennett's plan."

Margaret called Detective Conner and arranged a 3:00 p.m. appointment for Sunday afternoon at the police station. Paul drove, while Margaret continued reading. They checked in to the Hilton Garden Inn before meeting Conner.

Sunday May 27, 2012

Detective Conner said, "We usually like to conduct murder investigations ourselves. But, we welcome your help in examining the role of counterfeit drugs in Mary Jewel's death."

"We'll tell you anything we learn related to the crime," Margaret said, "As an ex-detective, I understand you cannot divulge what you've discovered."

"True, but we'll give you information related to the drug aspect of the crime, but you should keep it confidential. We believe the FDA has stopped their investigation so you won't have any competition." Conner said.

"That's typical. We plan to find out the source of the counterfeit Celexa. Did the FDA tell you who they interviewed?" Margaret asked.

"No," Conner said.

"Brian Jewel gave us copies of the autopsy report and the table summarizing the analysis of mysterious deaths, so we have that information to start," Paul said.

"Can you tell us the pharmacies where the six mysterious deceased had purchased the Celexa before they died?" Margaret asked.

"We can do more than that for four of them. My associate June Devins who is spending time with her family today, prepared a file of the drug evidence that you may find helpful," Conner said. He handed Margaret an USB drive. "Call her if you have questions." He gave them June's and his business cards.

"Two appear to have purchased their Celexa from internet sites and not their regular drug store in Kitty Hawk. The FDA has asked us

108

to help them find the source of the drugs for the two who died in Kitty Hawk. If you have some free time while you're here perhaps you could find out for us."

"We'll try. We'll need the names and contact information of the next of kin of the two deceased," Margaret said.

Conner handed her the data she requested. "How long do you plan to stay?"

"At least a week," Margaret said. "We've enlisted Dr. Jean Bennett to help us determine if Greenville Pharmacy had any role in selling counterfeit drugs."

The group talked for fifteen more minutes, and the two visitors departed for their hotel to review the Kitty Hawk files and plot strategy for finding the source of the Celexa.

Paul said, "I'm looking forward to taking my angel to dinner at her favorite Duck restaurant."

"Hon, if it isn't raining or too cold, I'd like to sit outside on the deck to get a better view of the sunset."

"We can sit wherever you want. I can't wait to eat the Grouper St. John."

"I'm more interested in Jean's plan for handling Greenville Pharma than in the food. Everything I've had there is great."

Margaret had her wish, and they sat on the deck. They sipped Chardonnay, waiting for their guest. They had perfect weather for outside dining with the wind lower than five mph and temperatures in the high 70s. Jean arrived five minutes later.

After exchanging greetings, Paul asked, "Would you like to order a drink?"

Jean said, "No, I'm on call tonight. My husband and kids are jealous since they had to stay home and have hamburgers. I'm ordering crab cakes. Would you like to hear about my plan for Short's firm?"

"Before you begin, Detective Conner asked us to find out the source of the Celexa for the two patients who died at Kitty Hawk.

Conner thinks they might be internet sites. We hope you can help us." Margaret said.

"I'm familiar with them. I'll call both of them tomorrow and find out and get back to you." Jean thought it strange that Conner didn't ask her directly?

"For your first question, I plan to use my contacts at the hospital to find out about Short's company. If they don't manufacturer or sell counterfeit drugs, we have to move to other sources."

"How?" Margaret asked.

"Simple, tell them the hospital wants to expand their sources for compound drugs, and they have asked me to search for new firms. I've already cleared this approach with the hospital's president. He helped me put together an information package I'll use to convince Short to tell me about his firm. I know this excludes you both from the interview, but it will enable us to get direct evidence of Greenville Pharma if they sell counterfeit drugs."

"Jean, you seem to be ahead of us. I had assumed you'd provide us with information, based on research, not undercover work," Margaret said. "I agree with your approach, especially if Greenville Pharma is innocent, we can move to other firms."

Paul asked, "Do you plan to use a recording device or take notes?"

"I plan to record the interviews. What have you learned from the books I recommended? Ask me questions, if you have them," Jean said.

Paul said, "Thanks for the drug industry book. The drug testing procedure sanctioned by the FDA seemed archaic to me. Testing a new drug against a placebo, rather than against a drug being used to treat a disease will not advance the effectiveness of new drugs."

"True, it could result in the licensing of a new drug less effective than the old drug." Jean said. "Drug companies will rely on marketing, including TV ads, to sell the less efficient drug. TV ads are illegal in most countries."

"Having the drug companies perform tests on their own products concerned me," Paul said. "It is an inherent conflict of interest."

"The company could fudge the results to achieve FDA approval," Jean said.

"The industry's arguments against importing drugs from Canada and other nations are just a ploy to extort money from U.S. consumers," Paul said.

"True, it would not be hard for the FDA and Homeland Security to develop checks to stop importation of counterfeit drugs," Jean said "But they won't as long as big Pharma bribes Congress with campaign contributions."

At 9:30 in the morning Jean called, "Margaret, I have the information of the Celexa source for the two who died at my hospital." Margaret put the phone on speaker mode. "One's husband said it was an internet pharmacy but he didn't know which one. He checked her laptop and found the exact name and internet address. The second patient's son said he had ordered the drugs himself and gave me its contact information. I'll send you an email with the data."

"Thanks. That was fast. We'll see you Wednesday after your interview," Paul said.

Jean called John Short on Monday morning, "Dr. Jean Bennett here. I'm from Kitty Hawk General Hospital. Our hospital and several of my medical colleagues are looking for new compounding pharmacies to lower our costs. We identified your firm as a potential candidate from your website. I'd like to set up an appointment with you this week on Wednesday."

"Thanks for considering us. Let me look at my calendar. Is 10:00 a.m. okay? That'll give you time to drive here from Kitty Hawk at a reasonable hour."

"Yes, I look forward to our meeting."

Margaret called Dave Conner late Monday morning, while Paul forwarded Jean's email to him, "Dave, it's Margaret Hoffman. My husband has forwarded an email from Dr. Jean Bennett identifying the internet sources for the counterfeit Celexa drugs for the individuals you asked about."

"Let me check." Dave smiled in surprise at the rapid result. He read the email, and said, "Thanks."

"Is there anything else we can help you with?" Margaret asked.

"Not right now."

After the conversation ended, June asked, "What was that all about? We could have asked Dr. Bennett."

True, but I wanted to test Hoffman and O'Hare. They passed. I now have confidence to give them other assignments."

"Good, we both work too hard and don't spend enough time with our families," June responded.

Dave sent a new email to Pete Dunlop that included the Canadian Drug websites and gave credit to Dr. Bennett, Hoffman and O'Hare for discovering them.

Wednesday May 30, 2012

Jean reviewed the Greenville Pharma website to learn more about the company. It was privately held, without the reporting requirements mandated for publicly held corporations. The website graphically displayed the firm's growth rate over twenty-five years and the major drugs they sold. Jean could not find information on new drugs or plans for market growth.

After Short and Jean Bennett completed their introductions at the start of their meeting, Jean repeated what she had said on the phone concerning her interest in Greenville Pharma. When finished, she said, "I reviewed your website. But it didn't provide information on one of our major concerns your firm's viability. The hospital doesn't want our drug supplies interrupted by a cash flow or employment problem."

"We use our website for marketing. This PowerPoint presentation shows our finances and historical growth rates, cash on hand, employment levels, and stability."

After the presentation, Jean said, "I'm impressed. I'll tell the hospital I have no concerns related to your potential. Please tell me the drugs you compound, including those not listed on your website, so we know the breadth of your offerings."

Short retrieved another PowerPoint presentation that described their portfolio of over one hundred and fifty compounded drugs. "These drugs are available for overnight delivery, provided the customer has a prescription, if required."

After reviewing the offerings, Jean said, "We purchase many of the drugs your firm sells. So that solves one problem. How long would it take to develop a new compound?"

"It depends on complexity of the compound, but we have a successful history of meeting new orders." Short gave Jean another PowerPoint presentation with examples of the time to create thirty-six new special-order compounds.

"Does Greenville Pharma produce generic drugs whose patents have expired, such as Celexa, Xanax, or amoxicillin?" She noticed Short frowned before he answered.

"No, we don't manufacture generics. We planned to when we first started, but since then we discovered we couldn't compete with the cheap labor of China and India. When we're finished, I want you talk to our chief pharmacist Brad Winthrop. He can provide you more details of our drug production and quality control procedures. He'll give you a tour of our facilities."

"I had a question on quality control, but I'll let him answer it," Jean said. "My last question is on references. Can you give us the names of five hospitals to contact?"

"Yes. But I'd like to call them and ask their permission first before I do. That information should be available by the time you complete the tour with Winthrop."

Short led Jean to Winthrop's office.

After the introductions, Jean asked, "Can you describe your quality assurance procedures?"

Winthrop said, "We use our International Standards Organization 9001:2008 Quality Management Procedures." He showed Jean a set of documents. "These describe our QA methodology, you're welcome to review them here, but you can't take them. I have a Power Point presentation summarizing the documents. We're confident all the drugs we produce are of the highest quality. We adhere to the FDA Good Manufacturing Standards and have an independent quality assurance department to ensure the drugs meet all FDA requirements."

Jean listened as Winthrop discussed each of the thirty pages of the presentation. When completed, Jean said, "Very impressive."

Winthrop handed her a copy of the QA presentation. "Show your colleagues, if they have concerns."

"We would like to buy prescription drugs at lower prices than charged by the manufacturers holding the patent. We understand there is a secondary market where firms purchase drugs on the wholesale market at low prices and resell them to medical and retail organizations at higher prices. Does Greenville Pharma participate in the secondary drug market?"

"No." Winthrop wondered, should he inform Jean of his resale company – Orlando Distribution. But he didn't want Short to discover his role in that firm. Before Winthrop decided, he said, "John Short and his late wife didn't enter the secondary wholesale market, because they believed they couldn't guarantee the purity of the drugs, nor compete against the oversea vendors. Dr. Bennett, I'd like to show you our manufacturing and testing facilities."

After spending thirty minutes on the tour, Winthrop had decided. "While we're not in the secondary market, I can recommend an honest firm you might use, Orlando Distribution. I have their contact information in my office."

Jean thanked him and drove back to Kitty Hawk to brief Margaret and Paul.

Settled into her office, Jean turned on her recorder and laptop, opened the Dragon Speaking speech to text application, and created a text file of her interviews. She edited the files, copied them to an USB drive, and printed them. She called Margaret and Paul and said, "I suggest we meet in your hotel room so I can brief you."

"We're here now," Paul said.

After handing them the printout and the USB drive, Jean summarized her visit. "Except for the mention of Orlando Distribution, I discovered nothing to link them to Mary Jewel's death. Short was adamant they don't produce generic drugs, such as Celexa. Orlando Distribution may be a source for buying secondary market drugs, which could be counterfeit."

Does North Carolina keep a database of death by counterfeit drugs and a list of counterfeit drug sources?" Margaret asked.

Jean replied, "We have data on death by poison, but it does not separate out counterfeit drug fatalities. The Carolinas Poison Center reports on poison calls and fatalities by county. They produce an excellent biannual summary report. In the last two years, the center received over 218,000 calls about poison events. In 2010, over 1,200 died from poisonings in North Carolina. Opioid overdoses accounted for over seventy percent.

"Many of the opioid deaths are from counterfeit drugs laced with fentanyl. Many of the counterfeit prescriptions for cancer, and heart disease deaths are not recorded since not every death has an autopsy. These unrecorded deaths may be caused by naive patients and uninformed doctors who order drugs from internet or overseas sources without knowing their danger.

"We have to learn about Orlando Distribution, but I can't meet until Friday afternoon. I have a full day at the hospital on Thursday and work until 2:00 p.m. on Friday," Jean said.

## Chapter 21 FDA Investigates Counterfeit Websites

Monday, June 4, 2012

Dunlap disgusted, printed the email containing the two Canadian Pharmacy website addresses. For more than a decade the FDA had problems with websites selling illegal and counterfeit drugs. Their Office of Criminal Investigation worked with state and Federal agencies investigating Google for accepting overseas internet site ads for selling and shipping illegal drugs in the U.S. Finally, in 2011 the FDA fined Google $500 million dollars for accepting the ads.

Dunlap accessed the two websites and developed cyber warning letters, stating that the FDA has tested Celexa pills they advertised at 40 mg levels that contained 60 mg of the drug. The letter said it is illegal to import counterfeit prescription drugs into the U.S. The letters asked the website companies to respond within fifteen working days of how they planned to correct their illegal actions. After a week-long FDA review, the agency emailed the warning letters to the websites on Wednesday morning, June 13, 2012. Based on experience, he did not expect replies.

Dunlap hoped the FDA would include these websites in the Operation Pangea V's international scan of sites selling illegal and counterfeit drugs scheduled from September 25, 2012 to October 2, 2012. He found satisfaction in knowing that eighty-one countries took part in the 2011 version of Operation Pangea and shutdown 13,500 websites.

## Chapter 22 Short Police Investigation – Phase 2

Wednesday, June 6, 2012

Early in the morning, Detective Conner asked June, "Did you set up the interviews with Short's neighbors?"

"Yes, we meet them all in a Greenville Starbuck's starting at 11:00 a.m. with Lynn Paul," June said, handing him the schedule.

1. Lynn Paul – Owner of a book store, 11:00 a.m. Wednesday, June 6
2. Joe Morris – Dentist, 1:00 p.m. Wednesday, June 6
3. Ronda Henderson – Housewife, 3:00 p.m. Wednesday, June 6
4. Jim Manly – Retired, 11:00 a.m. Thursday, June 7
5. Janet Andrews – High School Teacher, 1:00 p.m. Thursday, June 7

"I've prepared a list of questions. Look them over and hand-edit them," Dave said.

After reading the revisions, he said, "They look great."

In the nearly deserted coffee shop, they met Lynn, a thin, tall woman with gray hair. "Thanks for meeting us. We need to record the interview. How well do you know John Short?" Detective Conner asked.

Detective Devins turned on a recorder and placed it on the table.

"Just as a casual neighbor," Lynn said. "My husband and I don't really know him. I've never seen him in my book store."

"How often do you see and/or talk to him?" Conner asked.

"Several times a week, going to or coming from work, or gardening. The conversation was restricted to hello, goodbye, or an exchange of compliments on our gardens or something trivial."

"Have you observed anyone enter or leave his home?" Conner

asked.

"Yes, after his wife's death, they were all women. I never saw a man."

"We'll show you several pictures. Tell me if you know them," Conner asked.

Detective Devins showed her Barbara Young's image.

"I know her, I've seen her once several years ago when I walked my dog in front of my house. She stopped her car and asked if I knew where Dr. Short lived. Our street numbers are hard to find. She told me he had invited his students to a barbecue. I noticed her leave later in the afternoon, after the other guests had gone. She floored her car and sped out with a grimace on her face. I wondered what had happened. I'll never forget her."

Detective Devins then showed her Helen Morse's photo. "Do you recognize her?"

Lynn said, "No."

"Would you testify in court about what you just told us about Barbara Young?" Conner asked.

"Of course. Can you tell me why you're investigating him?"

"I'm sorry. That information is confidential."

After talking for five more minutes, they excused her.

After lunch, they talked to Joe Morris, a dentist in his early forties.

Detective Conner, asked, "How well do you know John Short?"

"I don't know him at all. Occasionally I see him coming home or leaving his house. But usually I'm at work or on the golf course when I assume he's home."

Disappointed, Detective Devins handed him the pictures. "Have you ever seen either of these two women?"

"No."

Detective Conner ended the interview.

The third interview with Ronda Henderson took place at 3:00. The attractive brunette housewife in her late thirties arrived a few minutes early. After greeting each other, Detective Conner asked, "How well do you know your neighbor John Short?"

"Very well. His deceased wife and I were close friends. My husband and I socialized with them often. It all ended after she died."

"Why?"

"We liked his wife, Liz, but barely tolerated him."

"Can you expand on your comments?" Conner asked.

"We believed he cheated on her. Jeff, my husband, saw him with other women. Liz told me she suspected it. John didn't treat her as a loving husband. Frequently, he'd lose his temper over trivial matters and yell at her."

"Did he physically abuse her?" Conner asked.

"Liz never said he did. But, when she told him she had a private detective follow him, and showed him compromising photos, his reaction scared her. She thought he'd kill her. John wasn't mad at her for divorcing him, but because she demanded he resign from the company and give her control. Her promise to buy out his share didn't make a difference and infuriated him. Liz told me he had only participated in searching for new clients and occasionally developing processes for creating new compounds. Liz said that he didn't understand most of the manufacturing processes, the logistics of purchasing inputs, supplying their products to the customers, and the qualifications of their staff. Liz feared he'd bankrupt the firm within a year if he took control after their divorce and she'd be penniless."

Detective Conner asked the next question carefully, so he'd receive an honest unbiased answer, "Did her death shock you?"

"Yes, she jogged with Jeff and me and appeared in great shape. I found it hard to believe she died of heart failure," Ronda said.

Conner probed carefully, "Do you think the divorce discussions stressed her?"

"No, I'm a social physiologist. In my opinion, raising the

possibility of divorce as a viable option reduced her stress."

"So, you don't think she died of heart failure?" Conner asked.

"No, at first I didn't question the cause of her death. But Jeff convinced me Short might have murdered her."

"How?"

"Short's a chemist and owns a drug manufacturing firm. So he knows poisons." Ronda raised an eyebrow. "Short cremated her two days after her death, without an autopsy. My husband told me he couldn't believe her death wasn't murder."

"Did your husband talk to the police?" June asked.

"Yes, but they didn't believe him."

"Would you testify in court to what you just told us?" Conner asked.

"Of course. You should talk to Jeff before a trial."

They talked for ten more minutes. Conner thanked her and asked her to call him if she remembered any other important information.

When they drove back to Kitty Hawk, June said, "We had an excellent day, the DA will love our interviews."

"Poor Short, he should have made friends with his neighbors. We'll need to get a search warrant to analyze his wife's cremated remains. If he killed her, then murdering Mary Jewel is his normal reaction to adversity."

Detective Conner welcomed Jim Manly, Short's fourth neighbor, at 11:00 a.m. in Starbuck's on Thursday. "Jim, how well did you know your neighbor, John Short?"

"My wife and I socialized with them before Liz died. I liked them. After she passed, I found out he wasn't as kind to Liz when they were alone as he was in mixed company. My wife told me the week before Liz died, he scared her. Liz thought he might kill her during an argument discussing their divorce. Strange, she died a few days later."

Dave continued his questioning. One statement made June struggle not to smile. "Because of the rapid cremation, I wondered if he killed her."

Conner asked, "Would you be willing to testify in court, about what you have told us?"

"Of course, I wouldn't mind having a new neighbor."

June and Dave enjoyed a healthy lunch as they waited for their last interview with Janet Andrews.

To his first question, Janet answered, "I've only lived in my house for three years and really don't know him."

They talked for fifteen more minutes, when Conner thanked her for seeing them.

As they drove home Conner said, "Short will never win, especially, if the DNA evidence goes against him."

"Maybe we'll find out tomorrow," June said.

"I'm not so sure. The lab has a large backlog."

The next morning, Dave and June documented the five interviews and waited for the DNA results.

Wednesday, June 13, 2912

Dave smiled as he answered a call from the DNA testing office. "I've emailed the DNA analysis, but I thought you'd like to hear the results ASAP. Helen Morse's underpants are full of John Short's DNA."

They called the DA and informed her of the neighbor's interviews, the DNA evidence, and more suspicions that Short murdered his wife.

"Several of the university and neighbor interviewees believed Short murdered his wife since he had her cremated two days after her death. We contacted her funeral home, and they told us they divided the ashes between Short and his two children. Since Short's a chemist, he should realize we would find poison minerals in the ashes. He might have disposed of his portion." Detective Conner said.

She replied, "Email me everything, and I'll prepare an arrest warrant for John Short and a search warrant for the ashes from him and his children and for Short's house."

Dave said to June, "It will take the DA until late this afternoon to get the warrants signed. I'll arrange staffing to execute the warrants."

## Chapter 23 Hoffman & O'Hare Investigate Orlando Distribution

Friday, June 1, 2012

Jean met Margaret and Paul in their hotel room to research Orlando Distribution. Jean suggested Paul log onto the Florida's Department of Business and Professional Regulation (DBPR) database. She said, "Since under Florida law, its data is public information. The DBPR will help find Orlando Distribution's location and owners."

Orlando Distribution is a closely held corporation. Paul said, "I'll look into their ownership. It's probably held by a chain of shell corporations so it will be difficult to identify the real owner."

"I'll travel to Florida and buy meds from them so we can test if they're still selling counterfeit drugs," Jean said.

"We'll go with you," Margaret said. "When do you want to leave?"

"As soon as we can. I'll call them now and try to set up an appointment for Monday."

Monday, June 4, 2012

The three flew from Norfolk, Virginia and arrived at the Orlando airport in the late morning.

Jean entered the Orlando Distribution office at 2:00. A voluptuous blonde with shoulder-length wavy hair greeted her. "Hi, I'm Cynthia. You must be Dr. Jean Bennett to see Mr. Raino. Follow me."

Jean could not help but notice her blouse had three open buttons revealing the tops of her large breasts. She turned and walked toward an office door. Jean saw a skirt so tight around her hips it left no doubt as to her sensuality. Before she introduced him to José, Jean thought Cynthia's job must be to market their drugs.

Jean couldn't help but notice how José looked at her when Cynthia introduced her. If she wasn't on a quest, she'd have challenged him. But she smiled when she realized it would help her get the answers she wanted.

"Dr. Bennett, how can I help you?" José wondered if he could convince her to join Cynthia and him later that evening.

Jean explained that her hospital was looking for a less expensive stable wholesale source of drugs, including Celexa and Plavix.

"Orlando Distribution is a ten year old establshed firm. We now sell over \$52 million worth of drugs annually on the wholesale market."

"How do you operate?" Jean asked.

"We search for price differentials between the wholesale market and drugs offered for sale by organizations that have excess drugs compared to their needs. We buy the lower priced drugs and resell them."

Jean cut in, "Are your sources publicly available?"

"No, they are proprietary. If I told you our sources, you could buy from them directly, destroying our business." José didn't want anyone to know how much of their supply came from three major sources. First, from a drug company he had set up in Costa Rica, second from India and China, and third from patients who purchased drugs by convincing their physicians to write unneeded prescriptions paid for by insurance. Many patients supplemented their income through regular sales to wholesale firms.

"How do you store the drugs between receiving and distributing them?"

"We use the original manufactures instructions for keeping them from spoiling," José said. "This picture shows our three-thousand square foot climate-controlled warehouse where we house them." The next few slides displayed various compartments that store different drugs, including refrigeration units.

Jean walked through the Power Point presentation of her hospital and asked questions to impress José about Kitty Hawk Hospital's interest.

José accessed his computer and wrote the prices for Celexa and Plavix on a notepad, tore off the page, and handed it to Jean.

He said, "Get Kitty Hawk Hospital to send us an order. These prices are good for two days."

"I'll ask our purchasing department to transmit the order."

José decided not to proposition Jean since he didn't want to jeopardize capturing a new well-financed customer.

Jean excused herself and called the hospital president and told him Margaret and Paul promised to reimburse the hospital for the purchase. He authorized the order. Orlando Distribution shipped the drugs to the hospital the next morning.

While Jean interviewed José, Hoffman and O'Hare spent Monday afternoon examining publicly available internet sources on Orlando Distribution and José Raino. They searched Florida state databases, Dunn and Bradstreet, Facebook, LinkedIn, and Been Verified.

Over a three-hour period, they found José Raino had little experience in pharmacy work. His history included three indictments for illegal drug trafficking, but Florida courts never found him guilty. He had spent a few months in jail in his early twenties for a shoplifting misdemeanor.

José had divorced two wives and had no children. He had held various non-skilled and sales jobs over his forty-five-year life.

José worked for Orlando Distribution since its inception. The firm only had three other employees. Two of whom worked in the climate-controlled warehouse. The last employee, Cynthia Smothers, worked in José's office. They discovered she lived with him.

They learned Cynthia acted in local Orlando theaters. Several of their internet sites displayed her picture.

"No wonder José has her for a roommate. With Raino's background, it's hard to believe the firm doesn't engage in illegal activity," Paul said.

"Hon, I agree, and he hired his girlfriend," Margaret said.

Paul continued the internet search of Orlando Distribution and learned information similar to that José had provided Jean. He found Florida Drugs owned one-hundred percent of Orlando Distribution. Miami Chemicals owned Florida Drugs. Brad Winthrop was the sole stockholder of Miami Chemicals. While the corporate ownership structure of Orlando Distribution wasn't a crime, it made the detectives suspicious of why Winthrop took such inordinate lengths to hide its true ownership.

"No wonder, Winthrop told Jean to buy drugs from Orlando Distribution. It makes sense now," Paul said.

Jean called Margaret and Paul after the interview, and they agreed to meet in their hotel room at 5:00 p.m. to exchange their findings.

Jean started first, "They have an impressive and sexy welcoming office manager who introduced me to José Raino."

"How was she impressive?" Margaret asked.

"The way she looked partially dressed, talked, and walked."

"Her name is Cynthia Smothers She lives with José," Paul said.

Jean summarized the meeting and explained how she ordered drugs from Orlando Distribution. When she finished, she said, "My husband will pick me up after we arrive at the Norfolk airport tomorrow afternoon so you don't have to drive back to Kitty Hawk. I've arranged for the toxicology center to test the drugs."

Margaret said, "Thanks we're anxious to go home. We'll leave early tomorrow so we don't miss the flight. We're tired, in two weeks Paul and I are going on a week's vacation to Quebec."

"Enjoy yourself. I love it there in the spring," Jean said.

Paul described their Orlando Distribution research. Jean promised to call them about the drug tests in the next two or three days. Margaret notified the Kitty Hawk police of the connection between Greenville Pharma and Orlando Distribution.

Thursday, June 14, 2012

On Thursday morning, Jean received a text message from the toxicology lab stating they had emailed her the drug test results. Since Jean was seeing patients, she couldn't access her email until 5:00 p.m.

Dr. Bennett sat at her desk with a cup of coffee and read the summary. Plavix was not counterfeit. The story on Celexa differed. While the contents of the drugs matched the manufacture's requirements, half of the 40 mg pills contained 60 mg of active ingredients.

After reading the detailed test analysis, Jean called Paul. Margaret listened in.

"Paul, the report says Plavix is okay, but half of the Celexa are counterfeit. I'll email you the report after our call." Jean outlined the details of the tests.

"This case gets more complex with every new lead." Margaret said.

"Since John Short's name isn't on any of the ownership documents, I wonder if he knew about the wholesaler," Paul said.

"Stu's revelations cleared Short. Our analysis now points to Brad Winthrop as a suspect. I'll call Dave and tell him," Margaret said.

"Dave, we've unearthed information that will interest the Kitty Hawk police."

"Wait until I get June. I'll record our conversation." After a quick pause, Conner said, "Go ahead."

Margaret summarized what they knew of Orlando Distribution and the drug testing results.

"Christ, are these people stupid. Caught once and still selling poison," Dave said.

June said, "This brings us back to Greenville Pharma, but with Winthrop, not John Short as the suspect responsible for Mary Jewel's death."

"Yes, but not as a murder suspect of Liz Short, his former boss, but only for distributing the counterfeit drugs that killed Mary Jewel," Dave said.

"Perhaps we can convince the DA to charge him with manslaughter," June said, "It might stop others from selling counterfeit drugs."

Margaret said, "I'll email you the test results."

"I'll notify the FDA," Conner said.

After the call ended, Paul said to Margaret, "Angel, great call. You've excited the Kitty Hawk police."

Dave told June, "We'll spend the rest of the day writing a rationale for charging Winthrop. After I read the test results and write a summary of our conversation, I'll call Pete Dunlap."

"Pete, I want to give you an update on the Mary Jewel murder investigation. Margaret Hoffman, Paul O'Hare and Dr. Jean Bennett have found a new source for counterfeit Celexa, Orlando Distribution in Florida."

He summarized their finding and forwarded the recordings and documentation to the FDA.

"That's very interesting. Pear Pharmacy told us they had purchased their counterfeit Celexa from Orlando Distribution. You can tell Hoffman, O'Hare, and Bennett of the FDA's findings, but tell them not to discuss it with anyone else."

"We need to tell our District Attorney's office."

"That's understandable, but don't arrest or execute a search warrant on anyone from Greenville Pharma or Orlando Distribution unless the FDA approves it."

"Understood," Conner replied.

"We'll give you credit for any arrests and convictions."

Both Dave and June smiled. "We still should write-up the findings on Winthrop and Orlando Distribution," Dave said.

"If we don't arrest him, and the FDA tries to steal the credit,

Margaret and Paul will write exactly what happened, and we'll look great," June said.

"I hope the FDA will honor their word."

## Chapter 24 Eve Strikes Again

Wednesday, June 20, 2012

Eve, while happy at avenging her ruined life, despaired at the lack of publicity connecting the assassinations to opioid drug companies. She assumed they either didn't recognize the tie between their staff's murders and their drug pushing activities or didn't care about sacrificing a few executives as long as the profits kept flowing.

Eve changed her approach. She decided to attack the political infrastructure that supported the atrocities of the opioid industry. Her first thought turned to members of Congress, but she soon realized that would be much riskier than her other executions. Eve chose lobbyists — conduits between the drug companies and members of Congress.

Eve accessed the Open Secrets database identifying lobbyists, to learn about lobbying and found the Phar/Health goods sector spent over $240 million in 2011, the largest of any major sector. Drilling down, she found a list of the largest influence-peddling firms and identified those who had significant Pharma clients. After accessing their website, she found a list of their staff engaged in lobbying by sector. With several hundred names, she cross-referenced them to those who lobbied for Simmons Pharma, the manufacturer of the opioids that enslaved her.

Eve identified three potential candidates. Since one was female, who lived in New York City, too far to investigate, assassinate, and return home the same day, she passed on her. Another had six children and a wife to support, since didn't want to ruin the innocent children's lives, she decided on a different candidate. Eve chose the fifty-two-year-old divorced lawyer, James Grass, who lived in Great Falls, Virginia.

Eve left her apartment at 4:00 p.m. on Thursday to avoid slow traffic on the Washington Beltway at the American Legion Bridge over the Potomac River. It still took over thirty minutes to get over the bridge.

Eve exited west at Georgetown Pike. Driving on the curvy road at a speed limit set too high for safety, she appreciated the stately homes in the hilly terrain. She turned right at River Bend Road driving parallel to the river. She followed her printed directions from MapQuest finally turning right on a dead-end street. She drove her car at 20 mph toward Glass's house. A closed black-cast-iron fence guarded his driveway. Unobserved, she turned around and parked so she could see his house. She waited.

The gated driveway thwarted her plans to place a tracking device on his car. After a half-hour, a black Lexus sedan turned right and went toward his house. Using a small pair of binoculars, she noted and recorded his license plate. Eve waited ten minutes after he entered his home and saw him leave with a large German shepherd on a leash. Glass opened the gate and walked toward her. Eve drove away realizing the dog would bark if she tried to attack Glass from his lawn, much less inside his house.

On her trip back to her apartment, she planned how to get to him. Eve would not see Joe all weekend since he was visiting his sister's family in Philadelphia.

She spent Saturday tracking James Glass. Eve arrived at Glass's home street at 8:00 a.m. and parked next to a tree-filled-empty lot. She wore her red wig and a brown eye disguise, and hid her figure with a loosely fitting sweat-shirt and pants. She wore a wedding ring and neglected to wear makeup to complete her role as a suburban housewife.

Eve sipped coffee from a Thermos, opened a book, and occasionally glanced at Glass's home. Finally, an hour after she arrived, Glass pulled out of his driveway and drove past. She followed him to a shopping center where he entered the Giant Supermarket. She left her car and noticed Glass push a large shopping cart into the store and walk to the vegetable section. Making sure no one was nearby Eve walked toward his car, bumped against it, and placed a tracking device inside the passenger-side rear fender. Her heart stopped pounding after she returned to her car.

After a dinner of rare steak, baked potato, and string beans, Eve opened her laptop and accessed the tracking program. Glass had left Giant at 10:00, drove home, and didn't leave again until 8:00 p.m. He drove four miles and parked at 10201 Colvin Run Road near the Great Falls Community Hall.

Eve learned the hall held dances for adults over thirty at least three times a week. She thought a perfect place to meet an aggressive bachelor. Eve regretted she had drunk the wine since she needed to be sober to drive without getting stopped. She wondered if Glass had a girlfriend to complicate her disposal of him.

If he went dancing on Sunday evening, she would join him.

The temperature on Sunday afternoon reached the mid-90s by 4:00. Eve spent the day in her air-conditioned apartment skipping her afternoon run since she had not recovered from a sprained ankle she suffered playing tennis with Joe several days earlier.

Every few hours she accessed the tracker. Glass had left the house a few times, but never went beyond the borders of Great Falls. Eve, expecting success, packed her Glock, silencer, and red wig in a large purse. Eve wore brown contacts and loosely fitting clothes.

At 7:00, her laptop alerted her that Glass's car moved and stopped at the Great Falls Community Hall. Eve smiled and drove to the dance hall. When she arrived, the parking lot next to the small white building had filled. She gazed at the cars and didn't find Glass's. Driving around she located his car two blocks north of the hall parked on the side of the road, under a large oak. Glass had retracted the hard convertible top. Eve turned around and parked a block south of the hall, ensuring she had visibility of its entrance. She put on her red wig and walked around the neighborhood.

At 8:30 she returned to her car, left her large purse, retrieved a small wallet from the glove compartment, and entered the dance hall. After paying the $5 cover charge, she limped to the bar and ordered a glass of club soda. She noticed several men staring at her. The old hall impressed her with its wooden floor divided into two large rooms. Customers, ranging in age from their twenties to their seventies, sat at tables or stood in groups in the first area bounded by the front door and the second area, the dance floor. She spotted Glass sitting at a table with another man and three women. None of them seemed like couples since they danced with more than one partner. Eve couldn't detect the looks, touches, and smiles between any of the pairs that showed they shared a loving relationship.

She gazed at Glass, wondering if he would leave alone.

Eve stood leaning on a wall next to the bar. Many unattached men walked up to her, "Would you like to dance?"

She always gave the same answer, "I'd like to," she said while pulling up her pants leg showing the ace bandage "but, I have a sprain that hasn't healed. I'm here for the music."

Eve watch Glass dance expertly to almost every song from the 60s and 70s – fast and slow rock. She saw that like most accomplished dancers, he only drank bottled water. At 10:15 she noticed individuals and couples leaving the hall. Not wanting to chase Glass when he left, Eve followed them. She walked to her car, sat in the driver's seat, and reached into her purse and retrieved her new Glock and silencer. Eve hid them in a billowing pants pocket.

Glass left fifteen minutes after she did. He walked alone at a slow pace that Eve realized she could beat. She left her car and limped rapidly toward Glass. He didn't notice her behind him. Eve caught up as he sat in his open convertible and was strapping his seat belt into its harness. He didn't hear Eve approach the car. Eve looked around. Seeing the deserted street she smiled and aimed the gun at Glass and pulled the trigger. A bullet entered the side of his head, squirting blood on the passenger seat. As he slumped toward the passenger door, Eve fired again aiming at the back of his head.

After picking up the shell casings, she walked back to her car and drove toward the Beltway.

Ten minutes later, a couple walking by the car saw Glass's motionless corpse leaning in a strange position. The woman said, "Another drunk who couldn't make it home."

The man moved in for a closer look, said, "He hasn't passed out, he's been shot," pointing at the blood, "I'm going to call 911."

With sirens blasting, the police arrived within five minutes.

Eve planned to drive east on George Washington Parkway and return to Maryland via the Chain Bridge, rather than crossing over the crowded American Legion Bridge on the Beltway.

She planned to throw the gun into the Potomac River while driving over Chain Bridge. She hoped it would be deserted on Sunday evening. As she approached it, she had to reduce her speed as she left the parkway for the bridge. While her lane had few cars, the other packed lane, moved at ten mph leaving DC. She had to revise her plan. Since the C&O Canal Park was closed after dark, she drove home with the gun.

Before arriving home, Eve turned on the news radio and panicked after she heard a report of the shooting.

On Monday morning, after a fitful sleep, worrying about disposing of the gun, she woke up at 6:00. She dressed in jeans and a blue sweatshirt and drove to Lock 21 (Swains Lock) hoping there would be few hikers that early in the morning. Eve parked her car in an empty lot. She walked northwest on the tow path. After covering a half-mile, she left the path and walked to the wide river and separately tossed the gun, shell casings, and silencer as far as she could. Relieved, she drove home looking forward to hot coffee, orange juice, bacon, and eggs. She arrived at work on time.

That evening the disappointment she experienced after every opioid murder returned. The Monday evening news accounts speculated a jealous husband or competing lobbyist had murdered Glass.

Eve began to doubt if her actions were worth the risk since the police never tied them to opioid manufacturers. If arrested, she'd go to prison for nothing since the assassinations didn't impact opioid production. Her happiness had become dependent on Joe and his children. Eve didn't want to get caught and lose them.

A week later, Eve read a story on the fifth page of the *Washington Post*, Tim Stables, the murderer of Dr. Cleary, Eve's tormentor, had agreed to a sentence for second degree murder of up to thirty years. He would be eligible for parole in ten years. Shocked, Eve believed Dr. Cleary's murder and her behavior morally justified. However, the police and the courts didn't. Could the legal system treat her the same way, ending her freedom and life?

# Chapter 25 Brad Winthrop Retires

Monday, June 8, 2012

Raino's call telling Winthrop of the FDA's letter shocked him. He had commanded Raino not to sell counterfeit drugs. Either Raino didn't listen or couldn't tell they were counterfeit since he purchased them from India.

Raino's call raised the possibility the FDA could investigate Orlando Distribution if his answer didn't satisfy them. Brad had a difficult time sleeping, wondering if the FDA would knock on his door with a search warrant. If they did, they wouldn't find anything incriminating. But, he didn't know what would happen if they searched Orlando Distribution and Raino's home. After four days of indecision, he decided to abandon both Greenville Pharma and Orlando Distribution.

Winthrop wanted to amass $100 million before he retired, but given the danger of an FDA investigation, he understood $63 million should finance a pleasurable and women-filled retirement.

Winthrop retrieved a document he had written three years ago, detailing close-out procedures for Orlando Distribution. He felt confident that if he shut down the firm and destroyed their records, the FDA couldn't touch him.

Brad reviewed his passport to make sure he had over six months left, before the TSA stopped accepting it. He decided he'd leave between June 15 and June 20 to have enough time to liquidate Orlando Distribution. Brad realized he couldn't sell his stock in Greenville Pharma to John Short. He had to take the financial loss, so as not to warn Short and the FDA he planned to leave.

Winthrop called Short at his home on Monday afternoon. "John, the business is running smoothly. A few of my friends have invited me to go deep sea fishing in Key West with them from Thursday to Sunday. If it's okay with you, I'd like to take Tuesday through Monday off."

"Enjoy yourself. See you next Tuesday."

Winthrop smiled as he knew he'd soon start a new phase of his life.

Tuesday, June 12, 2012

Winthrop drove to Florida in a white Chevy Malibu rental to tell Raino to dissolve Orlando Distribution. Winthrop feared he couldn't control Raino's behavior, but decided to give him a chance to show he could trust him. He packed a Glock he had purchased from a private owner in Virginia. He arrived in Orlando on a Wednesday night and checked into a Comfort Inn using false identification.

Early the next morning after eating a hot hotel breakfast, he checked out and drove to Raino's ranch-style house. He remembered the times he spent with Cynthia. The first time José asked him for a favor. "Sleep with Cynthia tonight. She likes variety in her sex life." Winthrop went on company inspections every two months on weekends and relived his first experience with her each time, just as José hoped.

Cynthia looked forward to Brad's visits. At 5' 10", three inches taller than José, with an athletic body compared to José's paunch, and since he had more concern for her satisfaction, she always enjoyed sex with him. José only provided pleasure half of the time.

Winthrop, wearing rubber gloves, let himself in with a key he had duplicated without Raino's knowledge. Wearing sneakers, he slowly walked toward their bedroom. The partially opened door revealed the sleeping couple. Brad entered the bedroom and touched Raino on the shoulder. "Wake up. It's time to leave."

Raino stirred, turned over, but stayed asleep. Cynthia woke up. She shook Raino awake. "Brad is here."

"Why are you here? How did you get in?" Raino asked.

"How did you sell the 60 mg Celexa pills as 40 mg pills?"

"We didn't. We purchased Celexa pills from many sources. Some must have been counterfeit 40 mg pills." Raino replied.

"It's time to close Orlando Distribution and enjoy our savings overseas," Brad replied.

"No, I'm earning too much and having too much fun to shut down the company."

"You have enough to retire having earned over $20 million in the last ten years. José, you have no choice. I'm the owner. You have to do what I say."

"How can I terminate the company? What if I don't do what you order?"

Brad reached in his jacket and handed José a fifteen-page document. "This is a step-by-step set of instructions on how to legally close. If you don't follow it, the FDA will eventually find one of your illegal activities, and you'll go to jail."

"The FDA's not that smart." José didn't appreciate Brad's unannounced entry and thought he was smarter than him. José's heart rate increased, his muscles tensed, and adrenalin flowed as he prepared to attack and overpower Brad.

"I'm not willing to go to jail for your naïve beliefs."

Brad seeing José's physical reaction placed his hand in his pocket, on the Glock, ready to fire.

"Tough." José jumped out of bed and lunged toward Brad. But he was too slow. Brad shot his gun through his jacket hitting him in the chest. The 9 mm caliber bullet exited and logged in the wall above the head-board. Blood spurted on the floor and the bed, missing Brad.

Cynthia screamed, "Don't kill me," several times, getting louder with each utterance.

"Quiet," Brad commanded. He looked at her nude body. Logically, he should kill her to prevent her from telling the police what happened.

But gazing at her captivating face, blonde hair, large breasts, and curved hips, he remembered the past, and decided she would make a satisfying companion to share his exile.

After several seconds of silence, Cynthia said, "I won't tell anyone. Besides, you did it in self-defense. I'll do and say anything you want, but don't hurt me."

Brad said, "Follow me to the living room."

Cynthia reached for a robe.

"You don't need that."

Cynthia smiled to herself. She thought if I satisfy him with a promise of pleasing him whenever he wants, I won't get hurt.

Winthrop, excited from the shooting, liked the power he now had over Cynthia and decided to enjoy her. He sat on the couch and said, "I like the way you suck me."

Cynthia kneeled in front of him and unzipped his pants and used her tongue and lips to stimulate him. After he climaxed, she continued to work on him. After his second orgasm, he lifted her head and said, "That's enough for now."

"If they find José here, they'll discover your crimes and arrest you."

"I know." Cynthia hadn't decided what was more dangerous, being arrested or traveling with a killer.

"I have a way to help us both stay free. Cynthia, come with me to a tropical paradise."

"Where?" Cynthia only had an economic dependency on José, with few emotional ties. Now, she understood she had a wealthier man to convince to become her partner.

"I'll tell you when we drive to the airport. Do you have a passport?"

"Yes, it's in the bedroom. I'll go with you." She had never left Florida, but José insisted she get one so they could travel to the Caribbean.

"Get it and pack for our trip using a carry-on bag. We can get you new clothes after we arrive."

Brad followed her into the bedroom and picked up the shell casing. After taking out his keys, he walked to the bullet in the wall, dug it out, and put it in his pocket.

"Give me your cell phone," Brad said.

Cynthia handed it to him and asked "Why?"

"I don't want the police to track your movements." He took out its SIM card and put it and the rest of the phone in his jacket pocket.

"Thanks," she said, smiling. "I never would have thought of that."

"Bring me your laptop," Brad said.

She retrieved it from the kitchen. Cynthia said, "We need to take José's private files." She went to the bedroom closet and returned with his laptop.

"What's on his laptop?"

"Records of illegal private transactions José hid from you. If the police find it, they'll arrest me."

"What are the main off-the-book transactions?" Brad asked.

"I'll start with the Celexa 60 mg transactions that got the company in trouble."

"Fine."

"I worked as the contact between individuals with excess drugs who wanted to sell them. After the FDA recommended against prescribing 60 mg pills, José ordered me to purchase them, and we'd repackage them as 40 mg pills."

"So, José lied about the source of the pills. I ordered him when we started, not to sell counterfeit drugs. Glad that bastard jumped me."

"José produced many different counterfeit drugs. I don't remember every one."

"Christ, we've been lucky the FDA hasn't caught the company years ago. Are there records anywhere else?"

"No, they're only on this laptop."

"I don't want you to tell me about the other illegal drugs Orlando Distribution produced or sold so I can deny their existence, if the FDA questions me. Reformat the hard drives on your and José computers to destroy the data.

Cynthia completed erasing the data. "It's done."

"We have to dispose of the laptops."

Cynthia realized this wouldn't solve her problems if the FDA interviewed her drug-selling contacts. They could find her if she stayed in the U.S. She planned to accompany Brad wherever he went, placing herself under his protection in exchange for sex.

Florida's landscape has a multitude of rivers, bays, ponds, swamps, and drainage depressions. Brad chose an isolated pond, and threw in his gun, the fatal bullet and casing, gloves, jacket with the bullet hole, Cynthia's SIM card, cell phone, and both laptops. He set the company closure document on fire and buried its ashes in the wet pond shoreline. Except for his rented car, he left no traces of his trip to Florida.

"Cynthia, we'll drive to my home in Greenville and get ready for our trip." Brad said. He hoped to secure her loyalty and body by bribing her with a rich, safe lifestyle.

"This should be an adventure for me. I've never been out of Florida."

"Really. It's only a short trip. We'll make it in two days. North Carolina is colder than Florida and the trees are different, but the eastern part is flat and contains many lakes and rivers.

They drove to Greenville rarely discussing the events of the morning. Instead, Brad, curious about his traveling companion, asked Cynthia about her past. Being verbal, Cynthia kept the trip from being silent. They had dinner at a Cracker Barrel in Florence, South Carolina and spent the night in a local hotel.

Several times during the drive, Brad thought of Raino. His death made liquidating Orlando Distribution in an orderly fashion impossible. He had to leave the country soon.

The couple completed the 640 miles to the car rental agency in Greenville in the early afternoon and arrived in Brad's home a half hour later.

Brad drove into his two-car garage and unloaded their luggage. Cynthia looked at the Honda Accord parked next to them before entering the house and said, "Nice car and attractive home. Let me look in the kitchen. I'll cook dinner."

"Thanks, you can find steaks in the freezer next to you and vegetables in the fridge."

"Do you have any wine?" Cynthia asked, hoping to relax him for a later seduction.

"No, I don't drink."

Cynthia thought, thank God, he won't have the irrational drunken rages José did. She had to listen to them and sometimes became a target of his physical abuse.

A half hour after they arrived, Brad said, "I'm going to take a shower."

"Would you like some company?" Cynthia asked.

He took her hand and walked her into the shower.

After drying each other, they went to bed. At 7:00 Cynthia looked at the smiling Brad and said, "I better get up and start dinner."

An hour after dinner, Cynthia said, "It's getting late. Why don't we go to bed?"

Cynthia spent the rest of the evening hoping to make Brad sexually dependent on her. She succeeded.

Saturday, June 16, 2012

The next morning after breakfast, Brad said, "I have to run a few errands. Can I trust you to stay here?"

"Yes, you're my protector. I hope you'll keep me out of jail. Brad, I'm enjoying our time together."

Brad smiled, "I'll be back in a few hours. Pack and be ready to leave when I return."

Brad left the house happy at his new relationship and solution to the problems Raino created. He drove to his bank and accessed his safe deposit box. He removed his passport, proof of real estate ownership in Ecuador, records of financial assets invested in that country, $3,000 in U.S. currency, and documents supporting his new false identity. Brad withdrew an additional $500 from the ATM in case they couldn't use their credit cards overseas.

Brad left the bank, and while still parked, made reservations for the first available seats for two round-trip plane tickets, flying Atlanta, Georgia to Quito, Ecuador on Tuesday, June 19.

After Brad left, Cynthia poured a second cup of coffee, sat on the couch in the living room, contemplating her past, Raino's death, and her future. While she had money with Raino, she experienced abuse, and he clung to her. She had missed her privacy, but traded it for his economic benefits. Cynthia never loved him. Cynthia's savings grew, and within a few years she expected to leave him and start an independent life.

Raino's death changed everything. Her job had ended. She couldn't access her savings. Brad had convinced her without José she may escape arrest, imprisonment, and live well. She bet on not getting caught and being charged with Raino's murder.

Cynthia smiled as she thought of Brad. He appreciated her body and sexuality. She planned to strengthen his affection using every technique she had learned in her teenage years. He had left her for a few hours in his home. Brad seemed smart enough to get them out of North Carolina so they'd escape arrest. Normally, alone in a new home, she'd look through every room locating valuables she could steal later if the relationship didn't work. She behaved herself so as not to scare Brad and chase him away.

When Brad arrived home, Cynthia's reaction surprised him. She grabbed him, gave him a big kiss and said, "I made us a tuna salad. Do we have time to eat?"

"Yes, it will save us a stop."

After they finished, they both cleaned up the kitchen and turned on the dishwasher.

They walked into the garage and Brad opened the door to the silver 2010 Honda Accord. Once on the road, Brad said, "We're going to Atlanta. In a few days we'll be safe, warm, and secure in a new home high in the Andes Mountains."

## Chapter 26 FDA Reopens the Investigation

Monday, June 18, 2012

The FDA reached a judge on Saturday who approved a search warrant for Orlando Distribution's headquarters, its warehouse, and the homes of José Raino's and Brad Winthrop. The warehouse search included an order for the FDA to seize Orlando Distribution's drugs for testing.

The FDA appointed Nancy Williams of the FDA Miami Field Office to lead the investigation. She assembled a team of FBI and FDA agents to start the four searches simultaneously at 7:00 a.m. on Monday. Since no one answered at either Orlando Distribution's headquarter, Raino's, or Winthrop's homes, they picked the locks. The FDA found two workers at the warehouse and served the summons before conducting the search.

Nancy Williams set up a command center in Miami to coordinate the multi-site operation.

The first FDA car started to pull into Raino's driveway, but stopped for dog walkers to pass, before proceeding and parking. The remaining cars parked behind the first car.

Agents ran to the back of the house to stop anyone from leaving. After they entered the house, a sickly sweet foul odor that smelled of rotten meat doused with cheap perfume filled the air. Several of the agents covered their faces.

The agents examined each room ensuring they were empty. Within a minute, they entered the master bedroom. The smell overwhelmed them. One yelled, "Dead male lying face-up on the floor in the master bedroom. Shot in the chest."

The lead agent looked at his decaying body and said, "Someone murdered him several days ago. I'll call the local police to get an ambulance here. We'll need to wait outside so we don't compromise the crime scene. Please put everything you've moved back where you found it."

He called Nancy Williams to report what they had found. She said, "Cynthia Smothers lived with Raino. Did you find any trace of her?"

"She's not here, and we just started the search."

"Send someone to talk to the neighbors and ask them the last time they saw her." Since Raino's neighbors were walking dogs, they received consistent confirming answers from the first three individuals. They saw Cynthia leave with a man in a late-model white Chevy Malibu early Friday morning around 8:30. They didn't have a good description of the driver since he wore a hat and sunglasses. He had pulled up the collar of his jacket to hide his face."

The agents asked everyone they talked to, "Did you see the car's plates?"

One said, "Yes, they were North Carolina plates, but I don't remember the numbers."

A second witness confirmed this observation.

"I'll put out an APB for them for Florida, Georgia, South Carolina, and Alabama. Have the local police arrived?" Nancy said.

"They just came."

"Wait until they give you the okay to restart the search. Call me after you finish."

The local police examined each room before entering the master bedroom to look for direct evidence related to the killing and to identify those in the house at the time of the fatal shot. They allowed the FDA agents to search the house after they had finished at 10:00.

The FDA staff left at noon. The lead called Nancy who told him, "Drive what you found to Miami and release the other agents from the search."

After entering Orlando Distribution's three-room headquarters, the FDA agents couldn't find José Raino or Cynthia Smothers.

146

The lead agent said, "They may arrive later. Let's search the offices, remove files, and wait for them."

At 7:45, the lead agent received a call from Nancy Williams. "The Raino home team found Raino murdered, and neighbors saw Cynthia Smothers drive away from Raino's house on Friday morning. I don't expect her to go to work. After you pack the files and electronics, stay there with another agent and send the rest to help in the warehouse. I've told them what happened to Raino. They expect you."

Nancy phoned the two agents at Orlando Distribution's headquarters three hours later and told them to drive to Miami. They left with an SUV full of the company's records and electronic equipment.

The original FDA search team arrived at the warehouse in a climate-control truck so they could drive the seized drugs to the FDA's Forensic Chemistry Center in Cincinnati in containers that maintained their viability.

The FDA search surprised the workers who let the FDA proceed, but tried to call José Raino on his cell phone. Receiving no answer, they sought to leave, but the agents told them, "You have to stay around and help us write up an inventory of what we take."

The lead agent welcomed the arrival of the others from Orlando Distribution's headquarters. He directed them to store the documents and computer equipment in one of their SUVs. The agents completed inventorying and loading the drugs by noon. Three of the agents found packed drugs boxes with the label "Costa Rican Generics." While they knew major international pharmaceutical companies had set up factories there, they didn't know Costa Rica had its own drug firms.

The FDA agents arrived at Brad Winthrop's home. Since no one answered the knock on the door, they entered the house.

After clearing each room, they found no evidence Winthrop had spent the night at his home. No one had slept in the beds, no one had used the sink and shower, and they noticed a clean and cold stove oven and burners.

They contacted Nancy Williams and relayed their findings. She told the lead, "Take another agent to the Greenville Pharma office after you finish. Maybe he stayed at a girlfriend's last night."

They took computers and paper files. They found nothing in his home related to Orlando Distribution.

The FDA agents questioned the neighbors. The first few hadn't seen him since Wednesday. But, the next one saw him leave on Saturday morning, "He drove a late-model silver Honda Accord with a blonde woman in the passenger seat. I hadn't seen that car or the woman before."

"Did you look at the plates?"

"Only that they were North Carolina plates."

Two other neighbors confirmed Brad had left his home on Saturday morning.

The Greenville Pharma receptionist told the FDA agents that Brad Winthrop had not arrived for work and was on leave fishing in Key West. The lead called Nancy Williams, "We couldn't find Winthrop in Greenville. Someone saw him leaving on Saturday with a blonde. He lied to his firm on where he was over the last four days."

With the search ended, Nancy Williams summarized their results to Detective Conner late in the afternoon. She stressed the murder of José Raino might imply Orlando Distribution's crimes extended beyond selling counterfeit Celexa.

Brad Winthrop's and Cynthia Smothers' disappearance told Nancy the murder could involve them since they may have realized their illegal drug schemes might implode. They killed Raino and fled to avoid being arrested. Nancy said, "We'll rely on the local Orlando police to conduct the initial murder investigation, unless the case expands. I need your police force to help find Winthrop. Are Hoffman and O'Hare still helping you?"

"Yes, they're great. Since they have no financial or jurisdictional constraints, they can do things normal cops can't. Hoffman was a Delaware detective before she and her husband wrote their first book."

"I know, I've read both their books. They're adept at locating felons who've disappeared. Can you ask them to help find Winthrop and Smothers?"

"I'll contact them. The first thing we'll do is try to find the license plate of the silver Accord. It won't be easy, with over three million cars registered in North Carolina. The Accord is the most popular car in the state," Conner said. The size of the task daunted him.

"I've issued an APB for Winthrop and Smothers for the entire Southeast. I'll notify the TSA to detain them if they try to leave the country," Nancy said. She wondered how long it would take her office to analyze the seized documents and electronics.

"Our DA has given us a search warrant for John Short, owner of Greenville Pharma. We didn't investigate Short as a source of the counterfeit drugs. We are charging him with rape and multiple cases of sexual battery with malice. The DA might charge him with first-degree murder, depending upon the results of the search. This case should not interfere with your investigation," Dave said.

"I agree. We examined Short and found the drug case didn't involve him. Good luck." Nancy satisfied with the FDA search, had nothing to do but wait for the documentation and drugs to arrive before resuming their investigation of what might become a significant counterfeit drug bust.

After the call with Williams ended, Dave said, "I need you to write an arrest warrant for Brad Winthrop."

"What should I include in the warrant?" June asked.

"Distribution of illegal drugs: Celexa under a false label, manslaughter of Mary Jewel and three others from taking Orlando Distribution's illegal drugs, and flight to avoid arrest."

"Should I include Cynthia Smothers in the warrant?"

"No, she might have involuntarily accompanied Winthrop, and we have no evidence she committed a crime."

After June finished, Dave edited the document and sent it to DA Shirley Sanders. He called her, and briefed her on the result of the FDA search. She emailed a completed search warrant two hours later. Dave printed it, and said, "We need this to get an extradition order for Winthrop from the governor."

## Chapter 27 Winthrop Learns about the FDA Raids

Saturday, June 16, 2012

Before he left his home on Saturday, Brad asked Cynthia, "Do you need new clothes?"

"Yes, since we left Florida. I couldn't really pack. I only have two pairs of slacks, two tops, sweat pants, and a large t-shirt. Plus I'm low on underwear."

"Where do you want to buy new clothes?"

"Chico's. It's the best store for travel clothes. Most of what they sell doesn't wrinkle when packed."

Brad said, "We're driving to Columbia, South Carolina, I'll find one on the internet." He used a disposable cell phone and located a store in the Trenholm Plaza. "Make sure you get a warm sweater, it can be cold at night in the Andes."

"I will. If it's a mall they should have stores selling underwear."

"The drive should take four hours. You have a small and shabby carry-on. If they have a Coach store there, I'll get you a new bag"

When they arrived, Brad drove around the parking lot until he found a luggage store. "Cynthia, you stay here, I'll be back in a few minutes. I don't want anyone to see us together."

Cynthia at first thought, he might be paranoid, but I don't care, I want to get out of the country.

Brad returned in ten minutes, with a blue leather suitcase that fit the carry-on requirements of the airlines. He showed it to Cynthia.

"It's beautiful. I should be able to pack twice what I brought from Florida."

"That's why I got it. Don't spend long in each store. We don't want people to remember you." He gave her three-hundred in twenties.

"Don't charge anything, nor give any identifying information. If they ask for your address, just say, 'I don't give out that information.' If they insist, walk out of the store and come back to the car."

As she walked toward Chico's, she wondered if the car would be there when she returned. After buying clothes in less than ten minutes, a personal record for her, she looked toward the car and smiled seeing it hadn't move. Ten minutes later after purchasing underwear, she returned to Brad and tried to give him the leftover cash.

"Keep it. Do you have much cash with you?"

"No. Only a little over a hundred with the money you gave me."

Brad handed her another ten twenties "You might need it, and I don't want you to use your credit cards until we're out of the country."

"Thanks, do you want to know what I got with your money?" Cynthia flashed a sensuous smile.

"You can show me when we get to the hotel," Brad said, after the tone of her voice excited him.

Brad drove to an Applebee's and ordered two takeout dinners. He drove to a Days Inn, and they carried the old luggage and new purchases into the room.

Before eating, Cynthia said, "Let me model them for you." She sensually took off all her clothes and tried on a set of the new underwear."

As she changed into her second set, Brad said, "I can't wait." He took her arm and went to the shower.

After they ate dinner, Cynthia said, "I'll model the other clothes at the next motel."

Brad fell asleep, exhausted after eating, assured in seventy-two hours he'd enjoy his new safe life in Ecuador. After checking out, he drove to Mountain View, a suburb of Atlanta near the airport, and stopped at a Best Western. Over the next two days, he couldn't get enough of Cynthia's modeling. Brad's behavior reinforced her new belief he'd never leave her.

Cynthia liked driving with Brad. He laughed at her jokes and always explained where they had been and where they were going. She found many similarities between the flat and watery landscape in Florida and where they drove in the Southeast, except for different vegetation and a few rolling hills. They had driven southeast of the southern Appalachians.

Monday June 18, 2012

Before going out to purchase a take-out dinner on Monday evening, they watched the 6:00 p.m. news. Ten minutes into the program, the commentator reported on a FDA execution of search warrants related to counterfeit drugs that involved the murder of José Raino, the president of Orlando Distribution, a wholesale drug company. Winthrop froze. The anchor cut to an Orlando reporter who said the FDA and police were looking for two individuals, Cynthia Smothers, who had lived with the murdered Raino, and Brad Winthrop, who owned Orlando Distribution.

Brad contorted his face into a hateful frown and shouted, "How could they find out about us in a few days?"

Cynthia remained quiet.

The reporter flashed their pictures on the screen and asked for help in apprehending them with the usual warnings not to approach them since they might be armed and dangerous. The FDA alleged the Orlando Distribution had sold counterfeit Celexa, a drug leading to the death of several of its customers. Cynthia became nauseous and feared her bright future over.

Brad looked at his new addiction, "We need to change our plans. The TSA will look for our passports. Since the police and TSA have our pictures, we need to disguise ourselves. Cynthia, wait here, I'm going to my car."

Her face turned white, her pulse raced. After he left, she started shaking uncontrollably. She knew he'd leave her, without transportation or cash, to answer for José death. Fear overwhelmed her.

Winthrop retrieved a carry-on bag from the car's trunk to help him with his transformation.

Cynthia's heart relaxed. She smiled as she heard Brad insert his key card into the door lock.

Winthrop had put on a blonde wig to hide his brown hair and inserted blue contact lenses to lighten his brown eyes. He used makeup to age his face. Brad always dressed sharply, but took off his creased gray pants and light blue Oxford shirt and replaced them with wrinkled blue jeans and a loose red cotton sweater. When he finished, he asked Cynthia, "How do I look?"

"If I didn't know you, I couldn't recognize you."

"Good, now it's your turn. Wash your sexy wavy blonde hair, comb and dry it so it's straight."

When she finished, Brad said, "Much better, you don't look as sexy. Wear clothes that minimize the size of your breasts,"

She retrieved the old gray sweat pants and the extra-large blue t-shirt, embellished with the name and illustration of Key West. She changed her uplift bra to a soft one that let her breasts surrender to gravity.

"Great, you could pass for a middle-aged housewife. Don't put on your regular makeup. I'll do it with mine to make you look older. You'll attract less attention, and men won't remember you if you're plain." After he finished, he smiled. "Wash your makeup off before you go to bed."

Cynthia looked in the mirror and laughed. "No one will recognize, or remember me."

"That's the point."

"Do you wear contact lenses?"

"Yes."

"Do you have the prescription?"

"Yes, it's on the box."

"We'll pick up a brown-tinted pair to go with your new hair."

"I have a brown-tinted pair. When not working, I act in local theater in Orlando. Will my new hair color be brown?"

"Either black or brown, we'll pick up hair dye at our first stop after we're long gone from Atlanta. Pack your things, we leave in five minutes."

As they drove away Cynthia asked, "Where are we going?"

"To get you brown or black hair coloring. Which do you prefer?"

"Black it's a better contrast than brown for my blonde hair." Cynthia thought they should be safe. She loved the adventure of traveling with Brad.

"Then will drive to a new motel, have dinner and color your hair. The next day we'll stop at a motel in Little Rock, Arkansas. Our last stop will be in a cabin I own in Arkansas."

"Won't the police find the cabin and catch us?"

"I doubt it. My second name, unknown to the police, is on the deed."

"That's interesting. What is it, in case someone we meet on our trip asks?"

"Brad Wilson. I have to tell you since it's your new identity. You'll be Mrs. Cynthia Wilson."

"I've always wanted to get married."

Brad smiled, thinking I'm already treating her as my wife.

"Why did you keep our first names the same?" Cynthia asked.

"If we used different first names, and someone called us by our original first names, we'd instinctively react, perhaps giving away our false identity. That won't occur with original first names."

Cynthia looked forward to life as a married woman.

Margaret and Paul watched the same national news as Winthrop.

Paul said, "Margaret, angel, I never expected the case to get so hot so fast with the information on Orlando Distribution we provided. Raino murdered, Cynthia Smothers and Brad Winthrop missing, and a major counterfeit drug crime that may involve Orlando Distribution."

"Hon, it's not the small crime of one person being murdered that we investigated. It looks like our role has ended since we proved Mary Jewel died from counterfeit Celexa drugs. I liked the travel and investigating the Pharmaceutical industry, but I guess it's over."

"We should call Brian Jewel and Conner and tell him our investigation has ended," Paul said.

"Yes, too bad this part of the story seems more exciting material for a book than the simple Mary Jewel case," Margaret said. "Hon, we can write the rest of the story, but our role will be reporters, rather than detectives."

"Let's enjoy our dinner. Angel, want another glass of Chardonnay?" Paul asked.

Margaret and Paul had just finished eating when Brian called, "Brian and Sandy here. Did you watch the national news?"

"Yes. We now know who supplied the drugs that killed your mother. Brad Winthrop, Orlando Distribution's owner, who worked at Short's firm," Margaret said.

"We never knew the investigation would end with a violent murder, kidnapping, and the killer disappearing. I hope the police catch him soon," Sandy said.

"So do we, but we've finished our role. The police will handle Winthrop's capture," Margaret said.

"Thanks for your help. We'll be scheduling a memorial service in Duck for my mother in a few weeks with my brother and sister and mother's friends attending. We hope you can join us and Paul can say a few words related to his friendship with her and your work on solving her murder," Brian said.

Margaret answered, "We'll look forward to it."

David Conner called early the next morning. "Nancy Williams, who's directing the Orlando Distribution investigation, wanted me to thank you both for the information you provided. She said, 'It changed the case from a minor to a major investigation, with life-saving implications for the U.S.'"

"We're glad to help," Margaret said. "Too bad our role is over since we know how Mary Jewel died."

"Perhaps not," David said. "There is another reason I called." Margaret and Paul looked at each other. "I assume you may have watched last night's news about Winthrop."

"We did," Paul confirmed.

"Nancy Williams wondered if you could help them locate the two missing persons: Brad Winthrop and Cynthia Smothers. Your writing on search procedures impressed her."

Paul mouthed "yes" to Margaret, realizing they may be directly in the action.

"Of course, always eager to accommodate a fan. But, we're on a short trip to Quebec until Sunday. We can start on Monday."

"That's fine. It must be fun to be retired and take a vacation whenever you want. I didn't know American cell phones worked in Canada.

"They do if you pay for an upgrade. As authors, we don't have complete freedom. Margaret and I are signing books at ten stores," Paul said, "Will we still report to you, with the standard payment of zero salary and no expense remuneration?"

"The financial provisions will be the same, but I'm not sure who will give you assignments."

"Since Winthrop lived in North Carolina, we'll start our investigation there. We'll stop by and see you on our drive to Greenville. We want to talk to John Short," Margaret said.

"When can we expect you?"

"Next week on Tuesday," Paul answered.

"Come to our office, and we'll deputize you to officially represent us. Please don't talk to Short until you see me."

Margaret said, "If we're deputies, can we carry guns? Winthrop has already killed. We shouldn't have to face him unarmed."

"Yes, you can carry guns in North Carolina, but I don't know the laws in other states. I'll email you a copy of the arrest warrant for Winthrop. You'll need it if you find him in another state. The local police might ask for it before they arrest him." Dave said as he ended the conversation.

"Angel, it appears Conner will arrest John Short soon."

"Yes hon, but maybe we'll assist in arresting Brad Winthrop."

## Chapter 28 Simmons Pharma Asks Hoffman and O'Hare to Help Them

Monday, June 25, 2012

Warren Pauley, Corporate Chief of Security called Robert Simmons, CEO of Simmons Pharma.

"Another killing. We lost James Glass, a successful lobbyist who worked for us."

"Hell, this had to happen when our profits have never been higher. Stop by and brief me at 10."

Warren entered his boss's office well prepared, with a one-page table of the company's murdered staff, which he handed to Simons

"This table summarizes the seven murders. The police found the latest, James Glass, shot through the head Sunday evening in Great Falls, Virginia four miles from his home. He wasn't an employee, but he lobbied full-time for us. It's too early to question the efforts of the Great Falls police to solve the crime.

"I've added another column summarizing the local police's reaction to each killing."

"The killings are now in three states. I see no updates on the earlier murders." Simmons said.

After reviewing the table, he ordered Pauley to, "Contact the local police, ask for updates, tell them the table shows a conspiracy to kill Simmons Pharma's employees, and ask for their help."

Warren emailed the six local police stations, attaching the table, explaining its significance, asking for their help, and stating he'd call them in the afternoon.

## Murdered Simmons's Employees

| ID | Name/Date and Time Murdered | Simmons Pharma Position | Location | Local Police Evaluation | Suspects |
|---|---|---|---|---|---|
| 1 | Michele Jones 4/25/2012 | Saleswoman | Philadelphia, PA | Non -sexual assault running in park. No witness or enemies. | Ex-husband |
| 2 | Ron Avon 5/16/2012 | Salesman | Rockville, MD | He had enemies, jilted girlfriends and jealous men | None |
| 3 | George Ball 5/18/2012 | Drug Production Manager | Monmouth Junction, NJ | Robbed and shot in home in New Jersey | None |
| 4 | Harold Roman 6/11/2012 | Comptroller | Lincroft, NJ | Ex-wife and ex-girlfriends | Several |
| 5 | Ann Pace 6/11/2012 | Chief Scientist | Lincroft Township, NJ | No non-family enemies | Ex-husband |
| 6 | Martha Russo 6/14/2012 | HR Specialist | Monroe, NJ | Mugged and strangled while running in park. Suspects include former staff she fired. | Examining ex-staff |
| 7 | James Glass 6/17/2012 | Lobbyist | Great Falls, VA | Police not contacted | NA |

At 4:00 p.m., Warren told Simmons, "They had similar responses. We have nothing new. While the table hints at a conspiracy, we don't have the resources to investigate murders outside our jurisdiction. They suggested calling the FBI."

Simmons, said, "Follow their recommendation. Call the FBI."

Warren scheduled a meeting for 2:00 the next day in the FBI's Newark, New Jersey office.

When he returned from the FBI, Warren told his boss, "Our table didn't impress the FBI. They said it only showed seven murders but not a conspiracy. They told me to get that information, and they'd open a case."

"Have you ever read the real-crime Hoffman and O'Hare books?" Simmons asked.

"Yes. Why?"

"Call them and see if they'll investigate the murders."

"What can I offer them?"

"We need them. If our staff finds they're targets of a serial killer, they'll quit and the company will crash. Offer a million plus rights to use what they find in a true-crime book."

Warren whistled, and said, "Okay!" He didn't realize this amount was small compared to Hoffman's and O'Hare's profit on each of their two previous books.

Warren called to set up an appointment to meet Margaret and Paul. Mindful of his rebuffs from the police and the FBI, he decided not to divulge the full reason for the meeting. "Hello, this is Warren Pauley, Corporate Chief of Security at Simmons Pharma. I want to talk to Margaret Hoffman and/or Paul O'Hare."

"This is Margaret. I'm on speaker phone."

"How can we help you?" Paul asked.

"I'd need to meet to discuss a series of events at Simmons Pharma that should be a great topic for a true-crime book."

"What events?" Margaret asked.

"I don't want to say over the phone, but it involves murders of several of our employees. Are you available to meet me tomorrow? I can come to your home."

Margaret and Paul glanced at each other. She said, "We won't be at home until Sunday night." Margaret said. She gave him the address. Can you make it by 1:00 on Monday? We can meet at our house in Ocean View, Delaware."

"Sure, I'll take the company plane and fly to the nearest airport."

"That's Salisbury, Maryland," Margaret said.

After the call, Paul said, "Angel, before we meet Pauley, we need to learn about Simmons Pharma and try to find out why they want to talk to us."

Margaret opened her laptop and began their research. Paul typed a summary of what they found on his laptop. They were a high-growth company going from $2 million in sales in 1995 to over $3 billion in 2011. Their key products were opioids.

Simmons Pharma has a large marketing department that sells drugs to hospitals, drug stores, and directly to physicians. They have an educational department that teaches free week-long courses to health care professionals on how to eliminate pain in their patients' lives. The company covers all costs for the courses including transportation, lodging, and food. They hold the courses in exotic locations like Hawaii, New Orleans, Florida, and at ski resorts.

After two hours of research, Paul said, "I've learned enough. There is no difference between them and the pushers on the streets of Baltimore. They just dress better, have a more expensive clientele, and enjoy a risk-free income, since Medicare and medical insurance companies write the checks."

"Hon, I agree. Should we cancel the meeting?"

"No. What he says may help us in writing our next book," Paul said. "I don't want to miss the chance to get Simmons Pharma's quotes into the new book."

"I wonder if they're the company that turned innocent, athletic, and beautiful Eve Jewel into an opioid addict." Margaret said in disgust.

Monday, July 2, 2012

Upon meeting them, Pauley said, "This is a great location. Perfect views of the bay."

"Thanks. We love it here." Margaret said. "You were vague on the phone yesterday. I assume you want to discuss the murders?"

"Yes. Someone or several persons killed seven of our employees or contractors in the last two months. As Director of Security, I have to find out why." Warren handed them company marketing literature bragging about the growth of the company and its major products. "I want to give you background on Simmons Pharma." Pauley stressed Simmons's role in eliminating major suffering.

Both Margaret and Paul thought of the millions addicted to narcotics caused by Simmons marketing plans as he talked.

When he finished the company propaganda, Warren gave them his table and said, "This shows seven murdered employees. We believe it isn't a coincidence. The last two columns include what the local police believe are the motives for the murders and any suspects they are investigating. They refuse to examine any connection between the murders."

Margaret said, "Jealous lovers or jilted spouses commit many murders. Most police departments will investigate those options before embarking on a conspiracy theory."

"Motive is critical in finding a murderer," Paul said. "Do you have any one in mind for the killings? If you do, why did they kill? Did you ask the FBI to get involved?"

"I'm concerned our competitors are murdering key staff to weaken our future growth and increase their market share. Yes, we talked to the FBI. They said until we can show them a conspiracy, they won't take the case."

"Did you try to establish one?" Margaret asked.

"No, that's why I'm here. Our company wants to hire you to find the killers, whether there is a conspiracy on not. We'll pay you a million dollars plus expenses, and you can use whatever you find in your investigation in your next true-crime novel." He noticed Margaret and Paul raise their eyebrows.

"That's a very generous offer," Margaret said smiling. "We're in the midst of a major investigation. Paul and I need to talk the offer over in private. Is it okay if we call you tomorrow morning?"

"Yes."

Margaret's skill in ending the conversation left Warren thinking he had convinced them to work for Simmons Pharma.

After Warren left, Margaret said, "Like many cops, who saw the horror of opioid addiction, I wanted to close these legal drug companies and send their executives to jail. It might be the reason the local police didn't share Warren's enthusiasm for investigating a conspiracy. Someone may have wanted to set an example for others, to make Simmons Pharma pay for legally killing patients."

"I'm glad we aren't going to help them. Millions have become addicted and thousands have died," Paul said.

"I'll call Pauley in the morning."

"I agree. I won't be as diplomatic as you."

At 9:00 a.m. Margaret called on her cell phone.

"Margaret thanks for calling. Will you and Paul help us?"

"No, we have discussed it and have to decline your generous offer. We have too many commitments. We wish you luck in solving the murders of your employees."

They never heard from Simmons Pharma again.

## Chapter 29 John Short Arrested

Tuesday morning, June 19, 2012

Besides dealing with the FDA on the Orlando Distribution investigation, Dave Conner worked with DA, Shirley Sanders in preparing search warrants for John Short's properties.

The Greenville DA and the Kitty Hawk police divided the workload between the two jurisdictions. At 8:00 a.m., the Greenville police began to search Short's and his children's homes in Greenville. At the same time, the Duck police, assisted by the Kitty Hawk police, searched his beach house. The Greenville police retrieved files, electronic equipment, and the urns containing the cremated remains of his ex-wife, Liz Short. They delivered the evidence, except for Liz's ashes, to the Kitty Hawk Police station since both jurisdictions agreed to compile the evidence of the murder case of Short's wife, the sexual assaults, and the rape of Helen Morse, in Kitty Hawk. The DA's from both counties had confidence they had strong enough pre-search evidence, and the testimony from the attacked women to convict Short.

New evidence that could lead to a murder charge rested in Liz's untested ashes. A detective from the Greenville police drove the urns containing the ashes to the toxicology laboratory in Raleigh.


Late Wednesday afternoon, Dave Conner received an email from the toxicology laboratory. The ashes contained a significant amount of arsenic, enough to kill Liz.

Dave called both DAs. In a conference call, he relayed the results, and suggested, "You should charge him with first-degree murder for poisoning his wife."

"I plan to, but it will be harder to prove than the rape case," the

Greenville DA said.

"I know, we'll try and develop other evidence," Conner said.

The Greenville DA said, "We want you to handle the interrogations in Kitty Hawk since you're more familiar with the case than our police. I'll send a representative to observe. Let me know when you'll start."

Two hours later, June, who had spent the day examining the laptop from Short's Duck home, told Dave, "I found a directory named 'My Friends Activities'. It contains a history of twenty-two women. Short attempted to seduce them since he left teaching at the university. He wrote that he used force against Helen Morse and three other women."

"It's a significant find. His file supports Helen's and the other women's statements. Send me the three other rape victims' names. If Short pleads out, we won't need them. Email me the incriminating directory and send it to both DAs. Outstanding work, it's getting late. Go home, and we can plan tomorrow's work early in the morning. You and I'll interview Short in the afternoon."

Wednesday June 20, 2012

Shirley Sander's confidence grew as she read the "My Friends Activities" file. She prepared an indictment that included: two cases of second-degree rape, twenty cases sexual battery with malice, and one of first-degree murder for poisoning his wife. Shirley showed the indictment to the judge on call. She asked for and received an arrest warrant.

Dave Conner felt relieved when DA Sanders called, "I'm emailing you and our Greenville contacts the charges and an arrest warrant for John Short."

"Thanks, June and I will pick him up from the Greenville police as soon as we can get to Greensville." Conner said.

"Thankfully, John Short will be off the street," Sanders said. "I've set a court appearance for tomorrow. We will ask the judge not to grant bail. Have a nice drive. Your office conducted an excellent investigation. Don't miss Short's appearance in court."

"We won't. The Greenville police will help us arrest him. I've told the Greenville DA we'll interrogate him this afternoon and try to get a confession."

"Good luck."

Within a half hour the detectives had started the drive to Greenville. On the way, they called their Greenville police counterparts, "We should arrive at your station in an hour. Did you receive an email of the arrest warrant and indictment?"

"Yes. We'll bring it to his house when we arrest him. A patrol car drove by and verified he's at his house. He's parked where he can see Short's driveway, but Short cannot see him. We'll meet you there for the arrest."

When they arrived, they saw the patrol car and two unmarked cars parked in front of the house. "They don't want to give him a chance to flee," June said.

"Guess not."

The arrest went without a struggle. But, Short gave a sharp response to the charges. "The sex I shared with those women was consensual. I did not murder my wife!"

"You can call your lawyer and have him or her meet us at the Kitty Hawk police station in two hours," Dave said.

Short called his corporate lawyer, explained his arrest, and said, "Get a good criminal lawyer to meet me at the police station in Kitty Hawk at 4:00."

They had an uneventful drive back to Kitty Hawk. The accused and the police didn't talk during the trip.

The interrogation started at 4:15. Dave and June, John Short, and his lawyer Bobby Sullivan attended. The DA from Greenville observed through a one-way mirror. He had called Shirley Sanders earlier, and they both agreed to listen because of the complexity and importance of the case.

Before the session started, Bobby warned John Short not to answer questions unless he approved them. The initial questions confirming Short's identity, his address, and employment did not bother the lawyer.

"John Short, we have evidence you preyed on vulnerable, divorced, and available lonely women. Did you know Helen Morse?" David asked. "She has accused you of raping her."

"Don't answer that," Bobbie said in an exaggerated Southern drawl.

"We seized your computer in Duck while executing the search warrant. Do you still want to remain silent on whether you know Helen Morse?" June said.

Short looked at his lawyer and hoped they hadn't accessed his activity files.

The lawyer shook his head yes.

"Yes," Short replied.

"You had twenty-two interesting files on your system. I'll read part of what you wrote concerning Helen. 'She was one of my smartest, beautiful, and sensual students. I have to have her...'. Skipping a few lines, you wrote, 'I'll drive to Manteo, run into her and ask her to dinner.' You wrote you planned to seduce her as soon as she invited you into her home. She must have frustrated you since it took five tries. That's when the attack took place. You drugged her, and when you kissed her and tried to take off her clothes, she resisted."

"Hold on," Bobby said. "How do we know a cop didn't type this information after you seized his PC?"

"Short is very risk adverse. He had his files backed up by a commercial IT security firm. We copied the files from that firm's disk farm. She handed Bobby the file that identified the sources as Carolina IT Security, Inc. The file had the start date when you typed the first text and the date recording the last entry." Short held his head in his hands and shook.

Bobby said, "I'd need to take a break and talk to my client. We didn't anticipate this evidence."

"Let me take you to a room where you'll have privacy," Dave said.

Bobby took the transcript of John Short's enjoyment of Helen Morse, into the room. "Let me read this before we talk," Bobby said.

After five minutes, Bobby asked, "Did you write this?"

"Yes."

"Is it true?"

"Yes."

"Are the twenty-one other files written in the same vein stating you enjoyed each one?"

"Yes."

"This can't get in front of a jury. If it does, the judge could sentence you, given you age, to what amounts to a life sentence. We have to plead out this charge. I'll ask them what they'll offer. Let's discuss the murder charge. Did you kill you wife?"

"No, I wonder how they came up with that charge."

"Usually, the police interview your associates, neighbors, and friends to discover your relationships. If they find you had a strained relationship, they'll make you a suspect. They then look for more concrete evidence. If they find it, they charge you with murder."

"Like most marriages, our relationship wasn't perfect, but I loved her."

"Did you enjoy any of these twenty-two women in the file when you were married?"

"No."

"Did you cheat on your wife?"

Short hesitated, "Yes."

"The cops will know that and use it in court."

"The punishment for first-degree murder in North Carolina is death by lethal injection or life imprisonment. I don't want you to answer questions related to that charge. Let them prove it. We don't have to prove your innocence."

Short walked back to the interrogation room with bent shoulders, looking at the floor, showing his fear and guilt.

Bobby started the conversation, "What can you offer to avoid going to court for the rape and sexual battery charges."

"We can't negotiate a plea agreement. You have to talk to the DA's office. We'll tell the DA of your request. We need to discuss the murder charge," Dave said.

"John will not answer questions related to that charge until the DA responds to our plea request."

Dave Conner realizing Bobby had decided not to talk further ended the interrogation.

The police kept John Short in jail overnight until the bail hearing at 10:00 in the morning.

The Greenville DA decided to wait until after the arraignment and the bail hearing before replying to Bobby's request for a plea agreement.

At the hearing, the judge had the charges read and ask Short "How do you plead?"

Following Bobby's instructions, Short replied, "Not guilty."

Shirley Sanders said, "We need to remand Mr. Short. He has unlimited resources, has terrorized many women over the last twenty years, and has property overseas in the Balkans, with countries that do not have extradition treaties with the U.S."

Bobby responded, "We request that Mr. Short, who has never been arrested, is a pillar of his community, be released under his own recognizance, until the trial."

Sanders said, "We strongly disagree, Mr. Short is a high risk for fleeing the country."

The judge replied, "I don't want to keep any accused in jail awaiting trial, whether they are rich or poor. The state has means to ensure he won't flee. I've set bail at $2 million, required he surrender his passport, restrict him to stay in his house in Duck, and wear an ankle bracelet to ensure he doesn't leave."

Dave Conner and June Devins left the hearing satisfied John Short could never harass or attack another woman.

## Chapter 30 Search for David Winthrop

Monday evening, June 18, 2012

Brad Winthrop drove west on Interstate 20 from Atlanta, stopping at Birmingham, Alabama.

The Alabama hills and small mountains impressed Cynthia since it was her first experience with rugged terrain.

They stayed overnight. Brad cut her hair short and Cynthia dyed it black.

"Don't worry, when we're safe you can grow it back. Cynthia, you're still sexy," Brad said. "I'll get us dinner."

In disguise, he drove to a McDonald's and picked up three Big Macs, two fries and two diet Cokes.

When he returned, he said, "It's not gourmet food, but I'm sure no one will remember me at the pick-up window."

Cynthia waited until her hair dried and was sure the color was permanent before she resumed her campaign to make Brad dependent on her.

The next day, after they left the motel, Brad drove through a different McDonald's and purchased breakfast. After finishing their meal in the parked car, they drove six hours to Little Rock, Arkansas. Brad registered in a motel and picked up dinner at another McDonald's. After a vigorous night, and another McDonald's breakfast, he left Cynthia at the motel. Brad walked to a low-price used car lot and paid cash for a six-year-old Ford. The dealer registered the car in Brad Wilson's name, purchased plates from the DMV, and installed them.

Brad returned to the motel, checked out, and asked Cynthia to follow him in the Ford. He drove to another used car dealer and sold the Accord for cash. The couple then spent over two hours driving to

Mena in the Ouachita Mountains in Northwestern Arkansas.

Cynthia stared at the trees and small steep mountains during the entire trip, something she had never experienced. This land was so different from Florida. "Is all of Arkansas as hilly and forested as this?" she asked.

"The terrain gets more rugged the further west we go. Tree covered mountains surround Mena. If you like to hike, you'll love my neighborhood.

Brad stopped in Mena and purchased groceries and supplies for a three-week stay.

After looking over the food, Cynthia said, "This will be a step up from our recent cuisine."

"It should be. My friends might complain that we have no wine. But since Mena is in dry Polk County, we'd have an excuse," Brad said.

Cynthia said, "Brad, Mena is an old town compared to most of the growing cities in Florida. There most of the buildings are new. In Mena, they look small and old."

"Like many places in Florida, Mena is a tourist town, but with a much smaller market. The population is around 6,000, but you'll get to like the wilderness outside Mena."

They arrived at their final destination in the afternoon, a two-story home in the mountains northeast of Mena. He had confidence no one would disturb them while he made plans for their escape to Ecuador.

Sunday, June 24, 2012

Since Dave Conner had told Margaret and Paul not to question John Short about Winthrop until Tuesday, they built a profile of Winthrop's life from childhood to the present.

The duo accessed the standard individual identification search sites for material. They found he was born in Little Rock, Arkansas forty-five years ago. His father taught English at the University of Arkansas. The family moved to Baltimore when the Towson campus of the

University of Maryland hired his father. Brad was seven. As a teenager he attended Towson and earned a degree in chemistry. Two years later, he earned a PharmD/MBA Dual Degree at the University of Maryland professional campus in Baltimore.

Fairfax General Hospital in Northern Virginia hired him for his first job as a management trainee. Brad married at twenty-two while in graduate school, divorced seven years later, with no children, and no arrest record.

After earning his graduate degree, he learned Brad led a career-oriented life. He held one job during the first five years of his marriage.

During lunch, Margaret said, "Hon, we should do the same for Cynthia Smothers since they may be traveling together."

"I agree. Can you do it while I finish with Winthrop?"

By 4:00 p.m., Paul had completed identifying the principal events in Winthrop's life. Margaret, since she started later, had made less progress on Smothers.

Paul said, "I'll work on Winthrop's location analysis for the rest of the week, while you finish Smother's history."

Paul learned the divorced Brad had purchased a timeshare for two weeks in July in his birth state, Arkansas, at Horseshoe Bend in Hot Springs National Park in 1997.

Paul assumed Brad liked hiking and fishing in the mountains. He learned Brad had opened a Facebook account in 2008. Brad's posts and comments with his Facebook friends showed he traveled to upstate New York, West Virginia, and western North Carolina in the last three years, to hike, fish, and camp.

Paul could not find a record of Brad traveling to the West Coast. Thus, after talking to Margaret, they both agreed, he wouldn't hide out in the west.

In 2009, Brad started posting in Spanish, bragging on Facebook he had learned the language so he could converse with the locals when he traveled to Latin America. He posted pictures of his travel destinations: Paraguay, Bolivia, and Ecuador. Paul copied them to a file for future reference. Both Margaret and Paul realized these countries would be his most likely destination. Even if they found him in Bolivia and Ecuador, these countries have extradition treaties with the U.S., but in the past, they had often refused extradition requests.

Margaret's research on Cynthia surprised her. The police had arrested her for prostitution to finance a drug habit in her teens, but she had become clean in her early twenties and stayed that way.

Cynthia had earned an associate in science degree in business administration when she was twenty-five from Valencia College in Orlando. She went to work at Orlando Distribution after graduation. Margaret found Cynthia only had one boyfriend, José, since working at Orlando Distribution.

The personnel search sites showed only Florida addresses. Margaret told Paul, who said, "That would be a handicap if she tried to avoid the police alone."

"Hon, I assume Cynthia, with a dependent personality, would not flee on her own but would adhere herself to someone like José or Brad to survive. I expected to find Brad and Cynthia traveling together."

Tuesday June 26, 2012

Margaret called John Short. "Hello I'm Margaret Hoffman. We met at Mary Jewel's funeral."

"Yes, I remember. How can I help you?"

"Brian Jewel asked us to investigate the death of his mother. We want to meet you to find out about Brad Winthrop. We're extremely interested in him since he has disappeared. The police want him for murdering José Raino, the President of Orlando Distribution. That firm supplied the counterfeit Celexa that killed Mary Jewel. We know he worked for you for twelve years."

"Are you aware I am out on bail?"

"Yes, but we don't want to ask questions related to your case, just those that will help us locate Winthrop."

"I'm staying at my beach house in Duck. Can you stop by tomorrow afternoon at 1:00?" Short thought, they'll give me a chance to get even with Winthrop, who may have erroneously connected Greenville Pharma with counterfeit drugs.

"Yes, we'll be there." Short gave her his Duck address.

Margaret and Paul drove to the Hilton Garden Inn that afternoon. At their hotel room, they wrote out questions they wanted to ask. After reducing the questions to a manageable number, they decided who would ask what. They agreed if one of their questions showed potential, they would follow it until they exhausted all leads.

The couple met with Dave Conner and June Devins Wednesday morning. Dave said, "Why don't you talk first and tell us what you found?"

"I examined Brad Winthrop's life while Margaret looked at Cynthia Smothers," Paul said. They summarized their findings for a half hour.

"I believe Smothers will accompany Winthrop and not flee alone," Margaret said.

Dave nodded his head, "That's true. We have two witnesses who saw her leave Winthrop's Greenville house with him last Saturday in a Honda Accord."

Paul said, "Brad probably fled to the mountains in Arkansas and will try to leave the country and go to Bolivia, Ecuador, or Paraguay. Those countries are unlikely to extradite them to the U.S."

Dave cut in, "If we don't get them soon, we never will."

June said, "Our witnesses told us they left in a late-model, silver Honda Accord with North Carolina plates. Smother and Winthrop have not charged their credit cards since Saturday."

"They must be using assumed names since they'd have to present a credit card to check into a hotel," Margaret said.

"The Honda Accord isn't registered to Brad Winthrop. There are thousands of cars fitting those specifications registered in North Carolina. There are too many to contact each owner to eliminate them until we find the one Winthrop drove, unless we find a few characters on the license plate," Dave said.

Margaret said, "We'll continue to look into Brad Winthrop. We've scheduled an interview with John Short this afternoon."

"I don't know how he'll respond to you. We have arrested him for rape, sexual battery with malice, and first degree murder. He's out on bail confined to his house in Duck," Dave said.

"We know. You two have been busy," Paul said.

"As have you and Margaret," Dave said. "After the initial investigation, we interviewed other women associated with John Short and found he had attacked at least twenty." He spent a half-hour summarizing the investigation of John Short. "Please don't tell him we found arsenic in his wife's ashes."

"We won't even tell him we talked to you."

Wednesday, June 27, 2012

Short woke up before 7:00, wondering if he had made the correct decision to have Hoffman and O'Hare interview him. He decided not to call his lawyer and hoped they would keep their promise not to ask him questions related to his current indictment.

Hoffman and O'Hare arrived on time. Short welcomed them and said, "Let's meet in the sun room. I brewed fresh coffee. I've looked into your history – interesting."

"Thanks for the coffee," Paul said. "Hope you liked what you found."

"Yes, I did, that's why I haven't canceled the interview."

As they had their coffee, Margaret complimented Short on his modern two-story house located several lots from the ocean.

She said, "We need to record the interview since Paul and I are poor at taking notes."

"Go ahead."

"We understand Winthrop worked for Greenville Pharma for

twelve years. When did you learn he owned Orlando Distribution?" Margaret asked.

"When I read about José Raino's murder, it upset me. Winthrop had asked me to start a distribution branch after my wife died. I said no in my strongest language. Distribution companies too often buy counterfeit drugs, resell them, and injure or kill their customers. Liz, my deceased wife, said Brad made the same request of her. The police found his company had sold counterfeit drugs but haven't implicated Greenville Pharma."

Short wondered if Brad had killed his ex-wife, since the murder of Raino showed he was capable of murder.

"Can you tell us about Winthrop's lifestyle?" Margaret asked.

Short spent fifteen minutes discussing what he remembered. Margaret and Paul listened carefully when he said, "Brad told me he loved Arkansas where he spent his early childhood. He visited a timeshare in Hot Springs National Park every summer until five years ago. Then he purchased a two-story-house with an in-ground swimming pool on over two acres of land in the western part of the state, north of Mena."

"Do you have the address?" Margaret asked.

"No, he never gave it to me. With a month's vacation, he went there every year. I know because I let him work from the cabin so he wouldn't have to spend every day of his vacation in Arkansas.

"Did he tell you how much he paid for it?" Paul asked.

"No, he never told me. Several years ago he started traveling to South America and told me he might retire in Ecuador or Bolivia, because of its low living cost, scenic beauty, and culture. He learned Spanish."

Paul thought this verifies what we learned from Facebook. He started on a fresh line of questioning. "Did Brad have a girlfriend?"

"Never had a steady one. He dated each one for a year or less. He never said why they split, and I never asked." Short thought, he had much in common with me.

178

Margaret asked the last question. "We learned Winthrop left his house driving a silver Honda Accord. Tell us what you remember about the car including its license plate?"

"Sorry, I've never seen that car."

"Thanks for your help. We'll send you a transcript of the interview, in case you want to change anything. Call us if you do."

Before Paul started driving, Margaret said, "I guess we have to visit Mena, Arkansas."

After the interview, they returned to the Kitty Hawk Police Station to brief Dave and June. On the drive, Margaret said, "Hon, with what Short told us, we may locate Winthrop and his car."

"Angel, Arkansas is a big state. We'll still have to get lucky."

In an interview room at the police station Margaret said, "Short told us Winthrop has a cabin near Mena, Arkansas. We plan to go there and search for him. It shouldn't take long in a small town."

Dave Conner said, "I'll call the Mena police and tell them you're coming." A few minutes into the phone call, Dave said, "I'll have our two deputies, Margaret Hoffman and Paul O'Hare, contact you when they arrive. Thanks for helping us, Chief Walker."

Dave looked at Margaret and Paul, "We've prepared your deputy badges." He handed them the badges. "This makes you official. I guess on this investigation you'll report to me. Please check in with John Walker when you arrive in Arkansas. June compiled an information package that might help, including pictures of Winthrop and Smothers, their family relations, and likes and dislikes. I'll send the same information to Walker."

# Chapter 31 Second John Short Interrogation

Wednesday, June 27, 2012

After Margaret and Paul left, Short called his lawyer Bobby. "I know who killed my wife."

"Who?" Bobby asked, wondering if Short would tell the truth.

"Brad Winthrop. Hoffman and O'Hare interviewed me about Winthrop, and I remember he had words with my wife before she died. She told me she'd fire him after she took control of the company. I opposed her move to take over the company as part of the divorce settlement. Perhaps that's why the cops developed the theory I killed her."

Bobby listened to Short as he explained why he thought Winthrop committed the murder. He said, "When my wife and I started arguing over the terms of the divorce, I moved out of our Greenville home and into our Duck home. I didn't have access to her to kill her."

"What about at work?" Bobby said.

"I didn't go to the office, but worked here in Duck."

"You have to prove your allegations and claims to the police. Want to talk to them?" Bobby asked.

"Yes."

Bobby called Detective Conner. "Can you meet Short and me at Short's Duck house on Thursday morning to talk about Liz Short's murder? He has information that will prove his innocence."

Thursday, June 28, 2012

Conner and Devins arrived at 10:00 a.m. Bobby said, "Thanks for coming. John would like to tell you who he thinks killed his wife."

They listened as Short went through his theory, only asking

clarifying questions.

"You mentioned you were with someone at your Duck home the week of your wife's death, but you didn't name the person. Your story isn't credible unless we can talk to her," Conner said.

"I was reluctant to name her because she is married. But, since I told her I could get the death penalty if convicted, she gave me permission. It's Regina Glory." He gave Conner her cell phone number and address.

When he finished talking, Detective Conner said, "We'll check your alibi. If it's true, we'll investigate Winthrop, but you're still our primary suspect. Are you ready to answer more questions about the murder charges?"

Bobby replied, "No. Perhaps after you investigate Winthrop, John can give you supporting evidence to help convict him."

After they left, Conner said, "We'll have to tell the DA, Short's comments will delay scheduling the trial. Let's talk to Regina Glory ASAP."

June Devins set up an appointment with Regina Glory for Friday morning. She welcomed them into her home in Greenville and offered them coffee. They both declined.

After turning on their recorder, Conner started the questioning, "We're here to ask you about your relationship with John Short. Specifically, how did you spend the week of June 1, 2002?"

"With John Short at his Duck beach house. We had a relationship for over a year. I was married at the time to my current husband. I told him about John and my relationship after the police arrested John. My husband had his own lover then, so he wasn't mad. Since our first child, we have ended our open marriage and are faithful to each other."

"What did you and Short do during that week?" Conner asked.

She said, "I won't tell you about our intimate events, but I'll mention the high points." Regina spoke, describing their average day and their trips to Norfolk and Williamsburg, Virginia.

June Devins ask, "Where did you stay on those trips?

"The Hilton in Norfolk and Wedmore Place in Williamsburg. I took pictures of the trip and looked at my photo albums to confirm John and I were traveling that week."

June said, "We'll check that out."

Regina gave them other verifiable information, including restaurants and tours they patronized. She said, "John used a VISA credit card to pay for everything."

"Thanks, we'll check out your itinerary," Dave said.

After they left Regina's, they drove to Janet Gray's house, whom they had interviewed earlier. On the trip, June said, "If Short has an alibi, we'll have to reopen the Liz's murder investigation."

After Janet Gray invited them into their living room, Conner asked, "You told us earlier, you thought John Short murdered his wife. That helped us in our investigation. Now, we need you to tell us if Brad Winthrop and Liz Short respected each other?"

"Poor Liz, she had problems with a hateful husband and a subordinate who pressured her to change the business model of her firm."

"What do you mean?" Conner asked.

"Winthrop told Liz their growth rate was too low, and that they should move into the wholesale drug market. She told him it was too risky. He kept pressuring her. After a month, she told him to stop, or he'd be fired. Winthrop threatened to go to her husband to overrule her. She said her husband agreed with her about not entering the wholesale drug business."

"How was it resolved?" Conner asked.

"It wasn't. Someone murdered Liz three days after their last conversation."

After Conner started the car to drive back to Kitty Hawk, June Devins said, "I'll set up appointments at the two hotels to verify Regina Glory's claim."

On Saturday Detectives Conner and Devins drove to Norfolk and Williamsburg. The hotel, restaurant, and tour management confirmed that John Short and Regina spent time at the locations she mentioned, including the date of Liz's murder.

Conner called the DA on the way back and told her, "We confirmed John Short could not have killed his wife. Our new suspect is Brad Winthrop." Dave repeated Short's alibi and their verification.

"I'll drop the charges. Now maybe we can get them to a plea bargain to avoid a trial. Can you bring him to my office on Monday morning?" Sanders said. "Yes, we'll notify Short's lawyer of the meeting."

On Monday, Shirley spoke first. "Mr. Short, we have good news for you. The state is dropping the murder charge that you killed your wife. But, I hope you understand the overwhelming evidence against you for the rape and sexual battery charges. Rape in North Carolina is punishable by up to fifteen years in prison. Since you're charged with two rapes, and because of your predatory nature, we can ask the judge to have you serve the sentences consecutively. In addition, we've indicted you for twenty cases of sexual battery with malice, each carrying a maximum sentence of 150 days. Served consecutively, that would be 3,000 days, or over eight years. If you go to trial and are found guilty, you could be sentenced to over thirty-eight years in jail."

Short, cautioned by his lawyer, knew his maximum sentence. But he still panicked when he heard the DA speak.

"At John's age, that's a life sentence. What can you offer to avoid a costly and disruptive trial?" Short's lawyer asked.

"If he pleads guilty to all charges, we're prepared to accept a fifteen-year concurrent sentence for the rapes, and five years for the sexual battery charges, totaling twenty years. He'll be eligible for parole in twelve years," Sanders said.

Short viewed Sander's proposal as generous and said, "I'll accept the offer."

After the meeting ended, and Short had signed the plea agreement, Conner and Devins stayed at the DA's office to modify the arrest warrant for Brad Winthrop to include the murder of Liz Short. Conner gave their draft to Sanders, who after making a few editorial changes, approved it.

She said, "This will strengthen our request for extradition if we ever locate Winthrop."

Conner emailed Margaret and Paul a copy of the updated arrest warrant.

Shirley Sanders walked Dave and June to their car. "Thanks for the outstanding work. Short will be in his seventies when he gets out, and he should be harmless by then," Sanders said.

"Do you think the sexual battery charges with malice would have been approved by a judge if we went to trial?" June asked.

Sanders smiled and said, "We'll never know and thank God it doesn't matter now."

## Chapter 32 Brad Winthrop's Escape Attempt

Wednesday, June 20, 2012

Winthrop used his laptop and untraceable internet connection to contact his property agent in Ecuador to ask him to email an application for an Ecuadorian passport for Cynthia.

"Since we don't have a marriage certificate, we'll have to use your real name on the passport. Ecuador will only issue you a passport if you have assets in Ecuador. I'm going to transfer ownership of my Atacames condo to you and open a bank account in your name so the government will be certain you can support yourself."

Brad emailed his property agent to implement the property transfer. The agent sent a return email to confirm Brad had sent the initial email and attached the required paperwork. Brad filled out the information, inserted his and Cynthia's signatures, and emailed the documents back to Ecuador. The agent returned a properly witnessed bill of sale stating Cynthia owned the property.

Cynthia found it hard to believe Brad had given her the condo and hoped it meant he loved her, and she could dismiss her fear of being alone and arrested.

Brad then accessed his Ecuadorian bank on the web and instructed Cynthia on how to open a new account. He transferred $500,000 in U.S. currency to her account. "Now you are a woman of means who should be able to get an Ecuadorian passport. I'll send the agent information on your Ecuadorian assets. If we get separated, contact my property agent. I've sent him your picture, both as a blonde and with black hair. He'll take care of you and locate me."

Brad handed her a paper with the agent's contact information.

"I don't know how to thank you," Cynthia said, feeling weak and happy, like a teenager who had been asked by her secret love to attend the senior prom.

"Just stay with me and make me happy, like you have been. I'm falling in love with you."

Brad's look almost melted Cynthia. Weakly, she said, "Me too. I'll never leave you." She meant it.

Brad received an email two hours later with the passport application. The email text stated it might take several weeks to a month to get the application processed. They returned the filled-in application identifying Cynthia's Ecuadorian assets and included a cell phone photo of her, to the agent via email within an hour.

When Cynthia saw the in-ground pool at the Brad's house, she said, "I'm used to a pool, but isn't the water too cold for a swim?"

"No. I filled it with water and turned on the heater. It should be ready to use tomorrow."

Cynthia looked at the mountains, smiled, and said, "This place is paradise. I can't wait to go swimming." She hugged Brad, showing her happiness.

Cynthia loved the hikes he took her on near his house. Cynthia read tourist pamphlets she found in Brad's bookcases. On the third day, she showed one to Brad, pointing at a section on the Black Fork Mountain Trail in the Ouachita National Forest. "Can we hike there? The scenery is breathtaking. Look at the photos of the surrounding area."

"I'd like to, but it's a national forest and Federal rangers might be looking for us. The Andes in Ecuador have more spectacular views and are five to ten times higher than the Ozarks. Wait a few weeks and you'll forget about these hills. We don't want the police to catch us and give us a view through prison bars."

"You're right." She felt disappointed but had to follow Brad's guidance if she hoped to survive.

Brad, deeply attached, and not thinking about going alone, tried to

186

prepare her for life in Ecuador. He gave her a set of interactive CD disks to teach her Spanish. In the second week, he insisted that before noon they converse in her new language. He cooked her Ecuadorian meals and had her read books on South America to acclimate her to the culture.

Their day became routine: breakfast, learning and speaking Spanish, swimming, lunch, reading and talking about Latin culture, a walk in the mountains, dinner cooked by Brad, and the evening watching the television news channels and movies. Brad felt relieved that his crimes and flight did not appear on the news after the first week.

Brad spent at least an hour a day bragging about his home in a gated community in Cuenca. The city had a metropolitan area population of over 600,000. The Andes peaks surround the city. "While it's near the equator, at an altitude of 8,400 feet, it has a perfect climate with temperatures ranging between the 60s and the 70s."

Brad would periodically show her pictures of her beach condo and his house on his cell phone. She loved the different views of the city and mountains from the house. She asked him to show her these pictures daily. Cynthia fell in love with the fantasy of living in a small country with extensive beaches on the Pacific Ocean, the rugged Andes Mountains, the Amazon rain forest, and a sizeable population of American expats. Brad's millions would ensure a grand life style.

Thursday June 26, 2012

Margaret and Paul drove back to Ocean View to extend their research on Winthrop to Mena, Arkansas, where they thought he might have fled. They poured over maps of the region. When they arrived, they planned to perform a grid search for his North Carolina silver Honda Accord. They would start with at the center and move to four cells comprising the areas surrounding Mena. Since they had pictures of the two fugitives as they drove, they would examine the faces of those on the street looking for a match.

Sunday, July 1, 2012

They flew to Little Rock from Philadelphia on Sunday, hoping Winthrop had not left the country.

Reading that Arkansas has no handgun registration requirements and has concealed carry reciprocity with Delaware, they packed their guns in their luggage, checked them before they entered the plane, and declared them to the TSA. Paul rented a car at the airport. They registered at the Ozark Inn in Mena and had dinner at the Branding Iron, a brief drive up Pine Ave.

"Mena reminds me of upstate New York and West Virginia. The landscape is similar to both states: ridges, trees, and small towns on rivers. But the culture resembles West Virginia, where the mountains are higher. Upstate New York's old towns have large Victorian homes and large deserted factories, which they don't have here. Mena reminds me of the tourist-oriented West Virginia towns of Davis and Elkins. Hon, too bad we won't have time to appreciate the state. The tourist literature showed great hiking trails in the mountains we'd both enjoy."

"Angel, we can return to research the book," Paul said. He looked at her lovingly, because he knew they both would welcome a week in the woods near Mena as a break from writing but would use it to research Mary Jewel's book.

They went to bed by 10:00, made a commitment to return in the fall and made love to celebrate their first visit to Arkansas.

The next morning, they visited Police Chief John Walker, an average-sized man in his late forties, who hadn't gained the weight that most desk-bound officers do at his age. He looked ten years younger. He welcomed them to Mena, saying, "Glad to meet an ex-cop and her husband. I've read your exciting true-crime books."

Margaret responded, "Thanks for the compliment. We look

forward to working with you."

"Good to meet you, Chief Walker. She's trained me to protect myself around criminals."

"So I read. Call me John, and I'll call you by your first names. You have a major search problem ahead of you.

Walker said, "We first searched for a house in Brad Winthrop's name, but couldn't find one. We assume he used a false name to buy the house. There are hundreds of homes north of Mena that would take weeks to search so you're wise to look for his car first.

"I circulated the information Detective Dave Conner sent to my staff. They've been looking for a car with North Carolina plates. So far, no one has found one. None of the staff recognized the pictures of the fugitives Conner sent. In fact, none of us ever remembers meeting someone from that state."

Margaret said. "The Kitty Hawk police have updated the search warrant. Besides the original charges, the state wants him for murdering his boss's wife, Liz Short, ten years ago." She handed him the updated document.

"We looked for Winthrop's car as part of our patrol duties. You might have better results if you structure your search."

"We plan to conduct a grid search of the town and sounding areas over the next several days," Paul said.

"Good luck. If you find the car or the fugitives, let me know. We can arrest them. We'll call you if we locate them."

After the meeting, they began the search in the southwestern quadrant of Mena since the hotel was at its southern edge. They spent the morning covering the streets in the sparsely populated neighborhoods. Paul drove over the area twice, hoping the car they were looking for had returned and wasn't parked in a garage. They didn't find a single car regardless of make with North Carolina plates. That afternoon they searched the northwest quadrant without finding the car. The next day they completed their search of Mena and examined the southwest quadrant on the map outside the town. It took them three days to complete their search of a twenty-mile area outside Mena. They were unsuccessful.

Saturday, July 7, 2012

Margaret said, "Since we can't find Winthrop's car, we should try and locate his property. Let's examine the county's property records where a purchase occurred between seven to three years ago. Short didn't seem that sure when Winthrop purchased real estate in the Mena region."

"I agree." Paul said, as he started searching Polk County property records on his laptop. "It would be much easier if we had an estimate of the house's price. He found several commercial websites designed to search for property ownership over the U.S. and several accessed the Polk County real estate database. After examining several files, he chose the Polk County Property Appraiser site and entered an advanced query search for 'Sales – Last Sale of Record/ Date of Sale for 2005 to 2009 for qualified purchases, and Last Sales only. His query returned 9,776 records, a number too large for a manual examination.

Paul restricted his search to 2006, 2007 and 2008 with the original constraints and added a property use code of residential and vacation residential, a swimming pool, a location outside Mena, and a site equal to or greater than two acres. This search reduced the number of records to twenty-six. He exported these records to a spreadsheet.

Margaret noticed one buyer with a first name of Brad and a last name of Wilson. He had lived at 703 E. Elm St, Goldsboro, North Carolina. Paul said, "Look at this guy, Brad Wilson. He's the only one from North Carolina. Let's call Dave Conner tomorrow and find out about him before we spend hours on the other names. I'm getting tired."

"I agree. You look tired. When we get in bed, I'll give you a massage until you go to sleep."

"I look forward to it. Hon, that's one of the reasons I love you."

Sunday, after a hotel breakfast, Margaret called Dave, "We completed a grid search of Mena and couldn't locate the Accord. The Mena police have also been looking for the car. They found nothing. We started looking at sales of property between 2006 and 2008, searching the characteristics Short gave us. We found twenty-six. One new owner, Brad Wilson is from 703 E. Elm St, Goldsboro, North Carolina. We need a background check and hope he's Brad Winthrop. We have his location but don't know if he's there. In addition to the arrest warrant for Winthrop, the local police might need an extradition order to arrest him. So, any incriminating information we give you, put in the order."

"I'll search the DMV database and call you back."

Dave Conner found a 2010 silver Honda Accord registered to Brad Wilson at the same Goldsboro address. Dave keyed in the Wilson's address to a locator database so he could ask the Goldsboro police to detain him if he was there. The response surprised him – "No Such Address."

Dave called his deputies and told them what he'd found, "An excellent chance he's Winthrop. Tell John Walker what you found and that I'm preparing an extradition request to send to him.

"Winthrop out-smarted himself. If he had chosen any state but North Carolina, it might have taken several days to complete reviewing the twenty-six candidates from the other states, and he might have gone unnoticed," Paul said.

Dave Conner said, "Despite their egos, criminals are not that smart."

Monday, July 9, 2012

Dave called the DA on Monday morning, briefed her on Winthrop's location and requested an extradition order.

The deputies returned to the Mena police station and briefed John Walker on what Dave Conner had found. "Our boss and the DA are developing an extradition request. Your governor should get it tomorrow, Tuesday afternoon. We'll give you a copy," Paul said.

"That's enough evidence for me. I could arrest him now, but without a physical confirmation it's Winthrop and Smothers, I'll wait. If we arrest the wrong people the publicity might alert the real ones. Winthrop and Smothers would flee the state, and we'd never catch them. Winthrop could have rented his home to a vacation couple. Even if it is them, without an approved extradition request, I might have to release him in twenty-four hours."

"We wouldn't want that," Margaret said.

Walker accessed the Arkansas DMV database and found Brad Wilson had registered a 2008 Ford Focus in Little Rock on June 19. He printed out several copies of the registration and handed one to Margaret. He gave the other to their desk sergeant who scanned the registration, emailed it to every Mena and Polk County patrol car, and posted it in the station.

"Periodically, I'll send a car to drive by his house to make sure he's there. We'll set up an observation post across the street later this afternoon if we can get permission from the owner. If he leaves, we can track and arrest him if he tries to drive out of the area."

"How can we help?" Paul asked.

"The road north of Winthrop's house winds three miles through the mountains without a cross street. Park at the first intersection and if you see him, let us know whether he goes straight or turns. Follow him discreetly until we catch up with you."

After they left, Margaret said, "Walker has a neat way of keeping us out of trouble and not interfering with their operation by sending us away from the action."

"True, but he wants to keep us safe. Let's get sandwiches for lunch, and a cooler to store more food and water for dinner and evening snacks. It won't be so bad. We can look at the fabulous scenery, and make out if it rains."

"I've never seen kissing your partner as a recommended search procedure, since most couples including us close their eyes when they kiss. We'd miss Winthrop if he drives by."

Paul sighed, "Okay, I'll bring my laptop and document today's activities for the book."

Margaret smiled, appreciating the intent of Paul's suggestion.

Walker contacted the Polk County Sheriff's office and briefed the sheriff on Winthrop's criminal past and potential location. Walker asked for support. They agreed the Mena police would setup surveillance on Winthrop's home, and the Polk police would supply backup support to detain Winthrop if he left his home. The sheriff identified four patrol cars Chief Walker would have at his disposal.

Brad answered the door around 10:00 a.m. after he saw a FedEx truck pull away from his driveway. He called Cynthia, and they opened the package. It contained her Ecuadorian passport several weeks earlier than expected. "We can leave anytime? Get me your luggage" Brad said. He handed her the passport.

When she returned, he said, "Open it."

After she did, he unzipped it and showed her a secret compartment on the backside of the open luggage. Brad opened it, placed her Ecuadorian passport, property and bank documents in it, and secured it.

"Pack your clothes. Don't lose the luggage and keep it near you so you don't have to look for it. We'll leave after midnight so traffic will be light, and we can get out of Arkansas before dawn."

"Great, but I'm going to miss this house. The scenery is beautiful here."

"True, but it's nothing compared to where we're going."

After lunch, Brad and Cynthia started on their daily walk into the hills behind the house. Both wore shorts, while Cynthia wore a tight tee-shirt that excited Brad who could not keep his eyes off her as she walked ahead. The sound of a car on the rarely used road several hundred feet below distracted him. He turned his head and spotted a police car driving past his house south toward Mena at less than ten mph. Strange, he thought, he'd never seen one there.

Forty-five minutes later as they descended the hill less than two hundred yards from his house, Cynthia said, "I just saw a police car creep past your house."

Brad's surprise turned to alarm. Did the police have him under surveillance?

An hour later, his fear turned to paranoia as he saw two cars pull into the driveway of the house across the road. Four men in their twenties and thirties wearing jeans and sweat shirts walked from the unmarked cars into the house, each carrying a bulky suitcase. An hour later he saw the cars hadn't moved. There were no lights on in any room. He thought that strange for an occupied house darkened by shadows from the hills.

He went outside to alert Cynthia who sat next to the pool reading a book. "Cynthia, the cops might be watching us from the house across the street. Come inside. It could be nothing, but close the blinds. We're not taking any chances, we're leaving tonight after it's dark, and we don't want to let them see us getting ready."

His words shattered Cynthia's euphoria. After checking the suitcase, she asked, "Should I stuff the cooler so we have something to eat?"

"Yes, make sure the blinds are closed in the kitchen before you fill the cooler. Only take prepared food, bread, mayonnaise, cold cuts, and water." Brad said.

After he finished packing and put five small bottles of energy boosters in his jacket, he said, "I'll go to the garage and load the car before dinner." He put black tape over the rear running lights.

Brad prepared their dinner, steak and potatoes, and waited for dark. At nine-thirty, he told Cynthia, "We want to convince them we've gone to bed. Go to the bedroom and before you turn on the lights, open the blinds. I'll join you after I turn out the other lights in the

194

house. Start undressing sensually, touching yourself. Make sure the cops see you nude. Run into my arms when I enter the room, kiss and embrace me and walk toward the bed, turning out the lights as you do. I'll close the blinds. Keep your clothes for the drive tonight outside the door. At five minutes before ten, we'll leave the room, crawl to the hall to get dressed, and leave by the back entrance."

Chief Walker, along with the other cops, had set up two binoculars in the front of the house focused on the front door and driveway. A small ridge covered with bushes blocked their view of the garage. Walker called Margaret, "We've set up a surveillance post across from Winthrop's house. How are you two doing?"

"Fine we're just sitting here. We've only seen two cars in the last five hours. We have enough food and coffee to last through the night."

"Good, if we see him leaving, we'll call. If our governor approves the extradition request tomorrow, we'll arrest them."

When one of the cops saw Winthrop with a woman with short black hair, he said, "Chief, I thought Cynthia Smothers had long blonde hair. Did Winthrop kill her and get another woman?"

"Get both their pictures in close-ups. We'll send hers to the North Carolina police to see if they know her," the Chief said.

The cop transferred the pictures to a laptop and Chief Walker narrowed in and expanded the image of their faces and compared them to photos they had on file of Winthrop and Smothers. "That's them. They just dyed her hair to disguise her."

Walker called Margaret and Paul and the officers in their patrol cars that they had confirmed the identities of the two suspects.

Since Brad and Cynthia never left the house after the first sighting and had closed the blinds, the observers were bored staring at a silent house all day.

At 8:00 p.m., Chief Walker told two of them to get some sleep so they'd be ready for the midnight watch. Dusk made surveillance difficult. By 8:30 the only clear images they had on this moonless night were in the lit rooms in the house.

Chief Walker noticed the lights go off in most of the house and stay on in one room. Since the other cop, Officer Bentley, couldn't see the garage, he glanced at that room. Both reacted when Cynthia started to undress.

"I didn't expect to see this," Walker said.

"No wonder Winthrop is going to bed early," Bentley said, as the couple embraced and turned off the lights.

"I guess they'll sleep till morning," Bentley said.

"Hopefully they will, but we still have to watch. They might have gone to bed early because they need to leave in the middle of the night or before sunrise to catch a plane," Chief Walker said.

At 10:00 p.m., with Cynthia in the passenger seat, Winthrop manually raised the garage door, careful to minimize any noise. He turned the car on and crept out of the garage and stopped, so he could manually close the garage door. He hoped they wouldn't realize he left until late in the morning. When he resumed moving at a few miles per hour, he took the left fork in his driveway leading to the back entrance to the house, out of view of the surveillance team. The right fork led to the front of the house. When he entered the road, he turned on the front running lights and drove at twenty miles per hour, hoping the cops would not look in his direction.

A quarter-mile from his house, Winthrop drove behind a hill separating his car's line of sight from the police stakeout house. He turned the head lights on and increased his speed to the safe legal limit of forty-five miles per hour. He soon reached the intersection where Margaret and Paul had parked and turned left.

Margaret sat in the driver's seat. Paul shouted, "Angel, it's a blue Ford Focus. It's them."

"I see their car. I'll let them go a few hundred yards before I turn on the engine."

Paul nodded acknowledging her and called Chief Walker. "John, a blue Ford Focus carrying a couple just turned left. We'll follow them."

"Christ, how did they get past us? We'll catch up to you. Don't get close to Winthrop's car. Let us stop him."

"Will do," Paul said.

After the call ended, Margaret said, "Hon, get my purse and take out my gun and place it in the cup holder." She smiled as she saw Paul had retrieved his gun from the glove compartment.

Walker called the sheriff and said, "The Focus turned left at the intersection. Tell your cars at the roadblock at position 'A' they are headed there."

"Yes. I will."

Walker sent the same information in a broadcast to all Mena police cars.

Walker woke the other two cops who dressed and followed him to their cars. Both cars left the house with flashing lights and soon reached fifty mph. They passed Margaret's car after she had driven four miles following Brad. When the police saw the Ford in front of them, they turned on their sirens.

Winthrop saw the flashing lights behind him and accelerated, reaching eighty. After he barely kept on the road turning on a mountain curve, he saw three police cars less than a half-mile ahead. They blocked the narrow road. Three cops with guns drawn stood on each side of the road.

Cynthia looked back in horror. She saw the police cars approaching and the trees flashing by her car. She knew she would die.

Looking to the right side of the road, Winthrop saw a sharp turn and a drop off, he knew he couldn't navigate so he turned left and drove into a flat surface sparsely covered with trees. The cops opened fire. Two shots hit Winthrop, who lost control and drove into a large pine tree. One shot hit Cynthia in the right shoulder. The air bags deployed, pinning both Winthrop and Cynthia to their seats.

The first officer to reach the car opened Cynthia's door and pulled her out and laid her on the ground away from the car. The second policeman opened Winthrop's door. When he checked his pulse, he declared, "He's dead. One shot in the chest and the other through the head."

Chief Walker arrived a few minutes later and seeing the crash called for two ambulances. Margaret and Paul arrived on the scene right after the Chief and walked over to him. Walker said, "You won't be able to question Brad Winthrop, but Cynthia Smothers should recover. She is either knocked out or has fainted. She has a flesh wound on her shoulder and it looks like no bones were shattered. Stop by the station at 9:00 tomorrow morning. We can go to the hospital. If she's alert, she should be able to tell you what happened."

After they returned to their car, Paul said, "Angel, at least we didn't get in a gunfight this time." He returned his gun to the glove compartment. Margaret placed hers in her purse.

"Yes, the Arkansas police were prepared and ready. Hon, you might never shoot your gun in anger again. Neither we nor the police got hurt," Margaret said.

On the drive back to the hotel, Paul dictated his version of the events on his laptop. He used speech recognition software to digitize it so he could edit its contents. After a quick edit, he'd printed it after they arrived at their hotel, and gave it to Margaret for her to improve and add any missing narrative.

Since it was past midnight in Kitty Hawk, Margaret called Detective Dave Conner at 8:00 in the morning Kitty Hawk time and described the chase, the survival of Cynthia Smothers, and the death of Brad Winthrop.

"Too bad, we'll never know if Winthrop killed Liz Short," Dave said.

"Not unless Cynthia Smothers tells us when we question her,"

Paul said.

"Call me after the questioning. I'll kill the extradition request since Smothers wasn't on it."

Cynthia regained consciousness in the ambulance with a major headache and pain in her right shoulder. When she went to reach for the shoulder, the EMT said, "Relax you've been shot. We dressed the wound, and you should be okay. We're taking you to the Regional Medical Center in Mena."

My God, she thought, I'm still alive but caught by the police. She started breathing hard, and her heart raced. If Brad's not dead, I'll never get out of this. "What happen to the driver?"

"Unfortunately, he died. Was he your husband?"

Thinking fast, she said, "No, the bastard kidnapped me several weeks ago. I'm glad he's dead."

The EMT showed no reaction but noticed her fast pulse and high blood pressure. After conferring with the emergency room, he said. "I'm going to give you a pain killer and something to relax you. You might go back to sleep."

# Chapter 33 Questioning Cynthia

Tuesday morning July 10, 2012

Chief Walker called the EMT in the morning and asked if Smother talked about the chase.

"Not much. She asked about the driver. I said, 'He died. Was he your husband?' She became agitated and said, 'No. He had kidnapped me several weeks ago. I'm glad he died.' I gave her a sedative. She fell asleep."

"Thanks," Chief Walker said, thinking she had experienced a terrible ordeal that almost killed her.

After the call to Detective Conner, Margaret and Paul went to the police station. Chief Walker said, "Smothers is awake and recovering. Her doctor said we can talk to her. I'll drive, but both of you should ask most of the questions."

At the hospital, Paul turned on the recorder.

Margaret introduced the three of them and began. "We're glad to see you survived. Your friend died from two shots. We'd need you to tell us what happened in Orlando and your travels until last night."

"First off, he is no friend. He killed my fiancé and kidnapped me after the murder. I've been petrified ever since." Cynthia remembered her local theater directors, cautioned her not to over act.

Walker had not told Margaret of the conversation he had with the EMT, but was glad to hear Cynthia make an independent statement of her innocence.

"Sorry, I wasn't aware of your relationship with Winthrop. Tell me what happened when Winthrop first entered your house in Florida," Margaret said.

Cynthia detailed José Raino's attempt to overpower Winthrop and the shooting.

"After the killing, Winthrop made me go into the living room, nude, and give him a blow job. He said the cops would consider me a suspect, and I should leave with him before I got arrested. When I declined, he said, 'You're coming with me, or you'll join José. You don't understand, I don't want any witnesses, and I like you.'"

"I'm sorry he kidnapped you. How did you spend the time until last night?" Margaret asked.

Cynthia spent an hour talking and answering questions. She liberally added Winthrop's outrageous sexual demands trying to impress the men in the room. As directed, she provided details of the trip to Atlanta, Binghamton, Little Rock, and Mena.

"We found out the FDA had raided Orlando Distribution when we stayed north of Atlanta on the evening news. Brad went crazy. We were supposed to fly to Ecuador the next day. I had planned to try and escape from him at the airport. He cut my hair and made me dye it black so I wouldn't be recognized. Since then and until we arrived at his house in Mena, he always wore a disguise."

She told them how he tied her to a bed every night after he assaulted her. Cynthia repeated Brad's promises of a splendid life in Ecuador.

Cynthia asked, "Can I have a glass of water?"

They took a short break, and then she continued, "Winthrop staged the sex scene in his home last night to impress any cops who might be watching us to throw them off guard. He had a gun and said, 'I'll kill you if you signal the police now or on the escape to Mexico.'".

"Mexico? We thought you were going to Educator," Margaret said.

"After the FDA raid, we had to go to Mexico to fly to Quito. Brad said we'd be stopped at a U.S. airport."

They asked clarifying questions for fifteen minutes, and then Paul asked, "Did Winthrop ever discuss his criminal past?"

"No, he told me it was better if I didn't know."

"Did he ever mention Liz Short's name?" Paul asked.

"He mentioned John Short, his old boss, but never Liz Short. Why?"

"She is John Short's murdered wife," Margaret said.

"I'm afraid I can't help you there."

"Thanks for your cooperation. We'll send a file of the interview to the FDA, the police in Kitty Hawk, and those in Orlando." Margaret said.

"That's fine. The hospital said they'd probably release me tomorrow, but I should check back daily so they can examine how my shoulder is healing. Am I free to leave?"

"Yes, you didn't commit a crime in Arkansas," Chief Walker said. "I'll have your luggage and purse delivered to the hospital."

"Thanks, I need my credit cards and clothes to survive here for a week, until the wound has healed enough to travel."

"Margaret, where are you and Paul staying. Do you recommend it?" Cynthia asked.

"At the Ozark Inn. We love it."

"Thanks."

On the ride back to the station, Walker asked, "Do you believe her?"

"Hard to tell. Her story was internally consistent. Since Winthrop died, no one can contest it," Margaret said.

Paul said, "Given her looks, body, and background, I figured she'd be in charge, not Winthrop."

"Background?" Walker asked.

"As a late teenager and in her early twenties, she had a drug habit and supported it and her life by being a prostitute. Cynthia quit that life and has remained sober for years. She knows how to manipulate men," Paul said.

"As Margaret said, no one can contest what she said." Walker said.

After they left the station, "Hon, since you're driving, I'll call Brian Jewel."

Sandy answered on the second ring and put the phone on speaker. Margaret summarized the events of Winthrop's attempted escape. "The case on your mother's death is closed. The two major participants responsible for it are dead: Brad Winthrop and José Raino. You can tell your family."

"Thanks. We never would have known how mother died without you and Paul."

"You're welcome. We enjoyed it, and we'll spend six months in Ocean View documenting the events for our new book."

"We've set the date for my mother-in-laws' memorial service for Saturday, July 21, three months after her death, in Duck at the family house," Sandy said. "Can you make it?"

"Yes," Margaret said. "We'll make reservations at the Hilton Garden Inn today. What do you want us to do?"

At the hotel, Paul emailed the interview to Detective Dave Conner and the Orlando, Florida police. He called Conner. "Toward the end of the interview, we asked Cynthia Smothers about whether Brad could have murdered Liz Short. She said she didn't know."

"Since he's dead now, we couldn't prosecute him if he killed her," Conner said, "Thanks for your support in the investigation. When can I expect to read your next book?"

"In about a year," Margaret said.

The Florida police reviewed the interview and phoned Chief Walker in the afternoon. "We've examined Cynthia Smothers's response to the detectives' questions and closed José Raino's murder case. Smother has suffered enough. We have no interest in bringing her to Florida."

Wednesday, July 11, 2012

Cynthia tired of the questioning and fearing she would make a mistake talking to Margaret and Paul at the Ozark Inn, made reservations at the Executive Inn. She felt her heartbeat rise and her breathing rate increase as she worried if the Arkansas cops had confiscated the documents confirming ownership of her new assets in Ecuador. After checking in, she opened her blue carry-on luggage, accessed the hidden compartment, and relaxed. The bill of sale for the condo, her passport, and the banking accounts had been untouched. Since Brad wasn't around to chastise her, she had a glass of wine with dinner.

José's lawyer called Cynthia. "Remember me? Jim Sullivan, I'm the corporate lawyer for Orlando Distribution."

"Yes. How did you find me and why did you call?" Cynthia first thought the lawyer knew about her activities and planned to blackmail her.

"Orlando TV televised reports of the car chase and José death. They said you had survived but were in the hospital. I called the chief of police of Mena to find you. While I'm sure your heart is broken over José's murder, as the executor of his will, I have wonderful news of your inheritance. You're Raino's sole heir. I won't be sure how much he left you until our accountant does a detailed review of Raino's assets, but it should be over $15 million including his real estate holdings."

Cynthia sat on her bed stunned holding the hotel phone to her ear.

Sullivan said, "Don't talk to the police anymore without me present."

"I won't. The local police and two North Carolina detectives have questioned me. They said I'm free to leave. I'll stay here until my shoulder has healed enough to travel. Do you know if the Florida police need to talk to me?"

"I'll find out."

Fifteen minutes later, the phone rang. "Jim Sullivan here, I have great news. The Orlando police received a recording of your interview. They have closed the case and commended you on your survival ability being held hostage by a killer. I have to talk to you later about José's will and how you want me to handle your money. I'll write up a proposal and email it to you."

"Can you check with the TSA and see if they are looking for me at the airports? I want to be able to fly home." Cynthia gave him her personal email address, ended the conversation, saved his phone number in her contact list, and smiled.

He called back in an hour and told her, "The Florida police has had TSA remove your name. You won't be stopped at any U.S. airport."

The next morning Cynthia rented a car which she had delivered to the hotel. She drove to a hair salon and had her hair bleached blonde. The hair dresser matched the color to her exposed roots. In the afternoon, she returned to the hospital to have the dressing on her wound changed. They told her it had healed well and she might not have to stay in Mena a whole week before leaving and warned her not to get it wet in a shower, or she would have to stay longer. On the way back to the hotel, she purchased a laptop.

At her hotel, she logged onto the internet and confirmed continued availability of her Florida checking and savings bank accounts and breathed easier when she found the police had not closed them and confiscated her money. The accounts still had a balance of over $100,000. Cynthia then checked her investments and felt euphoric since they remained untouched. On her way to dinner, Cynthia stopped at an ATM and withdrew $200 to add to her existing funds of $300. She didn't need the cash but just wanted to find out if she had access to her checking account.

Cynthia still worried the Orlando police might discover her role in Orlando Distribution's selling counterfeit drugs. She realized she had been lucky the police didn't arrest her in Arkansas. That night Cynthia transferred ninety percent of the Florida account funds to the $500,000 Brad had deposited in the Ecuadorian bank. She knew she could live well in her new condo, even without José's inheritance.

Brad had enthralled her with his daily stories about Ecuador. She decided to contact Brad's property manager and travel to Atacames, the site of her beach condo. She planned to follow Brad's lead and move to

Ecuador, hoping they would not extradite her to the U.S.

The next morning, she called the condo manager and tried to speak in Spanish but realized she couldn't understand him, and asked, "Do you speak English? I just started learning Spanish, but I'm still not fluent."

"Yes. How can I help you?"

"My name is Cynthia Smothers, and I just purchased a condo in your building." She tried to speak in steady tones even though she feared her ownership of the condo was a Brad hoax.

"Congratulations, you'll love it here. We have many American owners. I received your paperwork a few days ago."

Cynthia relaxed, "I plan to visit there in several days, flying into Quito. Can you send me directions how to get to the condo?"

"Yes, I'll email them to you. Do you know when you'll arrive?"

"No, but I'll send a return email with my arrival date when I decide."

"We are looking forward to meeting you."

Cynthia called Jim Sullivan, "Do you know how long it will take to transfer José's assets to me?"

"I can move funds from his checking and savings accounts now, but his real estate and financial investments will take longer."

"Can you transfer the funds to my Florida checking account?"

"Yes, give me your checking account information. José Raino had over $23,000 in his accounts."

"Thanks," she gave him the account information.

She used her American passport to book a flight the next day to Mexico City from Little Rock.

## Chapter 34 FDA Continues the Investigation

Tuesday, June 19, 2012

Nancy Williams organized the seized documents and electronic equipment the day after their delivery to the Miami office. Since counterfeit Celexa initiated the search warrants, she directed her agents to identify references to Celexa first.

José Raino had well-organized and easy-to-follow documentation. By the end of the week, the agents finished identifying the companies selling Celexa to Orlando Distribution and their sales to drug companies, pharmacies, public websites, and physicians. This data did not include purchases directly from patients, nor sales to patients, kept on Raino's laptop. Williams sent out notices to the purchasers to destroy their 40 mg pills since they may have 60 mg potency and might be fatal.

Raino's records showed sales to only two internet sites. Those Pete Dunlap had discovered to be the source of the Celexa purchases by the mysterious deceased patents in Kitty Hawk. Williams emailed Dunlap asking about the status of the two website's responses to his cyber warning letters. He emailed back that they had not answered, but they still had eight working days to respond.

Orlando Distribution had purchased drugs from eighty-two companies. Forty percent of the value of their purchases came from the Costa Rican Generics firm founded by José Raino, and twenty-two percent from India Drug Sales.

Williams instructed the FDA's Forensic Chemistry Center to test Celexa first. The lab notified Williams they had a ten-working-day backlog, and they should start testing on Tuesday, July 3. On Thursday, the lab reported that forty percent of the Celexa pills were counterfeit and had been sold to ten organizations. She notified the ten companies to send her the Celexa pills from the lot numbers the lab discovered and warned them not to sell these counterfeit pills to consumers.

Thursday, June 28, 2012

Nancy contacted the Department of Homeland Security and asked them to provide her with information on Costa Rican Generics, telling them of their role in selling counterfeit Celexa.

The next day she received a call from a DHS staff. "We called the drug firm with no answer. So we visited their address and found their building completely burned to the ground. The local police told me the fire occurred on Friday, June 22."

"That was seven days after Brad Winthrop murdered José Raino." Nancy said, wondering about Brad's connection with the drug firm.

"That's interesting. A Costa Rican cop told us José Raino owned the drug firm. He said the workers showed up for work in the morning and found someone had torched the buildings. The local police looked for the two factory managers, but couldn't find them, and feared they had either left Costa Rica, someone murdered them, or they had died in the fire. You won't have to worry about that company selling counterfeit drugs in the U.S. anymore."

"True, but if the managers are still alive, they may move to another country and start a new drug company," Nancy said, feeling they hadn't eliminated that source of illegal drugs entering the U.S.

Thursday, July 5, 2012

As Pete Dunlap suspected, he did not receive a response to the FDA cyber warning letter from the two Canadian Pharmacy websites selling counterfeit Celexa. The response was due on July 5 fifteen working days after the FDA mailed the letters.

Pete signed on to both websites on July 6. To his surprise, both had been taken down, an indirect response to the cyber warning letter.

Dunlap assumed they would set up the same website with a new name and perpetuate their sale of counterfeit drugs.

He emailed Williams notifying her that the websites no longer existed. Pete thought, so much for the FDA having the websites taken down during Pangea V.

## Chapter 35 Mary Jewel's Memorial Service

Thursday, June 21, 2012

Brian wanted the memorial to be a celebration of his mother's life and to help Eve and Stu adjust to her absence and recognize her as a guide to their future. Rather than interfere with morning beach activities, Brian originally scheduled the event to start at 4:00 p.m., to include dinner, and end whenever the last guest left or the bar ran out of alcohol. A four-piece soft-rock band had been engaged to start at 7:00 p.m.

At Brian's request, Sandy agreed to plan for Mary Jewel's memorial. She readily accepted the task since she hoped it would help Brian recover from his depression from her death. Sandy developed a list of invitees plus their spouses or significant others she and Brian knew. She wanted to limit the guest list to sixty. She asked Dr. Bennett and Wayne Watkins, Mary's lawyer, each for a list of ten local friends. After Sandy tallied all the invitations, the list exceeded one hundred.

Brian originally planned for the three children to split the cost of the catered event, but he realized his brother and sister might question its cost. As the executor of his mother's estate, he decided to charge the event to the Duck home maintenance fund.

Saturday, June 23, 2012

Sandy decided to make as many calls to the attendees while visiting the family's Duck beach house. In mid-morning, Brian had taken the children to the beach so they couldn't interrupt her.

Sitting at the kitchen table, with a freshly brewed pot of coffee, she first connected with Eve. "Hi, it's Sandy, we're going to hold your mother's memorial celebration of her life on Saturday, July 21. The agenda is simple, you, Stu, and Brian will speak on how your mother influences your current and future behavior. The speeches at the funeral dwelt on how she helped her children on the negative aspects their lives. We want these talks to be positive and not repeat what everyone presented earlier."

"I can do that. Thanks for giving me a month to prepare," Eve said.

"Brian wants to invite your friend Joe. It's time you introduce him to the rest of us. We've noticed you smile more and your voice broadcasts happiness, and we'd like to meet the cause. We have a room for you two."

Eve didn't answer for a half a minute. "I don't know if Joe can make it. He has to take care of his two children." Eve hoped this excuse would protect her. She hadn't told Joe of her opioid addiction, and feared if he learned about it, he'd drop her to protect his daughters. She feared he'd find out if he met her family or her mother's Duck friends.

"No excuse. We're setting up two dormitory rooms on the third floor, one for the girls and the other for the boys. I'm sure Joe's daughters would love a weekend at the beach."

"I'll see if he is available."

Sandy called Stu, who sat with Gayle in the kitchen drinking coffee and relayed a similar message. After he coordinated the date with Gayle, he accepted. Stu looked forward to their first family gathering since the funeral.

Brian and Sandy had originally planned for only four speakers: Mary's children and Paul O'Hare.

Not to have Mary's political life neglected, Wayne Watkins convinced them to ask the head of the Dare County Democratic Party to present her contributions to improving the county's political welfare.

When she called Paul to tell him of the date, he insisted he could not adequately summarize the investigation of Mary's murder properly, unless Dr. Bennett could address her role and the medical aspects of the case. She invited Dr. Bennett.

Dr. Bennett convinced Sandy to add Mary's best friend and tennis player, Jane Watkins, to provide local color on her life after she moved to Duck.

Brian originally thought each speaker would talk for fifteen minutes, but after listening to what the speakers had planned to say, he changed the start time to 3:00 p.m. on the formal invitations.

Joe had asked Eve over for dinner the day Sandy invited them. Eve understood she had to tell Joe more about her past before he found out on his own. Joe prepared a delicious summer dinner of barbeque baby back ribs, roasted vegetables, fresh corn on the cob, lemonade, and served mint-chocolate-chip ice cream for dessert. Eve waited until after dinner, the girls had taken their baths, and had been sent to bed before she talked to Joe.

"Joe, we've been dating for six months, see each other at least three times a week, and have a satisfying intimate relationship I want to continue. It is time you meet my family. An opportunity has come up that will allow you to meet them all," Mary said in one breath, afraid not to stop talking.

"Eve, I'm ready for that, but I didn't realize you were. When and where?" Joe smiled and his eyes couldn't stop focusing on Eve.

"Brian, Stu and I are holding a memorial celebration of life for my mother in Duck on Saturday, July 21. I want you and your kids to come. We'll stay at our Duck house." Eve looked at Joe's face as she spoke, wondering how he would react to what she was about to say.

"We want to go. My kids love the beach," Joe said. His grin and opened deep dimples showed his happiness.

"Before you accept, I want to tell you something about my past that might change your mind. I'll understand why you wouldn't want to see me anymore."

Joe's expression turned from adoration to concern. His grin vanished and his dimples flattened. He didn't speak, but waited.

"I've told you ten years ago, I got into a serious accident that smashed my left leg. The doctors fixed my leg after four operations. However, during the healing process, the pain overwhelmed me. My doctor gave me a thirty-day OxyContin prescription. I didn't realize it, but after five days the drug addicted me. After a year, my addiction was so strong and the pain of withdrawal so great, I never tried to get off it. When my prescriptions stopped, I stilled craved the drug. I found it easy to get the drug by shopping doctors or using the internet. My job paid me enough so I could afford the drug and didn't have to move to lower-cost heroin, the cause of many overdose deaths. After five years of disgust, I decided to end the habit. With the help of my mother, I enrolled in a treatment program and have been clean ever since. I don't drink because alcohol is the fastest way back to opioid addiction,"

Eve stopped and waited for Joe's reaction. She skipped part of the story, since she thought he didn't need to know about her sex life before they met.

Joe's faced relaxed, his smile and dimples returned as she confessed. When she finished, he said, "So that's why you don't drink? I thought you were a recovering alcoholic. I understand your concern, but I have the same problem of being addicted, not to opioids, but to the oldest drug in the world. Earlier, I told you I never drank because my parents were alcoholics and that whiskey destroyed their lives, and I didn't want to follow their example. That was a lie. I was my parent's child in my early twenties. I lived in a drunken haze, getting in car accidents and never being able to hold a job. Waking up in jail one morning too many forced me to change. I haven't had a drink in nine years. I married and had two perfect children. No way, I'll return to alcohol. So, we have something else in common that you shouldn't worry about."

Joe looked at her, embraced her, kissed her, released her, and said, "Eve, I've fallen in love with you."

"I feel the same way about you," Eve said. She kissed him again.

Brian's depression slowly vanished as he took part in the memorial's planning and worked as a full-time lawyer. Brian and Sandy used the event as an excuse to visit Duck on weekends, eat out, and interview prospective caterers. They chose Black Pelican Catering, because of its reputation, variety of catered items, and their satisfaction with the food they had eaten at the Black Pelican restaurant.

By July 20, Brian while still morose over his mother's death realized he had to accept her fate and to move on with his life.

Saturday July 21, 2012

Brian had set up a microphone and speakers on the deck several feet above the backyard. The caterers arrived early in the afternoon and placed thirteen round tables with eight chairs each on the lawn. They set up large tents to provide shade over each group of four tables, and placed three Porta Potties on the east side of the house. A beer keg and bar were located on opposite sides of the tables. Several catering trucks and servers arrived before 3:00 p.m. to serve hors d'oeuvres and drinks while the attendees waited for the speeches to begin.

The tables had no seat assignments, except for the two closest to the deck where the speakers and their guests would sit. Brian, Stu, Eve and their partners, and Joe's two children sat at one table. Brian assigned the other five speakers to the other table. Emma and Ruth sat with their father and Eve, since they didn't know anyone else at the event. Sandy assumed the young cousins would find seats together.

Joe surprised Eve with his discussions with the others at the table. He addressed everyone, asking polite questions and responding with extensive answers when they asked about his background. Eve didn't realize Joe, as a marketing specialist, had prepared answers to hypothetical questions to impress Eve's family just as he would have done with a new client. They all enjoyed his answer to Brian's question, "What do you do at Information Management Associates?"

Joe discussed his role of a marketer humorously describing how he identifies clients, develops marketing strategies, and contributes to writing winning proposals. Everyone seated, except Emma and Ruth, understood what he said.

Sandy hoped for a cool July afternoon, but the day reached the low nineties.

The invitation specified beach attire to forestall the guests from wearing formal clothes. Most of the attendees followed her advice, except for the speakers. The guests consumed copious amounts of beer and soda to replace the fluids they lost listening to the speeches.

Brian began the speeches followed by his sister and brother, tennis-playing neighbor, and Mary's political ally. They each had practiced their talks before their spouses or lovers, so the timing of their jokes elicited the hoped for laughter. They and all the speakers, except Paul and Dr. Bennett, who spoke last, followed Brian's direction to make the afternoon a celebration of Mary's life. By its nature, a summary of the murder investigation and the implications of the widespread invasion of counterfeit drugs weren't funny.

The dinner meal trucks pulled in the front of the house at 5:30 when the speeches were over. The caterer set up a buffet line on the west lawn. They served seafood and Carolina barbeque entries, corn on the cob, potatoes, Caesar Salad, and ice cream.

Margaret and Paul noticed many of the sweating guests had a slight stagger and a hungry smile as they approached the buffet line.

At 7:00, the band started playing soft rock. Many of the guest started dancing, holding on to each other, looking like long-lost lovers, but in reality were married couples trying not to fall down as they danced. Eve and Joe danced with each other and Joe's children, not missing a beat.

"Hon, we're still sober so we should have a safe drive to the Hilton." Margaret said.

# Chapter 36 Eve Retires

Thursday, September 20, 2012

Three months after Winthrop's death, Eve watched a two-hour documentary on the opioid crisis on public television. She usually stayed away from TV shows and books on the subject since they reminded her of her pain and fear of returning to addiction. However, after her last assassination of a Simmons related contractor, she had renewed her determination to remain sober.

The documentary started out with an exposé of several drug companies that produced not only the drugs, but their addiction inducing advertising campaigns, and the sweet-heart bonus deals with morally lacking physicians to prescribe the drug. The show portrayed the growth of the opioid addition to epidemic levels in the rural and suburban areas of the country.

In the last half-hour of the show, a reporter interviewed two companies involved in producing the drugs. Eve listened to this section to hear if they mentioned the employee murders.

Robert Simmons, the CEO of Simmons Pharma, first appeared on the screen. He gave an opening statement how legal opioid producers had pioneered eliminating chronic pain in the U.S. Simmons would not accept any blame for the growth in opioid addiction, stating the drugs were safe if used as directed on the prescription bottle. He then decried the vigilante behavior of those who blamed the drug companies for the opioid crisis and used their misguided view of justice as rationalization for murdering over fourteen employees or contractors of his company.

The number astonished Eve, since she only had killed four. The additional murders reassured her, she wasn't alone in protesting Simmons Pharma's behavior.

Eve hoped she and the others wouldn't get caught. However, over the last three months, she realized her actions would never force the drug companies to change their behavior.

Simmons complained about the rash of lawsuits filed by state and local governments and individuals against opioid makers who claimed the companies engaged in illegal and deceptive marketing practices. Simmons claimed these activities were educational with the purpose of informing the public. No one should live in pain. Eve noted the success of many of these suits and cheered when the TV narrator claimed they might put many of the opioid makers out of business.

While Eve realized she couldn't, she understood the lawyers suing the companies could stop the opioid producers by making the cost of staying in the opioid business too high to survive.

Eve had recovered addiction through efficient counseling and the love of her family. With her inheritance and economic future assured, she planned to become a social worker to help others. The University of Maryland's Professional School in Baltimore had accepted her application to enroll in the Masters of Social Work program.

Since Winthrop's death, she had been spending most of her weekends and a few weekday nights with Joe Kelly and his four- and six-year-old daughters. Eve loved that Ruth and Emma had begun treating her as their mother when they realized she made their father happy. A role she enjoyed playing.

Eve concluded that after spending the first week in August at Sea Colony in Bethany Beach with Joe and his children, she couldn't live without them. She enjoyed every day at the beach more than the previous one. Eve and Joe made breakfast and dinner together while the kids set the table. Their smiles, as they helped, infected Eve. They all walked to the beach together unless it rained or Joe played golf. They spent rainy days at the large in-house pool. Every beach day, they packed a picnic lunch of sandwiches, cookies, and water. Joe didn't like his kids to drink soda.

Joe played golf with two friends at Bear Trap Dunes on the third day. Eve treasured her time alone with Emma and Ruth. Since Joe left for golf early, Eve and the kids prepared the picnic lunch together and walked from their ocean front condo to the beach at 10:00. Eve made sure they all wore sufficient suntan lotion so none of them would be in pain by dinner. She took them to the ocean where the three stayed in shallow water and jumped in the waves. The children never left Eve, so she didn't have to worry about their safety. After lunch, the three sat under an umbrella. The kids went to sleep.

At 1:30, after playing golf, Joe headed to the beach. While Eve read *The Help* by Kathryn Stockett, Joe said, "Is there room for me on this blanket?"

"Yes," Eve said as she stood up to kiss Joe.

Her movement woke up Emma, who said, "Hi, Daddy." She smiled having seen her father embrace Eve.

Emma's voice aroused Ruth, who said, "Was golf fun?"

"Yes."

"We had more fun," Emma said.

Eve smiled and tried not to show her reaction to Emma's comment, which she agreed with.

"Glad you had an enjoyable time. What did you do?" Joe asked

The two kids started talking as once, relaying a minute by minute narrative of the morning's events: building sand castles, wading, eating lunch, having an ice cream cone, and playing catch with a Frisbee.

Joe beamed, since his plan to have Eve and his kids form a relationship without him present worked.

While walking back to the condo, Joe asked Eve, "Would it be okay if I played golf in two days? You could take Emma and Ruth to the beach."

Before Eve could answer, Emma said, "Yes, have fun with your friends."

"I agree," Ruth said.

Eve laughed and said, "Of course."

Saturday, September 22, 2012

Joe invited Eve to treat her for dinner at the L'Auberge Chez Francois in Great Falls, Virginia to celebrate his recent promotion to Vice-President for Business Development and the nine-month anniversary of their relationship. She had been there twice before she met Joe and considered it the best restaurant in the Washington area. Eve initially felt guilty at the dinner's cost until Joe told her he had received a twenty-five percent pay increase.

Eve anticipated reading the fixed-price seven-course menu that came with each entrée since Joe had told her about their next date. While she sipped her water, Eve became relaxed and happy as she read the menu. She ordered the Lobster Bisque, house salad, Parmesan-crusted wild Alaskan halibut, roasted potatoes, a house dessert, and coffee. She enjoyed homemade sorbet between her salad and entree.

Joe had more to celebrate than his new position. He tried to hide his nerves for the three days before they went to the restaurant. His order paralleled Eve's, except for an appetizer and entre. He had the snails from the vineyards of Burgundy, and for his entrée he enjoyed the veal scaloppini, with Virginia ham, crabmeat, mushrooms, and cream sauce.

As a couple confident and happy in their relationship, their conversation dwelt on their past weekend trips, the enjoyment of each other's families, and a winter trip to the British Virgin Islands they scheduled for February.

After the waiter removed the entree dishes, Joe reached into his left breast pocket. Eve didn't notice this move. But she couldn't miss Joe leaving his seat and kneeling on one knee.

Eve hoped he'll ask what she had wanted for the last six months. Torn between smiling and crying, she did both when he took out the ring, and said, "Eve, I love you. Will you marry me?"

###

## About the Author

Frank E Hopkins writes realistic crime novels and short stories portraying social and political issues.

Frank E Hopkins was raised in the New York City area, went to Graduate School at the University of Maryland, earned a Ph.D. in Economics, taught for ten years at Binghamton University in upstate New York, and returned to the DC suburbs. He moved to the Delaware beaches in 2001. Settings from all locations have been used in his writing. He has published five novels: *The Counterfeit Drug Murders*, *The Billion Dollar Embezzlement Murders* which won third place in the novel category in Delaware Press Associations 2020 Communications Contest, *Abandoned Homes: Vietnam Revenge Murders* which won first place in the mystery/thriller category in the Maryland Writers Association 2018 novel contest, *The Opportunity*, and *Unplanned Choices*. Frank's collection of short stories, *First Time*, was awarded second place for a single author collection in the Delaware Press Associations 2017 Communication Contest.

Frank is active in the Rehoboth Bay Writers Guild, the Eastern Shore Writers Association, the Delaware Writers Network, and Mystery Writers of America. He is also a member of the Berlin chapter of the Maryland Writers Association.

Website: www.frankehopkins.com

Author email address: frank@frankehopkins.com

Facebook profile: http://facebook.com/hopkinsfe

# Third in a Series

*The Counterfeit Drug Murders*, the third novel in the Hoffman and O'Hare Mystery Series, is a sequel to *The Billion Dollar Embezzlement Murders* and *Abandoned Homes: Vietnam Revenge Murders*. All three books have been structured so they can be read independently.

The Maryland Writers Association awarded *Abandoned Homes: Vietnam Revenge Murders* first place in the mystery/thriller in their 2018 novel contest. *The Billion Dollar Embezzlement Murders* won third place in the novel category in the Delaware Press Association's 2020 Communications Contest. This sequel does not continue a discussion of the crimes in *Abandoned Homes: Vietnam Revenge Murders*, but follows the lives of the two main characters of the book: Margaret Hoffman retired detective Delaware State Police, and Paul O'Hare, retired professor.

In the first novel, the couple meets and falls in love as Detective Hoffman leads the Delaware State Police team to solve the murders. Hoffman and O'Hare write a best-selling book about the revenge murders.

In the second novel, they marry and after Detective Hoffman retires from the State Police, they participate in solving the embezzlement, and become targets of the murderers in Greece on their honeymoon and on the Outer Banks of North Carolina.

In *The Counterfeit Drug Murders,* a close friend of the two detectives dies from tainted counterfeit prescription drugs. Further research indicates their friends' deaths are part of a larger tragedy, including the demise of several individuals from the same drug. The detectives vow to solve the cause of the death of their friend.

# The Billion Dollar Embezzlement Murders

The thriller sequel to *Abandoned Homes: Vietnam Revenge Murders* starts with the heinous murder of a participant in a billion dollar embezzlement of a Delaware company, the Liberty Credit Card Co. The action switches to the continuing romance of Margaret Hoffman and Paul O'Hare started in the first novel. They marry, have a successful release of the book they wrote about the abandoned home murders, and decide to spend their honeymoon in Greece.

The embezzlement continues as the crime's ringleader, Hank Strong, orders the murder of Jean Cummings, who discovered the crime. She avoids the first two attacks, at her home and at a mountain cabin in West Virginia, but fearing for her life she flies to Greece to enlist the help of Margaret and Paul to help solve the crime. As they become involved, an attempt is also made on the authors' lives in Mykonos, Greece and Duck, North Carolina. The action returns to the U.S. as the Delaware and Greek police get closer to solving the crime. The embezzlers make plans to leave the U.S. to live in a country without an extradition treaty with the U.S. Will the police or the embezzlers be successful in their quests?

**What readers think of *The Billion Dollar Embezzlement Murders***

**It Will Keep You Up All Night**.

Move over Elvirah and Willie. Frank Hopkins has created a pair of sleuths to rival the Higgins-Clark duo, adding the distinction of their being published authors. If you follow Margaret and Paul through this embezzlement scam, you will not only be rewarded with a gripping thriller, but you'll also take away an education in Finance and Geography. Hopkins's Ph.D. in Economics gives him the authority to fine-tune the shenanigans of his characters so as to distill them down to the understanding of everyman... You don't want to miss this one. Mary D. on June 22, 2019

**Cybercrime is real!**

This is a fictional tale of a very REAL, real world issue. Cybercrime and digital currency theft and manipulation. I always get a kick out of reading stories of these types of character. And our main "villain" in this case is enjoyable to read. Great writing, fast paced, and it's definitely a page-turner. I hate spoilers so I won't give any. Jnmorrison on September 4, 2020.

**Wow! A look into cyber-crime!**

Okay, this introduces the reader to a very realistic type of crime that could happen in the world we live in--or it lays out how it could. It is almost like a real-time peek into something very real. Written in a style that enhances the plot and the characters--giving the reader a somewhat detached view, it really comes together and keeps you entertained and turning the page. This is the type of book you want to read when you feel like a mystery or some drama. Grab a cup of coffee and open this one up. If you like mysteries, you're going to enjoy this ride. Addon on September 27, 2020

**Take a Ride with Hoffman and O'Hare**

They met in *Abandoned Homes*, and now they're back for more action. *The Billion Dollar Embezzlement Murders* takes us for a ride with Hoffman and O'Hare, the best pair of sleuths since Nick and Nora. The stakes are high. Bad guys get testy when there's a billion dollars at stake. Hopkins does a good job in describing action and in setting scenes and this book has plenty of action. Take a read and get involved with Hoffman and O'Hare. Jackson Coppley on June 8, 2019

## A Compelling International Thriller

Set partly in the U.S. and partly in Greece, THE BILLION DOLLAR EMBEZZLEMENT MURDERS is the second book of a thriller series featuring Delaware State Police Detective Margaret Hoffman (now retired), and retired professor Paul O'Hare.

Recently married, they're thoroughly enjoying their newlywed status and the bestseller success of the true crime book they wrote about the case they solved in Book #1 of the series. Now in Book #2 they've got a new case to solve and write about, the embezzlement of $1 billion from one of the top financial services firms in the country and the brutal murders committed to cover up the crime.

A complex, well-plotted, well-researched thriller that's vastly entertaining and enjoyable. The main characters are charming and likeable, and it's fun to follow them on their death-defying adventures – especially when they take us on a fabulous insider's tour of the Grecian Islands. Fascinating, authentic-sounding details about financial data, systems, and security, and the ingenious embezzlement plan.

Keeps you turning the pages – or tapping your Kindle – all the way to the satisfying conclusion. Definitely recommended. Kristy Dark on April 19, 2020

## Well Thought-out Crime Thriller

I really liked this book because of the embezzlement scheme being so interesting. The author provided just enough details to keep me guessing. The Greek setting was a nice touch. I will definitely go back and read the first book in the series now that I know the characters who are very likable. Reader88 on May 12, 2020

## It was a fun read on different levels

Not only was I invested in the story's characters, but I have been a lot of the places that were settings and found myself reliving past adventures. Well done! Fast paced. Great use of language. All in all, I am going to buy the first in this series which I had missed and keep with it. Excellent book! EH Ivans on August 31, 2020

**Great Read**

Margaret and Paul are back: married, happy and enjoying the good life in Greece. But, their bliss gets blitzed when a massive embezzlement scheme in their native Delaware is uncovered and follows them to Greece. As they assist their friend, they find themselves targets for elimination also. Frank Hopkins continues the fast-paced action for this pair we first met in *Abandoned Homes: The Vietnam Revenge Murders*. William Kennedy on July 22, 2019.

**Another great novel from Frank Hopkins!**

I was most impressed with the amount of research that Frank Hopkins must have done to write *The Billion Dollar Embezzlement Murders*. The technical aspects of embezzling that amount of money were well described. His depiction of Greece and its many islands made you feel you were there. Being a Delawarean, I was familiar with many of the other locales throughout the book, which added to the verisimilitude. And, of course, the plot was spot-on and moved quickly. Highly recommended! F. Weldon Burge on July 4, 2019

**A good read**

*The Billion Dollar Embezzlement Murders* held my attention from the first page to the very end. I liked the flipping between the different characters trying to solve the crimes to the perpetrators still committing them. The description of the scenery only adds to the enjoyment as the story journeys across the world. Amy on June 14, 2019

**Unique mystery!**

Just finished reading Frank Hopkins latest novel *The Billion Dollar Embezzlement Murders*. This mystery is filled with high-tech crime -- murder -- back stabbing intrigues and Greece. No putting this story down as it is a straight read through. Bill on September 20 2019

**They're Back!**

An unlikely pair at first, Frank Hopkins new dynamic duo, Hoffman and O'Hare are fast becoming super sleuths. Professor and cop, now writers, travel to Greece and uncover the crooks behind *The Billion Dollar Embezzlement Murders*. Crooks who also happen to be murderers. Frank Hopkins second novel featuring Hoffman and O'Hare has them in a fast-paced race to discover the murderers before they become the next victims. Amazon Customer on May 28, 2019.

# Abandoned Homes: Vietnam Revenge Murders

## IS A SUSPENSEFUL SERIAL KILLER CRIME NOVEL

U.S. involvement in the Vietnam War ended in 1975 when the U.S. abandoned its Embassy in Saigon. However, the hate developed during the war years, especially at major universities continued. Proponents of the war, fierce opponents of communism, acted during the war years to remove potential traitors from our society. Those against the war continued their opposition, begun in the 1960s, culminating in the riots and student killings at major universities, including Kent State, the University of Maryland and the University of Wisconsin-Madison.

Paul O'Hare, a retired history professor, uncovers a long-hidden domestic impact of the Vietnam War thirty-five years after the war ended when he finds a skeleton in the crawl space of an abandoned home in southern Delaware. The Delaware State Police investigation team, headed by Detective Margaret Hoffman, discovers two more skeletons, and the quest for a serial killer begins. Hoffman soon discovers the three skeletons had been graduate students at the University of Maryland during the 1970s as had Paul O'Hare, who becomes a major suspect. Eventually the State Police clear him, and he begins a romantic relationship with Detective Hoffman that includes conflicts between his anti-war sentiments and her experience as a Marine veteran.

The search for a serial killer reveals a complex web of interrelated former students, a crusading newspaper reporter, and CIA agents and double agents, in this fast-paced suspense novel.

The Maryland Writers Association awarded *Abandoned Homes: Vietnam Revenge Murders* first place in the mystery/thriller category in their 2018 Communications Contest.

**What readers say about *Abandoned Homes: Vietnam Revenge Murders***

## A Mystery on Many Levels

Frank Hopkins spins a tale that begins one place and takes you to another as the story unfolds. A photographer finds interest in old houses in the countryside where properties are low value and the houses are forgotten and left to decay. He steps on rotten boards exposing a skeleton and discovering the source of a deadly virus. So, we have an outbreak menace story, right? Wrong. As a smart, tough policewoman becomes involved, we have a cold case story about who the skeleton represented and now have a murder mystery. The murderers are alive and remain dangerous. The photographer and the policewoman begin a relationship and you want to know where that goes. Jack Coppley on November 4, 2017.

## I fell in love with the two main characters

Once I started this book I could not put it down. I fell in love with the two main characters. The story moved fast so you don't have time to get bored. The characters, the locations and the events were all believable. This is the third book of Mr. Hopkins that I have read and am now starting on the fourth. This gentleman is definitely my new favorite author. Bonnie P Cashell on January 4, 2018.

## Good Story, Especially for Delawareans!

This was a fast moving mystery and easy to read, with no dull chapters. I found the subject matter enlightening as well. Carol70 on February 5, 2018

## Frank Hopkins Scores Another Hit

Whoever said that reading was either for education or enjoyment hasn't read Frank Hopkins' novels. This second entry into a developing series has all the elements of a gripping detective yarn designed to keep you glued to its pages. At the same time you'll learn, as an old forties song goes, "A little bit about a lot of things." This latter point may be a coincidence, but the Hopkins style brings to mind crusty gum shoes of mid-century American noir, Sam Spade, Mickey Spillane and Perry Mason. Although his protagonist, Margaret Hoffman, may be more closely aligned with later women characters like Kinsey Milhone and Jessica Fletcher.

This novel spans the years from the end of the Vietnam War in 1975 to the present, and gradually reveals a murderous plot involving pro and anti-war factions resulting in a series of heinous crimes. Rat-infested basements and crawl spaces of abandoned houses reveal the grisly remains of the victims and soon connections are discovered among the skeletons.

Although himself a suspect at first in these crimes, Paul O'Hare helps Detective Hoffman unravel the mystery and the couple begin their partnership, professional and personal. If you haven't read either Hoffman - O'Hare Novel, read this one first for continuity.

Not only did I enjoy the edge-of-my-seat aspects of the book, I learned a lot about my own neighboring states. Frank clearly travels to his novels' locations doing exhaustive research. You'll travel south through sleepy towns in Delaware and stopping for lunch in an historic Virginia waterfront village. And as with all Hopkins' novels, you'll always know what his characters ordered from the menu. My suggested selection for you is *Abandoned Homes: Vietnam Revenge Murders.* Order it now while you're on the Amazon site. It couldn't be easier. What won't be as easy is putting it down. Mary D on August 28, 2019

## Skeletons in the basement and closet

Frank Hopkins has managed to reach back in time to rekindle old hates and awaken fears in his latest novel, *Abandoned Homes: Vietnam Revenge Murders*. Beauty, skill and toughness in the person of State Police Detective Margaret Hoffman, retired U.S. Marine, combine with modern police forensics to solve decades-old murders involving the CIA. Threading her way through the trail of skeletons, she falls in love with Paul O'Hare, a retired history professor, who initially discovered the skeletons, only to become a murder suspect. Follow the trail of mystery, motive and murder that abounded on college campuses of the 1970s. Amazon Customer on October 13, 2017.

## Unpredictable...Informative...Entertaining

*Abandoned Homes: Vietnam Revenge Murders* is a complex murder mystery which holds you captive from the onset. Hopkins' hero begins an unforgettable journey into the unknown with the discovery of a skeleton in an abandoned home. The story unfolds as he works in tandem with the Delaware State Police to ascertain the identity of the victim. It soon becomes clear that the political unrest of the Vietnam War is a pivotal piece of the puzzle. College campuses were a focal point of the peace movement and it was determined that the victim was a student at the University of Maryland during the 1970s. As a witness to the protest of the Vietnam War while attending the University of Maryland in 1970, Hopkins lends a personal aspect to his narrative, which is relevant in all of his books. Brimming with twists and turns! A Must Read! Linda D. on October 6, 2017.

## Another good read from Hopkins

Hopkins shows us his versatility with a murder mystery this time. The story develops when a retired college professor stumbles across a dead body in an abandoned home he's researching. First, he's a suspect by the investigating female State Police officer, he then becomes her lover. They follow leads across the Mid-Atlantic States to uncover a long-buried plot that began in the political unrest of the Vietnam War. Each chapter takes the reader deeper into this complex tale of intrigue. William Kennedy on October 21, 2017.

## Hatred between factions for and against the Viet Nam war didn't end when the war did

In Frank Hopkins' new murder mystery *Abandoned Homes: Vietnam Revenge Murders*, a retired history professor pursues an unusual but innocent hobby-investigating and photographing abandoned homes in rural Delaware. His discovery of skeletons in the abandoned homes sets off a search for a serial killer that endangers his life as it reawakens the raging conflicts that took place on college campuses during the Viet Nam war years. Carole Ottesen on November 17, 2017.

## Hard to put down!

Such a devious mystery! Frank E. Hopkins has a way of weaving an intriguing story along with characters that stick in your head. Kari on January 5, 2018.

## I enjoyed this captivating tale

Mysteries are not normally my genre, but the author kept my attention throughout. Can't wait to read his next book! Diana M. on January 5, 2018.

## Another great book by Frank Hopkins

Frank Hopkins' intriguing book *Abandoned Homes: Vietnam Revenge Murders* is a step-by step murder mystery. From the first page to the last, it is a fast paced story that is difficult to put down. The book starts innocently when Paul O'Hare, a retired history professor, stumbles upon skeletons in an abandoned house which he is photographing. Paul meets Detective Margaret Hoffman who is on the case using modern day forensics. Even though he becomes a suspect, Margaret Hoffman and Paul become lovers. Not only is this book a riveting tale of murder, but also has a great romance. Something for everyone! If you want an entertaining and unpredictable book, then this is definitely for you. S. Scarangella on March 11, 2018.

## Mesmerizing Murder Mystery

Mesmerizing is the word for this book. The mystery story line was exceptionally creative and from the beginning draws the reader in one direction, and veers off smoothly into others before its surprise ending. One could not help but sympathize with the corpses and surprisingly the culprits. The book brought back memories of our confused country over the Vietnam anti-war movement and my own College Park experience. My only complaint is that the "lovely" heroine policewoman's food choices were entirely too healthy!!!! Kathy H on March 15, 2018.

## Great mystery murder investigation

Excellent mystery with a strong female lead character. The Delmarva location setting and description are an interesting backdrop for this novel. A book you will not want to put down until the mystery is solved. Kathy L. on March 25, 2018.

### *Abandoned Homes: Vietnam Revenge Murders* is a page-turner!

In the late 1960s and early 1970s college campuses across the United States were sites of anti-war protests sometimes accompanied by violence as students and the country divided over the war in Vietnam. In 2008, when retired University of Maryland history professor, Paul O'Hare stumbles upon two skeletons in an abandoned home he's photographing in lower Delaware, he suddenly and inexplicably finds himself at the center of an intense and long-ranging police investigation. Paul is eventually cleared, but as the police uncover more and more evidence leading to the identity of the real killer, old enmities and enemies emerge from the shadows of Paul's past, making him a target right up to the story's dramatic conclusion. *Abandoned Homes: Vietnam Revenge Murders* is a step-by-step police procedural page-turner. Recommended for fans of realistic detective fiction, with a bonus if the reader is from Delaware and can recognize locations and landmarks! JM Reinbold on June 22, 2018.

## Nicely crafted murder mystery

A masterfully written police procedural, with finely defined characters and a well-paced plot. Hopkins has clearly done his research. And, as a Delawarean, I enjoyed his many references to lower Delaware and the beach area--many locales of which I recognize and have visited. The scenes of violence are handled with precision and with modicum gore. Two thumbs up. F. Weldon Burge on October 10, 2018

## Many of the locations in this book are easily recognizable to readers in the Mid-Atlantic area

Frank Hopkins' book, *Abandoned Homes: Vietnam Revenge Murders*, looks back at the turmoil, deception, intrigue, and anger of the late sixties and early seventies in this engrossing, hard to put down mystery. It won first place for a mystery/thriller novel in the 2018 Maryland Writers' Association novel contest. It is a thought-provoking, exciting mostly police procedural with a little romance thrown in. Many of the locations in this book are easily recognizable to readers in the Mid-Atlantic area. Eileen Haavik McIntire on July 5, 2018

**Stirs your curiosity**

If you are looking for a mystery that stirs your curiosity throughout, *Abandoned Homes: Vietnam Revenge Murders* is definitely one to purchase. From the beginning, Mr. Hopkins sets the stage with vivid images of rural Delaware through which he skillfully creates an intricate web of characters and plot twists that connect skeletons found in deserted houses to polarized views of the Vietnam War. You, too, will enjoy reading how the pieces of the puzzle fit together. A great read! JD, an avid reader on April 15, 2018

**Engaging**

Very engaging story and believable characters. This is also a Maryland Writer's Association winner, and Frank did a great job. F. J. Talley on June 17, 2018

**...a fast paced story of mystery and murder**

*Abandoned Homes: Vietnam Revenge Murders* is a fast paced story of mystery and murder. The author wastes no time with preliminaries and takes us directly to our hero who discovers several murders that have not been solved. He reports finding the bodies, one by one, but ironically, he finds himself a suspect. The story is set primarily during the heart of the Vietnam War during the 1960s and focuses on the conflict people feel about being involved in this war. This story held my attention throughout. Whether you're into murder mystery or not, I think you will enjoy reading this book. I highly recommend it. ruthziemniak on January 29, 2020